DJANGO'S
TUNETOWNSHUFFLE

I0544808

PHAROAH
CAIN

DUCK RIVER PRESS
www.duckriverpress.com

Third Edition

Cover Illustration by Maya Andres

Published by:
Duck River Press
Nashville, TN 37202
www.duckriverpress.com

ISBN: 0615594549
ISBN 13: 9780615594545

Library of Congress Control Number: 2012931494
Duck River Press, Nashville TN

"All human beings should try to learn before they die what they are running from, and to, and why."

James Thurber

AUTHOR'S NOTE

This work of fiction is set in Nashville during the early 1990's, the waning Analog days, before the Boom and before Technology changed the world and the Music Business in ways both good and bad.

Nashville was burgeoning, though for some of us it still felt like a small town. Perhaps because there were giants walking among us then, genuine legends with names like Cash, Conway, Porter, Waylon, and a handful of others whose presence alone made Country Music vital and significant.

Those were the days.

PS: Analog still sounds better.

PC

It was my great-grandfather who taught me about the smoke. Cornelius Vanderbilt Singing Wolf Shepherd was a full-blooded Paiute Indian who began living inside his mind long before I came into the world. Part poet, part oracle, part mystical shaman, he claimed to be the lone survivor of a cavalry massacre, adopted by my great-great-grandparents as they made their grim pilgrimage back East from Northern California after decades of disillusion in the gold fields.

While that legend may or may not be true, I know for certain he was a unique man who lived his life in two distinct halves: the first forty-five years as an eminent teacher and scholar, and the second half as self-anointed Chief of some lost and forgotten tribe that lived, fought and died in the mountains and valleys of his smoke-filled imagination.

He was christened Cornelius Vanderbilt, in the hope that such a fine name would bring good fortune to this heaven-sent child. Handsome, athletic, and possessed of a keen intelligence, still he was denied access to public schools and thus relegated to a private institution in Philadelphia, though he would later earn a Ph.D. in History from Columbia University.

Once armed with impressive credentials from the white man's world, Cornelius embarked on a personal and professional odyssey that took him back and forth across the country teaching in colleges and universities, all the while probing into the dark crevices of his own heritage. Along the way, he married one of his students and settled in her hometown of Charleston, West Virginia, where my grandfather Floyd Meadows Shepherd was born soon after.

Though widely acclaimed throughout academia, it was the research sabbaticals that led to his eventual undoing. Summers were spent out West investigating the few remaining Paiute reservations as Cornelius continued to trace his lineage. Ultimately, he discovered he was descended from a long line of medicine men and "keepers of the story," those revered wise men who could orally recite the history of their people, having committed tribal legacy to memory.

As Cornelius learned more about his people and ancestry, gradually the adopted traits of the white man began to fall by the wayside. One September, after a summer spent with the Paiutes in Idaho, his wife was shocked to see him arrive at the train station wearing buckskins and moccasins, his shoulder-length gray hair beaded and braided, and calling himself "Singing Wolf," a name he claimed had been given to him by an ancestor in a dream.

This new identity, combined with a recently acquired penchant for organic hallucinogens such as peyote and mescaline, hastened his abrupt discharge from the university as well as the untimely death of my great-grandmother, who merely grieved herself away in a few short years.

My grandfather Floyd, who was a young man when all this happened, renounced his father as a madman, then dropped out of school and headed south for the coal country where he married and raised four children, my own father being one of them. Papa Floyd never spoke to his father again and, as far as I know, never found in his own heart the same forgiveness he preached to others for the greater part of his adult life.

Years later, after my dad and mom married and I was born, Singing Wolf, who was by then in his late eighties or early nineties, came to live with us for the first ten years of my life until he died one summer evening, rocking in his chair on the front porch of our little frame house.

The few memories I have of the old man are still as sharp as the dry, harsh smell of the Prince Albert tobacco he smoked in his ancient elkhorn pipe or hand rolled with papers from the red tobacco tin nestled in the breast pocket of his faded overalls. It is the scent of the smoke I remember most: strong, bitter, and yet strangely comforting, a balm of familiar warmth that was as much a part of him as the wispy gray ponytails braided on either side of his eminent head. To me he was an exciting mystery and through the years I've come to love him even more, if that's possible, for surely in those days I believed him capable of walking on water.

He was too old and frail for me to sit in his lap so I would perch at his feet as he rocked and smoked, the ominous cloud of Prince Albert shading the light from the single bare bulb that hung at the far end of the porch as he held me spellbound with his tales of Indians and spirits and ghostly illusions. But even as the tiny hairs on my neck tingled with fright, I always knew that I was safe within the hovering, gray blanket of his magical smoke.

I'd sit for hours and listen as he told me the Coyote Tales, which were his favorites because they represented a time when all people were animals. He would carefully recite them just as they had been orally passed down for centuries. Always, the story would begin the same, in Paiute: "*Sumu onosu numeka nana quane ynas...*Once, long ago when we were all the same...*"

Many of the tales featured Coyote, the shape-shifting trickster, whose adventures were often at best bawdy, and at worst highly inappropriate, which made them all the more fascinating to a young boy. Most of the fables carried a lesson or moral, though I now suspect he invented a few just to astonish or scare the living Hell out of me. One thing is certain: it was on that porch where his spark lit the lifelong flame that would burn in my soul with a desire to create and tell stories, albeit most of them accompanied on guitar in three-quarter time.

That was a long time ago, but the old man is still with me. I feel his soft presence from time to time, whether I'm fumbling through my whiskey-soaked brain for the right word or rhyme, or just turning a corner into a dimly-lit honky tonk and running face-first into a thick gray cloud of friendly smoke. When he's there, when I can feel his gentle hand on my shoulder and hear the distant, easy laughter of his voice, I can smell that old familiar aroma, and I am overcome with peace, clarity, and the warm promise of sanctuary.

CHAPTER 1

Perched at the top of the brass pole, head back and arms outstretched, Cassidy looked like a circus queen waiting for the swinging bar that would take her out across the arena, high above the crowd and into the moving spotlights.

But then a crunching guitar chord and a burst of strobe detonated the air around her, turning her regal smile into a teasing pout as Cassidy gripped the pole with both hands and spread her legs wide to begin a slow, silky, downward spiral, the gleaming brass pole now an axis for the naked female planet orbiting the front of the black-lit stage. The mad shouting and sweaty applause almost drowned out the last few bars of "Beast of Burden," as bankers, bikers, lawyers and lunatics pushed and shoved at the edge of the stage, jockeying for a better seat, a closer look, a fleeting glimpse of immortality as Cassidy circled into view.

Nearing the floor, her lithe, tanned legs snaked beneath her as she not so much slithered but oozed the few feet to the edge of the stage. With a hand on either side of her golden breasts, she pushed them together to snatch a ten-dollar bill from the eager teeth of a wild-eyed Fort Campbell soldier as dollar bills filled the air around her, floating like butterflies before coming to rest at her feet.

As Keith Richard's guitar faded, Billy Gibbons' slide began knifing at the smoky air as Cassidy knelt on stage, hurriedly scooping up the pile of bills before sliding out of the spotlight and into the shadows while the roomful of madmen clapped, whistled, and begged for just one more precious peek.

Instead of dashing into the dressing room behind the stage, she walked straight across the floor to the bar where I was working, the crowd parting before her like the Red Sea as the Queen passed, arms crossed against her breasts, her fists full of crumpled cash.

It was against the house rules but so what? Cassidy broke rules about as often as she broke hearts, which was damned often. I should know, mine was one of them.

She dumped the bills on the bar and began slipping into her silver sequined bikini, the glorious breasts jiggling and swaying as she stepped into the tiny thong.

"They love me, don't they, Jake?" she giggled.

"Yeah, Honey," I said, handing her a Coke. "Everybody loves you."

Grinning like a schoolgirl, she turned and looked out across the strobe-lit room that pulsated in time to the bass guitar, pumping like the heart of a hunted animal. When she turned back to me, the smile was gone.

"Let 'em eat fish heads," she winked, then walked away on those perfectly sculpted legs, the cheeks of her tush starting a small revolution as they fought to overthrow the skimpy thong.

"That ees certainly some woman, yes, don't you think," more an observation than a question from Felipe, my Mexican bar back, as he dumped a fresh bucket of ice into the bin, spilling most of it in the sink and onto the floor. He'd only been in the States a few months but had already developed a talent for stating the obvious.

Cassidy hadn't gone far before two grinning suits waved her over for a table dance. One of the men held her drink as she peeled off her bikini and stepped first onto a chair and then to the table, where she stood and slowly shimmied inside a twelve-inch circle. The Queen had ascended her throne.

Onstage Porsche, a lanky dishwater blonde with an equal number of bad tattoos and bruises, was doing her best to keep the crowd interested, but it was tough work with Cassidy holding court just a few tables away. A crystal sheen of sweat glistened off her thin, translucent body as Porsche ground herself into the pole, hunching and kicking to Aerosmith's "Dude Look Like a Lady," a fitting choice, considering Porsche had once been a welder on an offshore rig before surrendering all things manly unto the knife.

But despite her great effort, the crowd of lovesick bozos began drifting away from the stage toward the table where the two suits sat like pillars of salt as Cassidy moved above them, totally in control and loving it. Porsche was pulling out all the stops now, determined not to lose the three or four guys left sitting around the stage. When a young fool stuck a single between her rock-hard breasts, Porsche squatted in front of him and folded the bill longways before sliding it into and out the bottom of her G-string. Then she rose and began executing a series of high kicks as she danced the length of the stage, smiling like Miss Poultry USA, the dollar bill snugly in place.

"That ees why...that ees why," shouted Felipe over the music, pointing at the stage as he swept at the spilled ice.

"Why what?"

"That ees why my Mah-ther told me never to put money in my mouth."

Out on the floor Bear was skimming silently throughout the crowded room, his head and eyes on a constant sweep from table to table. With his tight curls and black tuxedo he looked like Sonny Liston on the way to the prom. He had a sixth sense for trouble- he could almost smell it brewing and was adept at cooling a situation before anything boiled over. But what happened next caught us both off guard.

Cassidy finished her table dance and was stepping down to the floor when one of the suits ran his hand up the inside of her thigh, causing her to jump away, losing her balance. She landed on her feet but stumbled across the aisle and went crashing into another table, knocking it out from under Afro-Dite, a tall mulatto girl in the middle of her own table dance. Afro-Dite's legs flew up over her head and she dropped a hard five feet to the carpet with a *thud* that was heard all the way across the room. I knew she had to be hurt but she came up swinging and cursing anyway.

"Damn you, Girl," she hollered, lunging at Cassidy and throwing an overhand right that just barely missed, bouncing off the shoulder of a customer who foolishly thought to get between the two dancers.

Across the room Bear was already moving in their direction, so I locked the cash register and heaved myself over the bar, falling in a couple steps behind him.

"It's alright, Hon, it was an accident," said the brave patron to Afro-Dite, smiling and speaking gently in an effort to soothe her. And it did calm her, for about two-tenths of a second, until she took a half-step forward and drop-kicked him squarely in the crotch. His eyes shot red with pain as he collapsed to the floor in a heap, gasping for breath and trying not to choke on his bile.

"Asshole," she hissed, then made another move toward Cassidy just as Bear came up behind her and grabbed a big handful of hair.

That should've been the end of it, but it wasn't. Afro-Dite's head jerked, but only for a moment as the wig came off in Bear's hand, leaving him standing there looking bewildered at the hedge bush-sized mass of coiled, artificial curls.

"That's enough," I said, stepping in to catch a wide left hook with both hands, then turning it back into her and spinning her around, herding her back out into the aisle toward Bear, who still held the giant afro wig at arm's length as if it were alive.

Catfights are deceptively dangerous. Most women fight dirtier than men ever imagined, and Afro-Dite was as tough as any Marine I'd ever served with. She'd spent most of her adult life in the joint and even bragged that she'd done more time inside than outside. She wore that huge Cleopatra Jones wig that was straight out of the Seventies, but her sleek, almond body was absolutely up to date. And she would've been a stunner, too, if not for the primitive prison ink that started at the front of her left shoulder and ran all the way over and down her back. Bad ink, bad art, and bad news. Sometimes she wore silk jackets to cover it up, but the ink, like her nasty disposition, was always there, lurking just beneath the surface.

I was hustling her away when she stopped suddenly and snapped her head back, catching me solid on the end of my nose and crunching what little cartilage I hadn't managed to coke away over the years. Tears flooded my eyes and a torrent of blood went pouring down my shirt as I felt her wriggle away and turn back for Cassidy. Then I heard the brittle explosion of breaking glass.

Still trying to focus my eyes, I turned and saw Afro-Dite sprawled out on the floor, unmoving, blood bubbling from a three-inch gash at the top of her head, bits of dark, green glass lying shattered and sparkling wet all around her. Cassidy stood over her, naked and breathing nervously, her right hand wrapped around the broken neck of what had once been a magnum of Dom Perignon.

"Get your shit and hit the door, Girl. You got three days off and a hundred-dollar fine," ordered Bear.

Cassidy dropped the broken bottle neck to the floor, then turned and walked to the dressing room without saying a word. With one hand still clutching Afro-Dite's wig, Bear scooped up the dazed dancer with his free arm, hoisting her limp body onto his shoulder like a sack of fertilizer. As they passed me on the way to the dressing room, Afro-Dite raised her head and looked up with glazed, dizzy eyes.

"You...a...dead...Mutha-," was all she said, the rest of the word sliding off her cherry-red lips.

But I knew she wasn't talking to me.

My nose had almost stopped bleeding, so I headed for the back room to change shirts and grab a smoke. The adrenalin rush felt warm and electric, though I knew the next day I'd wake up unable to breathe, both eyes black, and a steady, painful throbbing behind my sinuses. But that was tomorrow, and I'd learned a long time ago not to bank on tomorrow. In this town it's either right around the corner or a long way off, depending on your luck at any given moment. And at that moment it was just another day at the office, another night in Music City, the place where dreams come true. Sometimes.

And sometimes they turn into nightmares. That night seemed like a million years ago, I thought, standing at the front of the cell smoking and listening to the dissonant jailhouse symphony: the clanking of steel slamming against steel, radios squawking, toilets flushing, the yelling of drunks and the wails of the deranged. On the floor behind me, two black gang members slept through it all like little boys.

I tried not to think about Cassidy. Then again, thinking is just about all there is to do when you're standing in a holding cell at four in the morning waiting to be brought up on Murder One. I lit another cigarette and thought some more.

Downtown Nashville in early August is a steamy plate of bright colors and thick, dull smells that simmer from mid-morning til late into the night. It's the burning stench of hot asphalt rising from streets that are always under construction. It's the gritty, dusty brick grit of sand and mortar from quaint old buildings being torn down or gutted to make way for modern-day monuments with all the character of a Burger King. It's the choking exhaust from tour buses, trucks, and trolleys filled with tourists in black socks and sandals making their yearly pilgrimage to worship at the shrines of the Unholy.

It's a wino propped against a newspaper rack in front of the Post Office, his hand held out from habit as he stands and weaves in a puddle of his own doing. It's five hundred lawyers, all wearing the same red tie, and secretaries in Walmart perfume and Reeboks, powerwalking down Church Street at lunchtime in search of the ultimate garden salad. It's a continuous flood of conventioneers, credit cards in hand, looking for coochie, music and directions. It's a street preacher with a stolen Gideon Bible spreading the word of Jesus in front of the Triple X Adult Cinema.

It's a songwriter from Oklahoma stepping off a Greyhound bus with a guitar and his life's savings stashed in his boot. It's a homeless woman with two kids, roaming the streets in the early morning hours, waiting for the public library to open.

It's an aging, coked-up country music star in a limousine, cruising lower Broadway and telling his life story to a fresh-faced, wanna-be girl singer, promising her that anything is possible here, that this is a magical place, a city of dreams, and that she, too, can make it if she'll work hard and listen, just *listen*, because he likes her more than he really should and he wants to help her avoid the pitfalls and traps that so many young girls fall into when they first start out here in Music City. Then he kisses her earnestly before easing her head toward his lap.

And after more years than I care to think about, I've somehow wound up at the very end of this ever-growing, all-consuming downtown monolith, pushed finally to the edge of the river at the corner of First and Broadway. I occupy the top floor of the century-old building that houses Acme Feed & Seed, a sprawling throwback to years gone by and the last remaining building in this part of downtown that has steadfastly refused to close its doors and turn itself into a fern bar. The owner, Mr. Pitts, is a character, now in his eighties, but still working downstairs in the feed store every day.

"Times may change but I don't," he said, when I asked him once why he didn't sell out.

He has a couple of sons who help him run the place and on the surface they all seem bound together not only by blood but by their fervent resistance to change and urban renewal. We'll see. Sometimes blood runs thin and attitudes get rearranged when people start waving money in your face and, God knows, there's an awful lot of money being waved around here these days.

But for now, the day-laborers still line up in front of the store at six a.m., some of them having shown up three and four days a week for the last forty years. Lately they've been joined by a half-dozen or so Mexicans who get relegated to the back side of the building, a move the Mexicans seem to take in stride as they are usually the first to be picked.

And you can still drive up to the front of the store and have someone load seed, mulch or fertilizer for you right from the curb just like forty years ago. A while back the city tried to put parking meters in front of the store, but they disappeared overnight, cut cleanly and evenly at the pavement. They tried again and the same thing happened.

"You can't fight City Hall but you can damn sure fuck with it," chuckled Mr. Pitts, as he and I surveyed the scene of the crime one morning. For the time being there are no parking meters.

The old building is an anachronism, a dinosaur struggling to survive with one ear cocked to the ticking of time. Maybe that's why I'm so fond of it. It reminds me of myself: old, outdated, out of touch, but too damn mean and stubborn to go gently into that good night.

They use the second floor as a warehouse but I have the third floor all to myself. Mr. Pitts gives me a break on the rent for keeping my eyes and ears open for burglars, though in truth it's a pretty sweet gig because now that this part of town has become a tourist Mecca, there are dozens of cops roaming Lower Broadway and Second Avenue at all hours of the day or night.

It's too bad I'm not a painter, because it's a big airy space with a fourteen-foot ceiling and large windows that wrap around two of the walls, from Broadway back down First Avenue. The First Avenue side faces east, looking out over Riverfront Park and the roiling, murky Cumberland River, a mud-gray amalgamate of sewage, gasoline, and factory waste that may or may not have been clean when it brought the first settlers here a couple hundred years ago. Today it's a highway for barges loaded with coal and sand as well as the riverboats and water taxis bringing tourists from the hinterlands and unleashing them like Huns on the downtown shore.

Some poet once said that a town needs a river to forgive itself. If that's so, then from the looks of it I'd say the Cumberland has soaked up enough sin and shame to forgive us all our trespasses both past and present.

That's not to say the muddy old river doesn't have its charm. In the winter, when everything down here slows to a dead crawl, I can stand at the window watching the barges going north and south, searchlights cutting from bank to bank, snowflakes falling and caught momentarily in their beams- it's nothing short of breathtaking.

But it's also a deceptively dangerous river, with a strong and violent undertow that can suck you down in an instant and spit you out dead and waterlogged five miles downstream. It's not unusual for some poor distraught soul to take a suicidal leap from Victory Bridge and not come up for days. And yet I'll look out the same window in July and see some lunatic slalom skiing, dodging beer cans and logs and waving at tourists on the General Jackson paddlewheel.

Most days the Cumberland and I share a tenuous truce. But when the dark times come, the times when my life gets as muddy as that old river, the late nights or early mornings when I've had too much of the whiskey pie, I'll lean against the window amazed at how it all came to this, how anyone could fly so high and then fall so far, only to wind up as I have, pushed farther and farther away from it all until I ended up here alone, my back at the edge of that river, fighting to keep from being driven into the water and sucked under. Staring up at the Victory Bridge, I wonder if maybe someday I, too, will climb that rusty steel rigging, opting for final action over last words, something unique, perhaps a triple-gainer-with-a-twist before embracing the muddy swill like some tired club fighter relieved to feel the canvas against the back of his head.

Thus far I've managed to keep the demons at bay, either by digging down deep or just fighting from instinct, preaching and promising and swearing on the ghosts of my great-grandfather, my dead friend Benny Watts, Hank Williams, or anyone else to whom I might have incurred some unexplained cosmic debt. So for the time being I live close to the bone and keep swinging at the smoke, running from bad luck, bad dreams and bad karma towards good whiskey and better days.

Besides, even the bleakest night is always followed by the dawn, and sooner or later the sun begins pulling itself up on shaky haunches, stirring the sleeping bums in Riverfront Park and spilling the forgiving sunlight into my east window and out the north, up Broadway and Second Avenue.

A few years ago, these streets were peopled with a community of artists, musicians, and craftsmen, interesting folks who lived and worked and hung out together every night. A quaint mixture of New Orleans, the Village and SoHo, the bars, shops and restaurants all fit together in a unique, unplanned pattern that gave the area its own peculiar identity.

But then the Developers came, and the land became lush with dance clubs and chain restaurants. The bookstores, coffee shops, and art galleries were soon replaced by the Hard Rock Cafe, which begat Hooters, which begat dozens of T-shirt and souvenir shops. The artists and creative types fled in droves while I stood at my window and watched it all take place, feeling like a helpless bystander at a mugging.

And now even Lower Broadway, the last bastion of true honky-tonking, has finally succumbed to the dreaded disease. Now there's only a couple of genuine, smoky little dives with dim lights and low ceilings nestled in the dark shadows of the Ryman Auditorium, waiting patiently but not silently for the creeping homogenization that will ultimately devour them one by one.

But for the moment, they are as alive as ever: loud, dirty, sweaty, sometimes dangerous, but still a haven for country music in its raw and primary form, a place where steel guitars still twang and twin fiddles ring through the neon night as dreamers play from the heart for tips and beer. Faded posters and yellowed eight-by-ten glossies from forty years ago line the walls and beer still costs a buck a can. The music is pure and uncut, and nobody goes there but cowboys, rednecks, bums, and the occasional has-been songwriter. Like me.

CHAPTER 2

Don't get me wrong, I haven't always been a bottom feeder on the music industry food chain. Several years ago, I hit the jackpot with a novelty song called "Sub-Urban Cowboy," recorded by Saddle Bronc Pipstein right at the tail-end of that woeful craze that saw half the country dressing in designer jeans with belt buckles the size of a hubcap, pointed-toe Tony Lama Ostrich-skin boots, all topped off with a feathered cowboy hat just slightly smaller than a beach umbrella. I wrote the tune in about twenty minutes, higher than a weather balloon, but it went to Number One in Billboard and Cashbox and stayed on the charts for twenty-nine weeks.

It was your typical Nashville fairytale. Three days before the record was released I had to pawn my guitar, a precious 1969 Martin D-35, just to pay the rent and buy a few groceries. Two weeks later my publisher handed me an advance check for ten grand against royalties.

"Never forget," he said, "In this town, the end of the rainbow is always three minutes away."

I got my guitar out of hock, put a down payment on a big Eldorado, (which I still have), then promptly went through the rest like shit through a goose. For the next two years, whenever it appeared I was almost broke, another check would arrive like manna from heaven. And even after all these years I still occasionally find a little surprise in the mailbox, not much, but just enough to remind me of the good old halcyon days.

I had absolutely no trouble adapting to life at the top. I was hanging out with stars, getting phone calls from Conway, Cash, Reed, or anyone else who had a record deal at the time. There was talk of a movie, and I just barely missed getting a nomination for Song of the Year. I partied a lot, wrote very little, and did more drugs than a Kamikaze pilot.

But like most things too good to be true, the song turned out to be both a blessing and a curse. "Sub-Urban Cowboy" was a novelty song, and I quickly got pigeonholed as a 'clever' writer, a label that can be the kiss of death in this town. Most people tended to view me as a One-Shot-Wonder and, after several failed attempts to follow up with another hit, I began to believe it myself. Pretty soon word got out that I was jinxed. *Muerte Negra*.

It was a short, fast ride, over in the blink of an eye, and even though I try not to be bitter, it still gripes my ass to think that when I die, if I'm remembered at all, it'll be for writing "Sub-Urban Cowboy." Some legacy, huh?

"I wouldn't bitch if I were you," said my buddy, Toad. "That song puts you in the top one percent of all the songwriters in history. If that ain't success, I don't know what is?"

I guess he should know. He's been plugging away on Music Row for twenty years without even coming close to a cut.

"Just you wait," he nodded, his whiskey-lit face glowing pink from his chin to the back of his uneven, bald head, "That song will come back around. Sooner or later everything does. You just gotta hang in and wait it out, you'll see. If I'm lying, I'm dying."

"I'm not so sure about that, Toad. That may be true for bell bottoms and lava lamps, but something tells me Urban Cowboy songs have gone the way of the Chiricahua. Besides, the last I heard of Saddle Bronc Pipstein, he was doing his second stretch in Huntsville for boosting catalytic converters."

For the next few years I tried starting over several times, dancing the TuneTown Shuffle whenever a new regime of honchos would arrive at the record companies and publishing houses, but eventually the frustration and rejection wore me down until finally I just gave up. The sad part is that I didn't give up all at once but rather a little bit every day, a piece at a time, until one morning I woke up and there was no poetry, no desire, no more fire in my soul. And even though I still like to think of myself as a poet, writing is no longer my life's work or mission, but something more akin to a well-worn, favorite shirt I put on from time to time to remind myself of who I am. Or was. And yet, despite it all, I'm not bitter.

"Better to shoot at the moon and hit a stump, than shoot at a stump and miss," is what my Granddaddy Floyd used to say.

At least I took my shot.

Of course, that was just one of a dozen winding roads I stumbled down before coming to a dead stop behind the bar at Jezebel's, the biggest and wildest strip club in Music City. It may not be the music biz but there are a lot worse ways to make a living than tending bar in a roomful of naked women.

The truth is, I took the job as a last-ditch effort to stay alive creatively, starting over again for the umpteenth time. Working nights would give me the freedom to write and pitch songs during the day, and working weekends would keep me from spending whatever money I might make. I know it sounds feeble but some of us old dreamers just can't kick the habit. It's almost as if the dream itself is the only thing keeping us alive.

Bear met me at the door the day I walked in with my hat in my hand. We were not exactly strangers. He'd tossed me out on my tail more than once a few years back whenever I'd get coked-up and whiskey-bent and my mouth would start writing checks my ass couldn't cash. I certainly remembered, but if he did at least he had the courtesy not to let on. A former defensive end for the Bengals, with his close, tight curls and neatly trimmed goatee, he was a dashing but deadly figure, moving fluidly, more like a dancer than a bouncer, and I couldn't help but wonder what kind of foreign substance I must have ingested to think, even for a second, that I could take him.

"Wait here, please," he said, in a voice as soft as an undertaker's, before gliding behind a partition and leaving me alone in the lobby.

It was a small room, with deep purple carpet accented by chrome molding and shiny black walls covered in framed 8X10's of strippers past and present, some of whom were appearing this week and some of whom hadn't seen a stage since Jimmy Carter was lusting in his heart. At least the place had a history, and I could appreciate that. I waited about twenty minutes, or long enough to check out all the pictures and mentally tabulate the three all-time most popular stripper names, those being, in descending order: Candy, Angel, and Tiffany.

Just as I was beginning to think I might need to shave again, Bear came floating around the corner, soft and silent, motioning for me to follow as he led me down a dark hallway of purple and black to a double door marked *Private* at the very end. He opened one of the doors and I entered a large office with a big mahogany desk with a facing loveseat made of deep brown leather. The rich, hunter green walls contained no stripper photos, having been decorated with expensive modern prints, and behind the desk there was no fat, cigar-chewing club owner, but a rather stunning, professional looking lady who looked to be in her late thirties, blonde hair tied perfectly in a bun, teal-green eyes behind tortoise-shell glasses, and all wrapped up in a dark blue business suit.

She rose from her leather chair and offered her hand.

"How do you do," she said, "I'm Aleta Thomas."

We shook hands as she brushed at a stray blonde hair that had escaped the bun to tickle at her cheek, and I wondered for a moment if she kept her life as tightly wound as her hair. Tony Bennett was singing in the background, just loud enough for me to make out the words to "I Wanna Be Around (To Pick Up the Pieces When Somebody Breaks Your Heart"). Aleta Thomas pointed a small remote control at the wall and clicked twice, banishing Tony from the room.

"Jake Shepherd," I replied. "It's a pleasure."

I was somewhat familiar with her story. She'd inherited Jezebel's from her dear, departed husband Burton "Boot" Thomas, a colorful, flamboyant figure who lit up the Nashville skyline one night in a Mercedes wired with enough dynamite to level the L&C Tower. Boot got his nickname from his love of fine, manly footwear, which was in itself ironic because after the explosion, the only identifiable thing the cops could find was a small portion of his full-quill, ostrich-skin Luchese.

He fancied himself a gangster and was thick with all the politicians in the Machine, which in those days ran not only the city but the entire state. Boot had his share of enemies, both in the underworld and on Legislative Plaza, but nonetheless his death came as both a surprise and a mystery, because in the fifteen years since, not one suspect had ever turned up.

Aleta, however, was another story entirely. The black sheep daughter of a prominent Belle Meade family, she was a runaway who'd crisscrossed the country a half-dozen times back in the Seventies before landing as a dancer at Jezebel's.

Legend has it that one night Boot filled her nose with candy and whisked her away to Vegas for a weekend. When they returned, she was Mrs. Burton Thomas. Her father, a distinguished Nashville surgeon, immediately disowned her, while her mother cleared the house of all Aleta's belongings and forbade anyone ever to mention her name in the family's presence. Both her brothers told everyone she had actually been adopted and that they, while pitying her, were not the least bit surprised.

Only her older sister Katherine stayed in her corner, a surprising fact considering Katherine and Aleta were total opposites. Katherine had been the model debutante, a genuine Belle of the Ball, and her marriage to Memphis golden-boy Carter

Robinson seemed nothing short of predestined, a natural union of old money and political ambition. They were the toast of the society pages for years, until a series of debilitating strokes left Katherine a bed-ridden invalid.

Robinson was an ex-jock from Memphis State, a boot-strap scrapper who'd managed to parlay a battlefield commission in Vietnam into a General's star before quickly retiring and entering politics. He'd authored a couple of best-selling books: the first, a detailed chronicle of the final years of the Vietnam War, the second just your basic, predictable, 'be-all-that-you-can-be' flag-waving tome, both of which had sent his visibility soaring. Now he was Senator Carter Robinson- popular, powerful, and perennially courted by his party for Presidential service, yet unique in his adamant refusal to run for higher office. He seemed content to remain a Senator, and his "Aw-shucks" image endeared him not only to Tennesseans, but to the folks in Washington as well. His work record was remarkable, in that he never missed a vote, and he'd never sponsored a bill that didn't get passed.

Even I liked him. And Robinson certainly had no bones with Aleta or her nightclub. He was a semi-regular when he was in town, sometimes holding court at the VIP table with a bunch of political types or foreign businessmen, yet just as often rolling up his sleeves to party with his old pals, usually ex-military types who drank hard, got loud and crazy, but rarely let their fun get too far out of bounds when they played footsy with the girls and tossed money around like confetti. He was always nice to me and he tipped well, so naturally he had my vote. Besides, we went to the same war together.

Like most rebels, Aleta was a survivor. After Boot's untimely end, she took over Jezebel's with a passion, remodeling, hiring feature performers, and creating a high-profile advertising campaign that eventually turned the joint into a multi-million-dollar operation that spun off additional clubs in Memphis and Atlanta. She was rich and powerful but kept an extremely low profile, all of which only added to her mystique. I respected her for that, but then I've always had a thing for black sheep.

She motioned me to the loveseat as we began the usual small talk that prefaces all job interviews, though in truth there really wasn't much to the job, since Nashville's antiquated liquor laws forbid selling alcohol in strip clubs. Customers have to pay to bring in their own booze and all the bartender does is serve set-ups. Pretty hard to screw up an order for Cokes and tonic water.

"What have you been doing since you left the music business, Jake?" she asked, leaning forward and propping both elbows on that massive mahogany desk. She was smiling omnisciently, as if she already knew the answer and just wanted to see if I'd get it right.

"Well, Ma'am, I've had some sales jobs and done some security work."

(Translation: I've sold burglar alarms, repo-ed cars, and worked as a security guard in a U-Store-It compound.)

"I see," she nodded. "If I remember correctly, you used to get pretty rowdy. Do you still drink?"

"Occasionally, Ma'am, but never behind the bar." (Translation: I won't drink at work but I'll probably go home every night and drink a twelve-pack, as well as anything else I can smoke, snort, or fish-for-in-a-bucket if I think I can get a song out of it.)

I watched as she looked me over with that cool demeanor, everything so prim and professional, and I tried to remember what she looked like fifteen years ago when I was sticking five-dollar bills between her tits with my teeth. If someone had told me then that I'd be sitting across a desk from her one day applying for a minimum-wage job, I'd have bought the house a round and then cut my own throat.

"Are you honest?" she went on.

What a question- it's the kind of question that, if you answer "Yes," as I certainly would, you can't help but think the other person automatically assumes you're lying. I should've gotten up and walked out the door but, as usual, I desperately needed the money. I had to play along.

"Ms. Thomas, I come from the old school of bartending that has three strict rules: don't steal, don't drink behind the bar, and don't sleep with the help."

She smiled a mouthful of polished white teeth as if that were just the most clever thing she'd heard all day.

"You stick to that, Mr. Shepherd, and we'll get along just fine."

And that's just what I did, at least until the day Cassidy walked in.

She came through the front door of Jezebel's looking as if she owned the place or was about to. Long, black hair falling below her shoulders, hazel eyes, full ripe lips, and a body any dancer would die for, I took one look at Cassidy and forgot every woman I'd ever met.

Almost from the start she became Queen of the House, taking it all in stride and managing along the way to make friends with most of the girls while skillfully ignoring or avoiding the few old-timers like Afro-Dite who were not so quick to follow.

A strip joint is like any other business, with its own particular pecking order determined in no small part by the amount of money a dancer brings in during a shift. Her first night there Cassidy made over nine-hundred bucks, more than twice as much as the other dancers. Of course, some of the harder girls made a little money on the side, the easy way, by paying the house a hundred bucks to take an hour 'dinner break' before getting dressed into street clothes and disappearing through the side exit by the alley for a quick rendezvous.

"The law says I gotta let 'em eat, so what can I do?" shrugged Bear, though I had the feeling that most, if not all of the hundred went into his pocket. What the hell, everybody in this business is into some kind of scam, and with all the cash floating around the room, it's only natural for someone to want a little taste.

But Cassidy was different. She had more charisma than all the other girls combined, and she knew how to use it. She was a master at reading a room and when she looked down from the stage and made eye contact with a guy she made him believe she was dancing for him and him alone. Once, while dancing, she blew a kiss in my direction and I walked around giddy as a freshman until I realized I was only one of about twenty guys who thought the kiss had been meant for him. By the end of the first week it was obvious that, while Aleta Thomas' name might be on the deed, it was Cassidy who owned the room.

"Any man who doesn't think Woman rules the world has never seen that gal dance," quipped Carter Robinson one evening, as he stood at the end of the bar. We were both watching Cassidy as she rewrote the book on pandemonium and crowd control. A hundred guys were spellbound at the foot of the stage and even Robinson had left the VIP booth for a closer look. I had to agree.

She sunk her hook in me the first time she walked up to the bar and ordered a Coke, her fresh-scrubbed face and cheerleader smile making her look like something out of an Elvis movie. I fumbled around spilling Coke all over the bar and myself before finally throwing up my hands and shrugging my shoulders at the mystery of it all, how a woman, any woman for that matter, could make me so silly and nervous. By the time I got the mess cleaned up we were both laughing.

"Sorry," I said. "I guess I'm a little off my game tonight."

"That's all right," she soothed, "Nobody said you had to be perfect."

I poured a fresh Coke and set it in front of her, then took a maraschino cherry from the garnish tray and placed it on top, along with a straw.

She picked up the cherry and set it on the bar.

"Those are very bad for you. Loaded with dyes and preservatives. But thanks for the thought."

"Want to see a trick?" I asked, picking up the cherry and pulling out the stem before holding it in front of her. I popped the stem in my mouth and put my tongue and teeth to work, applying the technique I'd learned from a bored waitress years ago. When I withdrew the stem a half-minute later, it was tied neatly in a knot. I held it up between my thumb and finger and beamed.

"You must get invited to all the big parties," she said coolly, then strolled away, leaving me standing there looking like ten-thousand assholes.

But that was all part of Cassidy's charm: cute and cuddly as a puppy one minute, then cool and unapproachable the next. Like most fools, I couldn't make up my mind which one I liked best.

Business had always been good but since her arrival it was better than ever, and I stayed swamped from open til close. Except for serving her an occasional Coke, I had little contact with Cassidy from night to night other than to catch a fleeting glimpse of her on stage, or to wave goodbye as she left at the end of her shift, usually with two or three other girls in tow. After closing, it always took Bear, Felipe, and me at least an hour to clean up the bar and close out the registers before I finally walked out the door at three-thirty or four a.m., tired, sweaty, sticky, and smelling like bar gravy. But one night, a Tuesday I think, was exceptionally slow.

For some reason there was just no business. By eleven o'clock Bear had let almost half the girls go home and even Cassidy found herself walking around with very little to do. After a while she wound up standing at the bar with me, sipping Cokes that I'd spiked with a little Jack Daniels from a bottle I kept locked in the cabinet for VIPs and special occasions.

Cassidy walked over to a bar stool and placed a small hand towel over the seat before sitting down.

"You afraid of catching something?" I asked.

"Vinyl puts bumps on your butt," she replied. "If you don't believe me, take a look at Anastasia."

I glanced up at the stage at Anastasia, a short, thick girl who had just bent over to touch her toes. Her rump looked like an outbreak of chicken pox.

"That's what I love about this job," I laughed. "I learn something new every day."

"Somebody get a shovel and let's bury this place," she demanded, waving her arm at the stark, nearly vacant room. It always struck me as to how lonely and depressing a strip club could be whenever there were only a handful of customers around. You could almost touch the sadness and quiet desperation that hung in the air like guilt.

"So," I said, every bit as bored as she was, "You want to recite your life story for me in twenty-five words or less?"

"Why not?" she laughed, taking another slow sip of her drink. "Let's see- Southern girl, small town, leaves home, big city, no job, no money, want ads, Now Hiring, big tips, time passes, here I am. Is that twenty-five words?"

"Give or take."

"Your turn," she countered, her smile melting my knees.

"All right," I paused. "West Virginia, small town, big dreams, big city, big success, big problems, big crash landing, big blank space, time passes, here I am."

Bear was in the back office so I slipped her another Jack & Coke. She ran her finger around the rim of the glass and looked up at me with cool suspicion.

"Are you trying to get me in trouble, Mr. Jake-the-Bartender?"

"I would never do that," I swore, placing my right hand over my heart.

"Well, I certainly hope not because I'm just beginning to think I might be able to trust you."

"Don't you worry none, Miss Cassidy," I drawled, affecting an over-the-top southern accent. "You can always trust ole Jake." I took a quick glance around the room before tossing back a shot of Jack myself. Screw the rules- like I said, when Cassidy's around, all bets are off.

She reached over and took a cocktail napkin and swizzle stick from the bar, folded the napkin several times, then tied it around one end of the swizzle stick. A simple white cocktail napkin had suddenly become a rose. When she finished, she leaned across the bar and motioned for me to come closer, the neon from the club lights making her eyes sparkle like Chinese lanterns.

"Here you go, Hot Shot," she smiled, handing me the bar flower. "You're not such a hard guy after all."

"Other women have told me that but it's usually when I've had too much to drink."

She slapped my face playfully and pouted.

"Don't be nasty," she chided. We were still close, our faces just inches apart.

There was a moment of awkward silence between us before we both finally looked away to the stage where one of the girls was half-heartedly humping to AC/DC's "You Shook Me All Night Long." Three or four young guys sat around the stage talking to each other, oblivious to the flesh that gyrated and hovered in the air just above their ears.

"I'm hungry," Cassidy said. "What time do you get off?"

Before I could answer, Bear walked over and told me to give last call. I hadn't seen him come out of the office and wondered for a second if he'd seen me down the shot. That was Bear for you, moving like smoke, quiet as death.

"I'll be through in about an hour. Want to meet me somewhere or you want to wait?"

"I'll wait," she called out, already on her way to the dressing room.

An hour later we were sitting in the International House of Pancakes, digging away at western omelets. We sat in the blue vinyl booth until almost sun-up, sipping coffee, smoking cigarettes and talking without ever taking our eyes off each other. She avoided specifics, other than to say that she'd been dancing for a couple of years, first in Florida and then Mobile, and that she came to Nashville because she had a friend who promised to help her break into music videos. Her plan was to dance for a few months and save some money to put together a portfolio. I'd heard different versions of the story from different mouths over the years, so by now my patented reaction was to just nod my head and say, "Good Luck." Then again, in this town you never know.

"And after the videos, next stop Atlantic City."

"You want to work in a casino?"

"Of course not," she laughed. "That's where the Miss America pageant is."

I figured the syrup had given her a sugar rush so I made no comment. But like I said, in this town...

We were both movie freaks, hers favorite being *The Way We Were*, with Barbra Streisand, which she'd seen eleven times on television before buying the video a couple years ago. Now the count was over thirty.

"I think it's just the most romantic story in the world," she said. "Two people who love each other so much but just can't seem to get it together and then, before you know it, Life has just kept going on and on until one day they run into each other and they stop and wonder, just for a second, what it might have been like if they'd tried a little harder, worked at it just a little more."

Her voice caught and her eyes clouded.

"That one scene at the end, when they're standing there on the street staring into each other's eyes, you know exactly what they're thinking, what they're feeling, and it's all just this great sense of loss, and yet, a sort of acceptance of the way things are. I've seen it a zillion times and I still start bawling every time I get to that scene."

She used her napkin to dab at invisible tears.

"I wrote a song that was in a Barbra Streisand movie," I said, hoping to lighten the mood a bit.

"You did?" she shrieked, her face illuminated at the very thought. "Which one?"

"Yentl," I answered.

"That is just so cool, Jake. What was the song?"

"Yentl On My Mind."

She tilted her head and thought about it for a moment, and I quickly realized I would need some better jokes and more recent reference points.

"Okay," she went on, "Now you tell me. What's your favorite?"

"Probably *The Wild Bunch*," I said, after a moment.

"I haven't seen it," she said, "But it's a western, right?"

"Yeah, it's the ultimate western. I like it because even the heroes are bad guys."

"How many times have you seen it?" she asked, as if that were the determining factor for any good movie.

"Not quite a zillion," I said, "But close."

"What's it about?"

"It's about a bunch of outlaws at the turn of the century who know that their time is about up, so they get together to pull off one big heist before riding off into the sunset. It's got William Holden in it, and Warren Oates, Ben Johnson, some of my favorite actors."

"Do they get to ride off into the sunset?"

I thought for a minute about the film's bloody climax, the long, slow-motion gun battle that wipes them out while exacting revenge for their slain compadre, dying like heroes instead of the outlaws they are.

"You could say that," I nodded. "Yeah, I guess they do."

She was looking at me in a way that made me think she understood exactly where I was coming from, though I knew she couldn't possibly. Looking back, I realize now it was at that moment I first began to feel close to her. I know it all sounds like a cliché, but then I live in a town built on bad clichés, bent metaphors and strained similes.

"You know, Jake, when you think about it, it's really kind of strange. When you're a kid they teach you all this stuff from the Bible, but most of it is hard to relate to because it all happened so long ago. Then, as you get older, you watch all these movies until finally one makes this big impression on you and it's like this movie becomes your own personal Bible, and you just sort of live by it, you know. It sounds silly, but that's how it seems to me anyway."

"That's a scary thought," I said.

"Well," she said, looking away, "the Bible is a very scary book."

It would make a great story to say that we finished our coffee and went back to my place and made love for hours, but the truth is we barely made it to the bed before we both collapsed into a deep sleep that lasted until the next afternoon. For the next few weeks we were inseparable. We went to work together, came home together, spent every waking hour together with no other goal in life than to make each other happy.

Cassidy brought something into my life that had been missing for a long time, a peace of mind that defied definition. I felt alive again, and more importantly, I began to quit thinking of myself as a loser. Little by little, I started to believe in myself again. I played my guitar without a drink in front of me and even began to write a bit. And best of all, for the first time in years, I slept peacefully, with no bad dreams, no napalm nightmares or apparitions of Benny Watts and his ghoulish smile reminding me of our future date in Hell. I could feel my spirit healing, see things evolving in a new and different light. For about five weeks.

And then, just as quickly as it began, she ended it. It came out of the blue, like a sucker-punch, swift and merciless, and when it was over she left no doubt she was never coming back. I tried every trick in the book, up to and including begging, but once Cassidy's mind was made up there was no changing it. When I pressed her for a reason she would simply say it had nothing to do with me, that everything in life has a natural course to run and that ours was finished.

"What about *The Way We Were*," I pleaded, "What happened to trying a little harder and working at it just a little?"

"Jesus, Jake, it's a movie for Christ's sake. Look, it's okay to blame me, it really is. I know I'm screwed up and I admit it, but it's something I've learned to live with. Right now, the best thing you can do is just give me plenty of room and don't push, so that maybe we can still be friends down the road."

She was rubbing my cheek as if I were a little boy.

"You know I think you're a sweet, wonderful man, Jake. It's just that I have to get focused on what my life is about, which is *not* running around naked in front of a bunch of drunk, slobbering jerks. Besides," her voice dropping an octave for effect, "we both know that in the long run I could never make you completely happy."

"That's Bullshit," I said. "And you know it."

But it was done. Toast. The same brutal honesty that first endeared her to me and made her naiveté and innocence so compelling had circled back around and cut me off at the knees.

After that we barely spoke in the club and I kept busy at the bar, trying gamely to keep my emotions in check. But it all came to a head one night when I stormed out from the bar and caused a scene at the VIP booth where Carter Robinson was holding court with Cassidy and three other girls. Robinson was stuffing ten-dollar bills in their tops and G-strings and copping a quick feel in the process. In hindsight, he was only doing what twenty or thirty other guys were doing at that very moment. The difference was that I was pissed at the world and he was the closest target.

"You can't do that in here," I shouted over some wretched Billy Ray Cyrus song that was way too loud.

"Who the hell do you think you are?" he bellowed, not at all intimidated.

"I'm the guy who's going to throw you out of here on your ass if you touch another one of these girls."

Robinson struggled to rise but I shoved the table against him, pinning him against the back of the booth.

"You sonofabitch," he hissed.

Before I could reach over and smack him, a firm but gentle hand on my shoulder pulled me back. I hadn't noticed Bear walk up but then again that's his deal.

"Get back behind the bar," he whispered.

"Wait a minute, Bear, he-"

"Get back behind the bar, *Now*."

I turned and sulked away, and everything would have probably cooled down had Cassidy not stormed out of the booth to come after me, grabbing my arm and spinning me around.

"You pull another stunt like that and your ass will be on the street," she threatened.

"Screw you, Lady. Why don't you pay out so you can go ball your Big Shot."

She slapped me hard and I grabbed both her arms and started shaking her. She screamed, and I recoiled in horror at my own anger, just as I felt Bear's grip again, only this time it was around my throat and this time it wasn't so firm and gentle. It was more like a vise. He pushed me against the bar and brought the palm of his hand up under my chin, lifting me up onto my toes, speaking slowly and deliberately to make sure his point would be well taken.

"I think it's time you took a few days off, Jake."

I went home and dove into a bottle of whiskey and stayed there for several days until I was sure I'd drowned every fragment of Cassidy's memory. When I came up for air I felt like a new man: born-again-hard, a little sick and queasy perhaps, but nonetheless determined to put her behind me and start looking ahead to better times.

But then everything went from bad to worse.

CHAPTER 3

We were slammed from the get-go that evening. My first night back and to make matters worse, I'd stayed up til daylight with Toad picking songs and telling lies until finally we drank ourselves sober. I'd gone home, taken a shower, and tried to sleep but it was way too hot and I was way too loaded, so I just lay there all day staring at the ceiling until it was time to go to work.

The Convention Center is only a few blocks from the club and that week it was playing host to hundreds of heavy equipment operators from the paving industry. By six-thirty we were jammed tight with four-hundred hard-drinking conventioneers. The thick air was quilted with smoke and carried the sour citrus smell of drink mixer, cheap perfume, and testosterone.

We had over forty girls on deck and every one of them was busy. Even Tammy, all two-hundred and twenty pounds of her, was doing one table dance after another. The couches in the back were full and small lines were forming at the end of each with guys waiting their turn for a particular dancer.

"Where's Felipe?" I asked Bear, as he passed the bar once. I was fast running out of everything.

"He quit last night. Say he couldn't handle the stress. Say he can make mo' money framing houses. Lemme know if you need help, but right now I best watch the room."

Yeah, right, I thought.

I'd only caught a glimpse of Cassidy during the night but I'd been too busy to even think about her. When you've got six waitresses running drinks and guys standing four deep at the bar, you get in the weeds quick and you stay there. I'd copped a hit of speed from one of the girls, but it only made me feel even more fried, and I wound up walking around like a zombie, working from habit and instinct.

Finally, about 1:30am, the crowd had thinned out enough for me to catch my breath. I waved Bear over.

"Can you watch the register for two minutes while I get some ice and straighten up?" I pointed to the three large drums overflowing with trash at the end of the bar.

He nodded and I grabbed a cigarette, lighting it as I began sliding the biggest trash barrel through the swinging doors and down the short hall to the back door. I felt in my pocket for my keys, then pulled the barrel through the door and out onto the ramp outside, letting the door lock behind me as it slammed shut. Leaning against the railing, I inhaled the smoke and the muggy summer night air, thoroughly exhausted and soaked with stinking sweat.

Taking a seat on the landing step, I looked up at the radiant Nashville skyline and thought about my wasted life and all the wrong turns I'd taken that had led me to this place and to this point in time. The walls behind me reverberated with a dull thudding as KC and the Sunshine Band invited the last few remaining customers to "Get Down Tonight." I took a deep drag on the cigarette and let out a tired, defeated laugh. If they could just see me now, wouldn't the folks back home be proud?

Head down, arms across my knees, sweat dripping, I began to preach to myself a mental sermon, a silent tongue-lashing that usually happens when I'm extremely tired or drunk, and which always ends with the perfunctory promise that tonight I'll go straight home and start writing again, that tomorrow is the first day of the rest of my life, a hit song is only three minutes away, that failure can never catch a man in motion, all that and a half-dozen other amphetamine vows I would never keep.

At any rate, I was immersed in all that self-absorbed, motivational bullshit when I heard a loud, scuffling noise that caused me to jump up and look around. There wasn't much of a moon but in the dim light I could see something moving around in the bed of Bear's old Dodge truck which was parked in the alley. Frozen in place, I watched and then breathed a sigh of relief when a wino rose to his knees like a phoenix in the bed of the truck. He shook the cobwebs from his dirty head, rubbed his eyes with his fists, then carefully climbed over the tailgate and stood on the asphalt and raised both arms overhead, easing up onto his toes, rocking gently back and forth like some ancient athlete who still knew the benefit of a good stretch.

He was in the middle of his wino aerobics when he spotted me on the steps of the landing and stopped abruptly. He took a half-step toward me, then thought better of it, turned and shuffled off down the alley.

I'd seen the old fart before but didn't know him and didn't want to. In my high-rolling days I used to think of bums as glorified romantic characters, Quixotic outcasts who chose to live by their own set of rules and shun society's sense of order. Modern-day prophets who kept deep secrets and infinite wisdom hidden behind crusty beards and dirty hats. But when my own life began its downward spiral, and I found myself getting closer and closer to the gutter, the idea quickly lost its allure. Most prophets don't piss themselves unless they're running for cover.

Bear was probably wondering if I'd gone AWOL, so I flipped the cigarette across the lot and got ready to dump the trash. The barrel looked even bigger than it had a few minutes earlier and I judged it to be at least a hundred pounds, and its size and shape made it damn near impossible to lift without risking a double hernia. I'd have to empty most of it by hand until I got the load down to a manageable weight.

I tried to open the door of the dumpster but it was jammed. Something heavy was lodged against it from inside, probably last night's trash. I thought of Felipe, the little shit, who should have been doing this in the first place, and I made a mental note to one day hunt him down and torture him for walking out and leaving me with such a mess. If the door wouldn't open, there'd be nothing left to do but climb inside the bin and move the garbage around until the door was free. Not a pleasant thought.

Backing up two steps, I took a short run and hit the door solid with my left shoulder while simultaneously pulling the latch down with my right hand. The door sprung open and knocked me on my ass, causing me to hit my head on the steel-pipe step railing as I went down.

"Dammit," I screamed, as streaks of pain darted around like pinballs inside my head. Tears were welling up behind my clinched eyelids, partly from the searing pain and partly from fatigue and disgust.

"I just want this night to be over," I whimpered.

Pressing the back of my head with one hand, I sat up slowly and leaned against the railing, wiping my bleary eyes with my t-shirt as I looked up at the dumpster and felt my heart stop in mid-beat.

Cassidy's nude body was hanging upside down, halfway out the dumpster door. Her fingernails scraped the asphalt pavement while her beautiful breasts swayed lifelessly at odd angles. A silver sequined G-string was entwined around her neck and tied in a perfect bow. Her eyes and mouth were open as if she were about to say something.

The events unfolding after that seemed to alternate between harsh reality and confused blur. About a dozen of Nashville's finest showed up and locked the front door. The customers were all told to take a seat and the girls were herded into the dressing room. The cops questioned everybody, taking statements, phone numbers and addresses from the clientele, half of whom were probably more afraid of the little lady back home finding out about their night on the town.

Two cops escorted Bear and the DJ into Aleta's office along

with Aleta herself, who had been quickly summoned from her beauty sleep at home. I was questioned by just about every blue suit in the building before being taken out and put in the back seat of a patrol car and told to "Sit tight."

Waiting alone in the blue-and-white, too numb to even think, I turned around to watch the swarm of cops taking pictures, making notes and searching the alley with flashlights. From where I sat I couldn't see Cassidy and that was fine with me. That final look was enough to last a lifetime. Even so, the reality of the situation hadn't really settled in. Maybe I was in shock, or maybe it was because I was just too tired and wired for this to be anything more than a bad dream. My body was crashing but my head was still revving at warp speed. Suddenly I was aware of the taste of blood in my mouth and I realized I'd been chewing on my lips. I needed a smoke in the worst way.

The sound of the engine turning over brought me back to earth and I jerked around to see a uniformed cop in the driver's seat. A young kid with buzz-cut hair, he couldn't have been a day over twenty-two.

"Where are we going?" I heard myself ask.

"Disneyland. Now shut up, Asshole. You have the right to remain silent and if I were you I'd do just that."

Even half-fried I could tell he'd waited a long time to use that line. As the car moved down the alley a sudden wave of panic brought me stone cold sober and fully aware of what was really going on, what all of this craziness was about, and more importantly, just where I fit in. I started to say something but decided instead to take Junior's advice.

When you look out at the world from a caged back seat everything moves in slow motion and you notice things, little everyday things you never really paid much attention to before. We drove down Church Street, a weathered business district that had been re-invented more times than Cher. As the red bricks drummed softly beneath the tires, I stared at a few vagrants curled up in office doorways behind shopping carts. At the corner of Fourth and Church, a lonesome cowboy stood smoking under a streetlamp, waiting for a new buddy. Slumped down in the back seat, with fatigue and weariness settling about my shoulders like an old damp Army blanket, I closed my eyes and listened to the intermittent droning in my head.

We parked behind the police station and the kid opened the back door of the cruiser. Since I hadn't been cuffed, I assumed this was going to be routine questioning despite Junior's abbreviated Miranda speech. He was strictly business though, right out of *Adam-12*, leading me up the steps and through the waiting room, past the front desk and down a short hallway to a door with a sign that read *'Property'*.

"In here," he pointed. "Empty your pockets."

The speed had finally begun to wear off, leaving me skittish and edgy, my nerves a knotted bundle of misfires and short-circuits. Not to mention the fact that Junior's attitude was beginning to wear thin.

"Let me guess," I chided, tossing my wallet and keys on the counter. "You were a squad leader in ROTC, right?"

He handed me a 3x5 card and a manila envelope.

"Fill this out and shut up."

This kid made Jack Webb look like a stand-up comic.

When I'm totally exhausted it doesn't take a whole helluva lot to piss me off. Besides, Junior was taking himself and his uniform way too seriously for my taste. I think what really bugged me was that he reminded me a lot of myself when I was a twenty-year old Marine Sergeant. But that was different. That was me.

I got right in his face.

"Listen, Sport, in case you don't remember, I'm here to try and help find whoever killed my friend. I'm not a criminal, understand, I'm a citizen, and unless you start treating me as such I'm gonna find the OD and see if we can't get you sent back to the academy for a week or two so you can bone up on your bedside manner."

When I get wound up, it's hard for me to stop.

"...So I suggest you take your snot-nosed attitude and find someone in charge for me to talk to, because I'm dead tired and I'm sick of looking at your baby-butt face. I haven't been charged with anything but if I have to be around you much longer I *will* be charged with *something*."

Junior stood very still and looked at me without blinking. I was sure he was thinking about what I'd just said, every word weighing like a brick of wisdom on his thick young mind. For the first time I noticed the gold name tag over the pocket of his dark blue shirt: BRUNDIDGE.

Finally, he spoke in a slow, mono-syllabic voice.

"How-does-Mur-der-One-sound-Ass-hole?"

And that's how I wound up in a holding cell at four in the morning with two sleeping Bloods curled up on the floor behind me like a pair of rattlesnakes. After what seemed like decades, I was taken out and escorted back through the main area and down another hallway to a small office and told to take a seat.

I looked around at the sparse room lit by pale fluorescent light. On the walls were two framed pictures, one of the mayor, and one of Johnny Majors, former coach at the University of

Tennessee. Scattered about were several other bits of orange UT memorabilia, the usual tacky stuff, coffee cups, notepads, etc.

In a moment the door opened and a big guy who looked more like an investment banker than a cop walked in carrying a Diet Pepsi and a blank yellow legal pad. He was taller than me, maybe six-three or so, bald, but carried himself as though he spent a lot of time and effort staying in shape. A dark thin mustache illuminated his tanned face, and I wondered for a second what he did to stay so dark. Probably a jogger, or maybe he owned a boat.

He sat down behind the desk and faced me, expressionless, like a proctologist looking at the first asshole of the day.

"Mr. Shepherd, I'm Detective Lyle."

He hadn't offered to shake hands. Maybe he didn't know I wasn't cuffed.

"I'm investigating the murder of Margaret Ellen Eskew. I'm told that you were recently involved with her, is that correct?"

It took a second or two to make the connection to Cassidy because she never used her real name, not even away from the club. She had always been adamant about being called 'Cassidy' and, since this is a town where twenty percent of the population has a stage name, it's really not all that unusual. But hearing Lyle refer to her by her given name made the situation all the more real. I squirmed a little when I spoke.

"Yes sir, we worked together. And we were involved romantically for a while."

"What happened?"

I could almost hear the cell door slamming shut.

"She broke it off."

"And how long ago was this, Mr. Shepherd?"

"A couple of weeks."

Lyle sat back in his chair and took a slow drink of Diet Pepsi. From another room nearby a radio was playing faintly. I could hear George Strait singing about making Amarillo by morning. It sounded like a swell idea.

"And just what was your reaction to this break-up, Jake? Is it all right if I call you Jake?"

"I'm sorry, what did you say?" I was still somewhere between Little Rock and Texarkana.

"I mean how did you take it? The break-up. What did you do? What did you say?"

"I said 'Okay'."

"You said, Okay?" he echoed, his creased eyelids squinting lizard-like. For the first time I realized that his pencil-thin moustache made him look like an Americanized version of Charlie Chan. And I still couldn't get past that tan. My guess was he probably *did* have a boat and was most likely a huge Jimmy Buffett fan. Parrotheads, I believe they're called now.

He stood up from his chair and leaned over the desk, his nose about three inches from mine.

"Let me get this straight," he whispered, his eyes welded into mine. "One of the most beautiful women in the entire city of Nashville, with one of the greatest bodies God ever created, this girl cuts you out of the kitty and you just say 'Okay'?"

"That's correct," I said, shifting in my seat and turning away from his hot breath. Lyle stayed in front of me and kept talking, getting louder with each word.

"Well, Jake, I hate to say it, but something tells me that either one of two things is happening here: One, you're lying. And two, or maybe and/or two- you just think I'm the dumbest sonofabitch in the world. Now which is it?"

"Detective Lyle," I began, carefully choosing the words, "I don't know you well enough to even venture a guess as to how dumb you are, but one thing I do know, Sir- I had nothing to do with Cassidy- I mean- Margaret Ellen's death. I want to know who did this as badly as you do."

He hovered over the desk, the bottom of his orange paisley tie almost touching his blotter. I cut my eyes to it and saw a coffee stain shaped like Florida near the bottom.

"Well now, I'm sure that'll be a great comfort to her family, Son. Maybe, if you're lucky, they'll overcome their grief long enough to nominate you for some kind of humanitarian award, model citizen that you are."

He sat back in his chair and wrote something on the legal pad, then clicked off his pen and stuck it in his shirt pocket.

"Jake, it looks to me like we're going to be here for a while. And fortunately, I just happen to have all the time in the world. So, I'll tell you what's going to happen: You are going to start at the beginning and tell me everything you know about the Eskew girl, and I am going to sit here and listen patiently to every word. And when you're finished, I'll go grab another soda and then I'll come back and you can tell me your story all over again just to make sure I don't forget anything and that you don't leave anything out."

It was hard to tell if he was playing good cop, bad cop, or both.

"And to be honest with you, Jake, I'd say there's a good chance you'll get to tell me your story at least two or three dozen times. You see, I believe the truth always bears out, especially through repetition. Now, you say you had nothing to do with this girl's death? I promise you, I want nothing more than to believe you. And I want to believe you so bad I'm going to give you all the time in the world to convince me. So let's get started."

And that's exactly what we did. I started at the beginning and told him everything I could remember about Cassidy, from the first day she walked into the club, how we got together, the break-up, how I had decided to get on with my life, everything I could remember down to the smallest detail, right up to the moment I looked up and saw her body dangling in front of me. Lyle never lost eye contact the whole time I was talking. When I finished, he half-smiled and adjusted himself in his chair.

"Tell me again."

So I told him the same story again, a little slower, but almost word for word. When it was over, he got up and left the room without saying anything.

It didn't take a mathematician to figure out I was in a world of hurt. All the conventional signs pointed to me and even I was hard-pressed to think of anyone who would want to harm Cassidy. We'd only been together a few weeks, but I felt as if I knew her pretty well, though admittedly, Cassidy was an actress and very adept at keeping her past and personal life vague. And I had purposely avoided asking too many questions so as not to appear to be prying. Her past was hers to deny if she wanted to. Besides, I didn't hang out in the highest social circles myself and over the years I've come to believe that almost everyone is running from something or somebody.

Lyle came back into the room with a fresh Diet Pepsi. I got mentally prepared for another round, then opted for a quick offense.

"Do I need a lawyer, Detective Lyle?"

"I don't know, Jake. Do you think you need a lawyer?"

"If you're gonna charge me with Cassidy's murder, then yes, I want a lawyer. And if you're not charging me, I want to go home. I've told you everything I know, twice, and I frankly don't know what else I can tell you, except that I'm in shock, I'm exhausted, I smell like garbage and I'm falling asleep on my feet. So, either lock me up or let me go home. Either way, I've said all I'm going to say without an attorney."

He looked at me for a long minute and then smirked as he rose from the desk.

"All right, Shepherd. You can go, for now. Just don't get lost on me because I'm sure we'll want to talk to you again real soon."

I knew that if a person stayed up long enough they could start to hallucinate.

"What?" I mumbled.

Lyle popped me on the head with his legal pad but I was so punch drunk I didn't feel it. The door opened again and there stood Brundidge, beaming like the President of the Sophomore Class.

"Officer Brundidge will take you home," Lyle said, then added, "Remember, don't take any sudden vacations."

I got up and followed Brundidge out the door without answering. The ride home was mercifully quick and uneventful, and I got out of the car in front of the feed store without saying a word to Brundidge.

"You're welcome, Asshole," he blurted, driving away.

Across the river the sun was already up and a warm sheet of humid air washed over my face. Electrical wires hummed overhead, and behind me engines and generators coughed and sputtered to life as horns and sirens called from the freeway, the first sounds of the city yawning and stretching to meet the day.

I stumbled up the stairs and into the shower, then fell into bed without drying off. It felt like ninety degrees in the apartment, but I didn't care. I slept hard.

CHAPTER 4

"Wake up, Boy. Come sit down."

My Great-Great Grandfather is calling to me in a dream. I see my ten-year-old self standing barefoot in the dirt yard, wearing cut-off jeans and no t-shirt. I step onto the porch and take my place sitting cross-legged at his feet. He nods and takes a deep drag from his elkhorn pipe before blowing a smoke ring that floats above my head and beyond.

"Sumu onosu numeka nana quane ynas...Once, long ago when we were all the same, Coyote was trotting through a canyon on his long journey home when he saw a flash of light up above him. He sneaked up the canyon for a closer look.

"What he saw almost blinded him, so he squinted until his eyes got used to seeing the forbidden parts of the two females he saw squatting on the ground. This was back in the days when the female private parts still had teeth. The flash of light Coyote saw came from the sun reflecting on those teeth. It was forbidden to look on the private parts of a female in those days."

He winked at me as I saw myself sitting motionless, eyes wide open and mouth agape, hanging on his next word.

"The two females that Coyote was watching were eating boiled rabbit. As they stripped the meat off the rabbit bones, they would throw the bones underneath themselves, and the second set of teeth would devour the bones."

He made a loud grinding noise with his teeth while I sat unbreathing, face cupped in my hands, elbows cemented to the insides of my knees.

Well," he continued, "Coyote was fascinated at what was going on, so he decided to throw a piece of thorny rose bush under one of the females. The stick was quickly chewed up, thorns and all. Coyote said, "Hea-te suda ma-ni," which means, Oh my goodness, how awful! Coyote then decided to throw a piece of shale rock under the females. From his hiding place he aimed carefully and- BANG! When Coyote hit his target all the teeth from the private parts broke out as they crunched down upon the rocks. And to this day, the female private parts have remained toothless."

As always, the billowing cloud of smoke accompanied by loud ringing laughter, ringing... ring...ring...

It was my phone. I picked it up and held it to my ear.

"Hello, Mr. Shepherd? ...Mr. Shepherd?"

If I'd been conscious, I'd have never answered but, lost in the dream, it jolted me awake and I picked it up out of reflex. Old habits are hard to break, and I guess all those years of waiting for Opportunity to break down and dial my number had left their mark.

"Is this Mr. Shepherd?" the female voice asked again.

I was already tired of being called Mr. Shepherd. It seemed nothing good ever followed that salutation.

"Yeah."

"Mr. Shepherd, my name is Charlotte Eskew. I'm Margaret Ellen's sister."

Again, it took a moment to make the connection to Cassidy. Even though Detective Lyle had referred to her by that name about a thousand times the night before, I still felt everyone was talking about some stranger I'd never met and yet was expected to know. I took a couple of deep breaths to get my brain in the proper firing order and shake off the remnants of the Singing Wolf dream.

"Mr. Shepherd?"

"Yes, I...I'm sorry...what can I do for you?"

She sounded nervous but determined as she continued.

"Mr. Shepherd, my parents and I would like to talk with you. We came to Nashville yesterday to identify my sister's body and we were hoping to sit down and speak with you before we drive home."

The fog had begun to lift inside my head. Something she said caused me to sit up and look around the room.

Yesterday?

It was daylight outside. I looked at the clock beside the bed and it read 7:35 a.m. My God, I had almost slept the clock around.

"Listen, Miss Eskew... I've already told the police everything I know. I...I'm sure I can't begin to understand how you must feel right now, but believe me...I swear...I had nothing to do with your sister's death. We had a very special relationship for a while but it was over and we were both getting on with our lives. You have to believe me, I wouldn't have harmed her for the world."

"We know that, Mr. Shepherd."

I wasn't expecting that reaction and it threw me momentarily. Sincerity will do that to you, especially if you're not around it that often.

"Mr. Shepherd, we're staying at the Music City Motel on Nolensville Road. We're getting ready to check out but there's a coffee shop across the street. If you could meet us there in an hour I promise we'll only take a few minutes of your time."

The grief in her voice was turning into a plea. I didn't want to hear her ask again.

"Of course, I will," I said. "I'll be there in an hour."

"Thank you, Mr. Shepherd, we do appreciate it. We'll see you then. Goodbye."

After making coffee I shaved, showered and dressed, then looked in the mirror and wondered if the Eskews would be able to tell I'd been asleep for an entire day. I started for the door but stopped cold when I reached the main living area of the huge, one-room apartment.

On the floor was an empty quart bottle of George Dickel. Scattered around were several pieces of paper torn from a legal pad, each containing several lines of unintelligible verse. But when I looked on the sofa and saw the splintered remains of my beautiful 1969 Martin D-35 guitar, my memory came rushing back in nightmarish color.

I hadn't slept the clock around after all. I barely remembered waking up sometime after dark the night before and plunging into the Dickel. There were flashes of myself ranting, raving, pacing the floor in blind madness. But that was all. Everything else was a mottled blur.

Picking up the busted Martin by the neck, the worn bronze strings and pieces of wood dangling like a cheap wind chime, I kissed the headstock of the guitar and gently laid it back on the sofa as if it were a drowned child. For a moment I thought of all the songs I'd written and played on it over the past twenty-five years, and I was reminded once again that all we can really lay claim to in this life are the memories. And my head was suddenly reeling with memories- memories of my precious guitar, memories of last night, and memories of Margaret Ellen Eskew. Heading down the stairs, I felt a weary loneliness settling around my heart.

My old Eldorado was sitting in the parking lot covered with dust, waiting patiently where I'd left it a few days before. Jezebel's was only a few blocks away, so it was always easier to take a cab or walk to work. Consequently, the car would often sit for days without being driven.

I'd bought the Caddy used with the first money from "Sub-Urban Cowboy." She was a real head-turner in her day: shiny black with a big 500 cubic inch V-8 and an eight-track tape player that still worked. Over the years she'd stayed true to me and never failed to run, and in return I kept her well maintained, changed the oil regularly, tune-ups, whatever she needed. The dust blanket was the price paid for living downtown without covered parking.

Heading south on Fourth Avenue, I needed music to ease the shakes. A friend of mine is a DJ at WSM radio, the home of the Grand Ole Opry, and in return for a couple of favors, he'd been gracious enough to put together about a half-dozen tapes from the vast library of music at the radio station. He'd started with the 1939 version of Bill Monroe's "Muleskinner Blues" and gone through more than fifty years of the best of country music. But Charlie had gotten in a hurry making the tapes and he hadn't labeled them, so I never knew just what I was going to hear when I put one in the tape deck. Fine with me. It's all good.

Reaching under the seat, I grabbed the first tape that touched my fingers and popped it in. Dave Dudley had just pulled out of Pittsburgh and was heading down the Eastern Seaboard after "Six Days on the Road." I hit the gas as I shot over the railroad tracks past Chestnut Street and almost went airborne, doing my level best to outrun the blues.

The Music City Motel was a relic of the past, small, run-down, the kind of place you can rent for thirty bucks a night but nobody ever stays that long. Back in the Fifties and Sixties, when the Opry was still downtown at the Ryman Auditorium, no doubt the joint was booked solid every Friday and Saturday night. But then the interstates came and the Opry dropped the rhinestone suits and put on a suit and tie and moved east a few miles outside of town where it still resides today.

Since Cassidy never talked about her family, I knew very little about them. She would only say she was from a small town in Georgia and that most of her relatives were still back there. I'd assumed she'd either grown up dirt poor, or worse, suffered a terrible childhood that she wanted to escape and put behind her. I never questioned her. It was her past and if she wanted to lose it, she could. After all, very few debutantes run away to become strippers, Aleta Thomas being the one known exception.

I picked out the Eskew family as soon as I walked in the door of the coffee shop, the three of them sitting at a table in the rear, away from the other customers. Mr. Eskew rose as I approached the table. He spoke without smiling or offering his hand.

"Mr. Shepherd, I'm Walter Eskew. This is my wife, Esther, and my daughter Charlotte. Thank you for coming. Please sit down."

I acknowledged the ladies and took my seat in the remaining chair. A worn-out waitress appeared instantly at my side to place a cup of coffee in front of me along with a menu, which I handed back to her with a nod and a Thank you.

Walter Eskew was tall and lanky, probably in his late fifties, with thinning grey hair and long, yellowed teeth. His skin was ruddy and his features were stark, like so many deep-country people whose lives are spent in an endless day-to-day struggle for two things: survival and salvation. His charcoal suit was cheap but neatly pressed and his white shirt and blue tie were worn but clean. With his deep-set, dark eyes he looked like a man to whom Life had given nothing, a man who had worked hard for everything he'd ever had and expected nothing more.

Mrs. Eskew was a surprise. She had a strong face, with high cheekbones suggesting perhaps third generation Cherokee, pellucid violet eyes and full lips. She was probably in her mid-forties and her simple, black cotton dress couldn't hide the fact that she was still a beautiful woman. Her hands were tanned and not delicate, with long, capable fingers, though her clean, unpolished nails were just slightly longer than you might expect. She wore little or no makeup and her shiny, black hair was tied back with a silver clasp. It was easy to see where Cassidy got her looks.

Charlotte was also a natural beauty who, surprisingly, resembled neither of her parents except for the obvious height she had inherited from her father. She sat erect and made no attempt to hide her stature as many women might have. Her long, auburn hair fell to her shoulders in gentle curls, framing a soft, porcelain face that wore the drained, weary look of the bereaved. Her pale green eyes were reddened, and she dabbed at the corners with a blue tissue. She, too, wore a simple black dress although evidently more expensive than her mother's. I caught myself momentarily wondering about her legs and was immediately ashamed.

She was the first to break the awkward silence, getting straight to the point.

"How well did you know my sister, Mr. Shepherd?"

I told them the whole story, taking careful pains to refer to Cassidy as Margaret Ellen. Speaking slowly, thinking before each sentence and trying to tell them everything while at the same time skirting references to the club or Cassidy's chosen profession, I talked about all the laughter and joy she'd brought me and the sadness that followed our breakup. Perhaps I whitewashed it a little, but this was a grieving family who deserved to be spared any further distress.

When I finished, Walter Eskew leaned over the table, drilling a hole through me with those deep-set eyes.

"Weren't you the last one to see her alive?"

"No, I was busy working and only caught a glimpse of her that night. To tell you the truth we hadn't really spoken in a couple of days."

Charlotte put her hand on her father's arm, an act that seemed to calm him almost immediately.

"Mr. Shepherd," she said, turning to me, "we didn't call you here to question you. I'm sure the police have done that sufficiently, and if they thought you were a serious suspect I doubt you'd be walking the streets right now."

I could've challenged that statement but I let it slide. I knew they'd already met with Lyle and I couldn't picture him portraying me as a harbinger of innocence. However, if Lyle didn't want to tell them I was the prime suspect, then I certainly wasn't about to. I still had the rest of the day to live through.

"Charlotte," I began, "Mr. and Mrs. Eskew, I can't begin to imagine what you all are going through right now. I've lost someone who was very dear to me, someone who came into my life for a few weeks and gave it a whole new meaning, and for that I'll always be thankful.

"But you've lost a part of your family, and I want you to know she was a wonderful person, with a heart as big as the universe. I truly feel that I'm a better person for having known her, and I promise I'll never forget Margaret Ellen for as long as I live. I just wish there was something I could say or do to make things easier for you."

Walter Eskew sat back in his chair and looked at me for a minute without speaking. He took a sip of coffee, then reached into his coat pocket and withdrew a familiar red tin of Prince Albert tobacco. Flipping open the top of the flat tin with his thumb, he pulled out a small pack of Tops rolling papers, opened them, and deftly drew out a tiny paper. Holding the paper in his left hand, he sprinkled a thin line of tobacco across it, licked the glue, then twisted it quickly with his fingers before bringing it to his lips. He placed the red tobacco tin back in his coat pocket and brought out a large wooden kitchen match, which he struck with his thumbnail.

I hadn't seen anyone roll smokes that facilely since my great-grandfather. In a moment the air at the table was full of the harsh smoke and for a split-second I was back on the dimlit porch so many years earlier, listening to Singing Wolf telling tales and teaching me about the Indians. Charlotte and Mrs. Eskew waved the wafting smoke from their faces but said nothing, waiting for Walter Eskew to speak.

"Mr. Shepherd, you talk of Margaret Ellen as if we should all be proud of her."

His words caught me off guard and yanked me back to the present.

"Now understand, Sir, I loved my daughter, but the truth is, I ain't a bit proud of her or anything she's done in the last few years. Margaret Ellen chose to walk the Devil's path and now he's taken her straight down the road to Hell, which is what happens when one turns their back on the Holy Spirit."

Charlotte and Mrs. Eskew looked as if they wanted to speak but knew better.

"Mr. Shepherd, I'm a man of God, and a great part of me wants to admit that my daughter died, not two days ago, but two years ago when she left home to follow Satan. Right now she's standing before God, and he, in His wisdom, will decide whether or not she will enter the Kingdom of Heaven."

I wasn't in the mood for a sermon but his voice carried a different tone, one of solemn regret, a pointed failure within himself. He certainly wasn't preaching.

"Be that as it may," he went on, "as the son of my own father, and as a man who dearly loved his child, I will not rest until her killer is punished."

He stubbed out the remainder of his homemade cigarette as his words settled about my shoulders with the fading Prince Albert smoke. Charlotte leaned toward me, her voice almost a whisper.

"Mr. Shepherd, a few weeks ago my sister sent us a great deal of money. Up until then she'd always sent home at least a hundred dollars a week, every week without fail. She told us she was modeling in department stores and traveling some. Margaret Ellen always had big dreams and we didn't think, or didn't want to think, that she was doing anything different. Then...like I said, out of the blue she sends home all this money."

Mrs. Eskew finally spoke for the first time.

"We may live in the sticks, Mr. Shepherd, but we know you don't make that kind of money in department stores."

Her voice was husky, almost sultry, like Lauren Bacall's. It fit her face but not her circumstance.

Walter Eskew stood up from the table.

"It's the Devil's money," he swore, as two or three tables turned to look in our direction. I realized I hadn't even touched my coffee.

"Daddy is right," agreed Charlotte. "It *is* the Devil's money, and we don't want it.

She placed a small manila envelope beside my cup of cold coffee.

"You take this money, Mr. Shepherd, and you use it to find out who killed Margaret Ellen. And when this runs out you call us and we'll get more. But, Mr. Shepherd- you find them and you see to it that they're punished for what they did, not only to her but to this family."

She was crying as she took her father's arm and led him from the table, leaving me alone with Mrs. Eskew.

I wanted to call out after them, tell them that I knew nothing, that I had no idea how to start, where to look or who to look for, and I was about to do just that when Mrs. Eskew reached over and gripped my hand in hers, the native beauty in her face now framed by a look of fierce resolve.

"Mr. Shepherd, my husband is a man of true faith. He believes in the Resurrection and follows the way of the Lord. But I feel I must tell you that before he found Salvation, he was the meanest, smartest, and hardest working bootlegger in North Georgia, and to this day he has a profound distrust of the police. He would not tell you this, but in his absence, I can assure you this family believes in an eye for an eye."

Her grip tightened, and I couldn't have averted my eyes from hers if I'd wanted to.

"Now, I don't expect you to believe or understand this," she went on. "But I am in tune with the other side, and I know that my daughter's soul is not at rest. Charlotte wanted to hire a private investigator, someone she knows and trusts, and we had all agreed initially, until your name came to me in a dream. I believe you can do this, Mr. Shepherd. I was told that you could."

"Mrs. Eskew, I...you should listen to Charlotte-"

"-I know," she interrupted, a faint smile fanning across her lips. "It's taken many years, but my family has learned to be patient when I feel strongly about something. Spirits don't lie, Mr. Shepherd. Nor do they make mistakes."

She picked up the envelope and placed it in my free hand.

"Find the man who killed my daughter, Mr. Shepherd. Please."

I watched as she walked outside to join her husband and Charlotte, watched them all as they piled into an old, dusty Chrysler sedan, drab green with dried red clay forever caked around the outside of the tires. They might have come from the hills of Georgia, but they drove away as stately as the Kennedys and not one of them looked back.

Once in the Caddy, I opened the envelope and found two stacks of bills wrapped in a scented sheet of pink stationery that read:

Dear Mama and Daddy,

Use this money to make some dreams come true.
I've met someone special and, in a way, he reminds me of you, Daddy. Don't worry though, I'm still your little girl and I'm still going to be Miss America.

Love to all, Margaret Ellen

Then I looked at the two stacks of neatly wrapped bills: Twenty-thousand dollars.

CHAPTER 5

I took the money home and hid it in a safe place, then spent the rest of the morning riding around trying to collect my thoughts. Driving east to Percy Priest Dam, the radio played softly as Claude King warned me not to go on "Wolverton Mountain." I couldn't help wondering if perhaps Walter Eskew didn't bear more than a faint resemblance to Clifton Clowers, the fearsome, protective father Merle Kilgore must have had in mind when he wrote the song.

Out on the lake the sailboats, skiers and jet skis were fighting for squatters' rights, gamely trying to breathe life into the waning days of summer while I sat on the fender smoking and thinking about that last night at the club. I knew I hadn't seen

Cassidy leave but I also knew that meant nothing. I'd been so far in the weeds behind the bar she could have left and come back a half-dozen times and I wouldn't have noticed.

Something else was bothering me too, something that had been gnawing at the back of my mind ever since it all went down. As a rule, dancers only left the club in the middle of a shift for one reason: to turn a trick. It was hard to picture Cassidy in that role, and I thought I'd been around her enough to feel pretty sure about that. Then again, I'd also been around enough to know anything is possible, and even I couldn't argue the fact that a great deal of Cassidy's life was a perpetuated mystery.

"That's private property," was an answer I'd heard more than once, whenever my curiosity would overrule my good sense and I'd start probing around in her head.

The logical place to start was by asking a few questions, so I drove to Cassidy's apartment to talk to her roommate, Heather. It was early afternoon so there was an even chance she'd be out of bed.

Heading west down Woodmont Boulevard, I hung a left on Granny White Pike, passing David Lipscomb University, a Christian college in a beautiful neighborhood of quaint houses just inside the Green Hills district. At first, I'd thought it strange that Cassidy would choose to live there, but I soon realized it was the perfect place for her: a world away from the neon lights, with trees, kids, and sidewalks, dogs, cats, grass and birds, things that I, too, had begun to miss after too many years of living downtown.

Heather's beat up Dodge sat parked in the driveway, it was either rust-colored or covered in rust, I couldn't tell which. I've always wondered why strippers, most of whom make anywhere from one to a few grand a week cash, always drive such miserable cars. Probably because they are supporting some worthless husband or boyfriend or girlfriend who's spending their money faster than they can make it. There are a few exceptions, of course, and Cassidy was one of them. Her shiny white Lexus Coupe had been impounded the night of the murder and was probably at that moment being dismantled for clues.

Heather came to the door in a purple silk kimono. She looked like she hadn't been awake very long.

"Jake?" She seemed surprised to see me. And I thought I caught a flash of fear in her eyes.

"I need to talk to you, Heather. Can I come in?"

She hesitated, then unlocked the door without saying anything and went back to the sofa where she had apparently been watching TV. She curled up on one end and I sat at the other since there was no other chair in the room.

I didn't know Heather all that well, even though we had worked together for some time. She was the quiet type, almost shy, but possessed of a centerfold's body and wild, peroxide-blonde hair that flowed down her back and made her doe eyes and heart-shaped face all the more sensual. Up close, her features were somewhat hard, but from a distance you could swear she was a homecoming queen until she turned around and you saw the intricate, multi-colored Harley-Davidson wings tattooed from one shoulder blade to the other across her otherwise flawless back. As far as tattoos go the artwork was perfect, but I'd always thought it was overkill, like putting a nipple ring on Venus de Milo.

"Are you okay, Jake?"

"I'm about as well as can be expected, Heather. How about you, are you holding up all right?"

"Yeah, I guess," she replied, without taking her eyes off the television. "I don't know, it's like there's this big fog around everything, like it's all just some kind of awful dream. You know, I still don't think it's really hit me that she's gone. I try not to think about it and yet, it's the only thing I think about. Yesterday I went through the house and picked up all of her things and put them in her room but it didn't help that much. I...I just feel like I should be doing something but I don't know what."

"I think those are pretty normal feelings, Heather."

Her face was still glued to the TV, but I could see the beginnings of crocodile tears making their way down her pale cheek before she broke down and put her arms around me, crying in hard, shaking sobs for several minutes.

"I'm scared, Jake. I haven't been able to sleep since it happened. I have to wait until daylight and then take a pill so I can sleep a little bit but I'm turning into a nervous wreck. Do the police have any suspects besides-"

She stopped suddenly and covered her mouth.

"Besides me? No, I don't think so."

"I'm sorry, Jake, I-"

"It's okay, Heather. I was the one who found her. We'd been seeing each other and then we weren't. Not to mention our little scene that night in the bar. As far as the cops are concerned, I had a motive. People get sent to the joint on less evidence than that every day."

Heather sat up straight and wiped her eyes.

"I know you didn't do it, Jake. I told them that."

"I know it, you know it, and I believe her folks know it, or at least they say they do. I just wish the boys down at Homicide would catch on and start looking for whoever really did this thing."

"Her sister called me yesterday."

"Charlotte?"

"Yeah, Charlotte. She said they would send someone to get Cassidy's things in a few days, said they were meeting with the police before they left to go back today. She also asked me about you, Jake."

She started to sniffle again, and I reached up and put my fingers against her cheek. It seemed to calm her.

"It's all right, Heather, I've met the Eskews. I'm sure the police have already been here, right?"

"They were here the morning after she died," she nodded, "They went through the whole house, took fingerprints and everything, and questioned me for about an hour. They spent a lot of time in her room, really trashed the place, and took a big box full of her stuff with them. I told them everything I knew about her, which wasn't much, I mean, Christ, we'd only been roommates for a couple of months. But to tell you the truth, I don't think they believed me."

"Don't take it personally," I said. "That's just their nature. Cops get lied to so much they eventually start to think the whole world is bullshitting them."

"Yeah, well..." she said, and turned back to the tv.

"Heather, you've got to help me. If someone doesn't find Cassidy's killer soon the cops are going to nail me just so they can sweep this under the rug and say, 'Case Closed.' Cassidy was a stripper, not some banker's daughter, and they want to wrap this up quickly and move on. They're not blessed with a lot of sympathy for girls like her."

She winced, and the look in her eyes told me I'd just taken first place in the annual foot-in-the-mouth awards.

"I'm sorry," I apologized. "That's not how I meant it, but I need to ask you some questions and I need for you to answer them as best you can. You can begin by telling me everything you told the police."

Still sniffling, she got up and went into the kitchen and came back with two Cokes. She sat back down and began telling me how she had met Cassidy at the club, how they had hit it off and become friends and eventually decided to get a place together. I wasn't surprised when she finished talking and I found myself with no new information.

"Was Cassidy seeing someone else?"

"No," she shook her head, "I don't think so."

"Don't try to protect my feelings, Heather. If she was seeing someone else, I need to know."

"I said *No*," she blurted, loud enough that I got the point.

"All right, then answer me this. Was she turning tricks?"

She turned abruptly and slapped me so hard I dropped my Coke. My jaw burned like dry ice.

"You Bastard-"

I grabbed her hand before she could hit me again.

"Look, Heather, I'm sorry, but I need some straight answers right now so I can try and put this thing together."

Without speaking, she rose and went back into the kitchen, returning with a towel to mop up the spilled drink. She was still crying, but softly under her breath.

"You can ask me all the questions you want, Jake, and I may or may not have the answers you're looking for, but I do know one thing," she said, wiping at the floor. "I know that Cassidy was crazy about you. You and I both know she wasn't like the rest of those girls in the club. She was miles above them. Most of those skanks are two steps away from working at some jack-shack on Eighth Avenue. Cassidy was class, that's why she was the Queen. Guys could see it a mile away and they went for it."

She was right, of course. I remembered how she could walk through a crowd of drunks completely untouched, remembered seeing men push and shove just for the privilege of sticking a bill in her garter. But the thought gave me more than a few mixed feelings.

"Then why did she all of a sudden stop seeing me?"

"I don't know why, Jake. Maybe Aleta told her to cool it. I know she called her on the carpet a couple of times for some petty shit- you know how some of those girls are, always bitching about something. You don't get to be Queen of the House without making a few enemies along the way."

"Cassidy never mentioned any problems with Aleta," I said, a little surprised at the idea.

"I never understood it," she resumed, "but Aleta just always seemed to have some kind of hard-on for Cassidy, which is strange considering how much money she brought into the place. My guess is that it was probably jealousy, maybe a little bit of the age thing too. Aleta always had to be in control, and that was hard to do with Cassidy. Who knows, maybe Aleta came on to her and Cassidy turned her down."

Heather lit a cigarette and sat back down on the sofa, waiting for the look of surprise on my face that wasn't long in coming.

"You mean-"

"You know how Aleta is, her whole life is a well-kept secret. Not that it matters, but sooner or later word gets around, even though in this business it's not a big deal."

My mind flashed on a mental picture of Aleta and Cassidy in naked embrace. I pushed the image out of my thoughts, but it took longer than I'd like to admit.

"Heather, do you think Aleta or one of the girls could've had anything to do with Cassidy's death?"

"Are you kidding? All Aleta would have to do is pick up the phone and it could get done like *that*," she said, snapping her fingers for effect. "For that matter, all she'd have to do is tell Bear and he'd do it without a second thought. The sonofabitch is so loyal you'd think she was his mother, for God's sake. That whole situation has always seemed more than a little weird to me."

What she said made sense and I chided myself for being so far out of the loop in the club, although that was the way I had wanted it, totally removed from all the gossip and silly politics. Always the loner, yeah, that's me.

"And as far as the rest of those bitches," she went on, "half of them are living with ex-cons, so who's to say? Some dude's old lady ain't bringing home as much as she used to... well, stranger things have happened, that's all I'm saying."

"What about Afro-Dite?" I asked.

"What about her?"

"Well, for starters, she made threats the night Cassidy laid her out. And you and I both know she's capable of killing somebody."

"Maybe, Jake, but I don't know. Afro-Dite blows a lot of smoke, but the truth is, I don't think she'd want to risk going back inside. She's got a baby now, and an old man."

"She seems lethal enough to me," I said. "I know I sure wouldn't want her holding my markers."

I had a hard time picturing Afro-Dite as June Cleaver, changing diapers, carpooling and PTA.

"But don't forget one thing," she added. "Afro-Dite wasn't working that night. I know that for a fact because I heard one of the girls say she was out with a sick kid."

"That's not an alibi," I said. "It just puts her outside the club, which only makes it easier to get Cassidy lured outside and then do the job. See what I mean?"

She nodded her head half-heartedly and put out her half-finished smoke.

"Like I said, Jake, anything is possible. I don't owe Afro-Dite squat but I don't think she did it. I don't know, it's just a gut feeling."

"Heather, did you tell the cops everything you just told me?"

"Hell no- you think I want to end up dead too? They can find whoever did it without my help. I learned a long time ago nothing good ever comes from talking to cops."

"As far as motives go, I don't think Aleta had any reason to kill Cassidy," I said. "Jealousy is a strong emotion but I don't think she'd kill because of it. And I sure don't think she had anything to do with Cassidy leaving me. Heck, Aleta barely knew my name and she always looked at me as just the lowest form of hired help. Believe me, I noticed."

"You're probably right but there's another thing to think about, Jake. Maybe Cassidy just needed to regroup because she was losing sight of her goal. You know what big plans she had. Christ, hardly a day went by that I didn't have to listen to her tell me she was gonna be Miss America, whatever-the-hell that meant."

Then her eyes narrowed and she leaned in closer.

"Or you know, Jake... maybe it was because she was afraid she could never hold on to you. Maybe deep down inside she knew she could never really be the person you needed her to be. You talk about 'girls like us'-"

"Heather, I didn't mean that-"

"-Let me finish," she demanded, rising in front of me, hands on her hips, lips trembling.

"You talk about girls like us? Let me tell you a little bit about girls like us. We start out with great big dreams just like all the other girls, the only difference is most of us are carrying around some kind of dirty baggage the other girls don't have to worry about, but that's okay because we've been carrying it around a long time and we pretty much deal with it because we know that's just the way it is.

"But there's something else that makes us different from everybody else, Jake. We know, deep down inside, that it's all up to us, just us, and that anything we get out of this rotten life is gonna come to us because we went out and got it ourselves with little or no help from anybody.

"That's why most dancers say there are only three types of men: suckers, tightwads, and assholes. The suckers throw money at you, the tightwads want it all for nothing-"

"-And the assholes?"

"They're the ones you end up supporting."

Her face was glowing red as she stood there shaking, in defiance not only of me but society in general. I felt like a jerk but I truly never meant to put her in the position of having to defend herself or her way of life. I mean, who am I to point fingers at anybody?

She sat back down on the sofa, calmer now, but not quite finished with me.

"The only problem, Jake, is when you meet the real deal, the genuine article, if you know what I mean. When you meet the right guy, it don't matter if he ain't got fifteen cents to his name. If his heart and soul are real, and you know it, then somehow you just never feel like you're good enough, no matter what you tell yourself. You start to see yourself for who you really are and you get scared. You just know something's gonna happen or someone from the past is gonna pop up unexpectedly and you eventually realize you're living every moment on a tightrope.

"So you do the only thing you can to hang on to some tiny piece of your self-respect- you bail. You bail out and go back to the same old bullshit game you've been playing since you ran away the first time. Think what you want, Jake, but that's what it's really like for girls like us."

I sat there looking at her, digesting everything she'd said and trying, at the same time, to apply it to Cassidy. I'd heard a condensed and much sweeter version of the tale from Cassidy herself, though at the time I'd just taken it for a cop- out. And while I never pictured us with the white house and picket fence, I'd always felt we had more going for us than just a month of good times. But hearing it from Heather put it in a different light.

"Did you see Cassidy leave the club that night?"

She shook her head and smoothed the kimono along the outside of her thighs.

"No, but as you know, we were slammed. I must have done fifty table dances. I made over eight hundred bucks that night. I don't know when she left, but she obviously did at some point."

"Did you notice her spending a lot of time with any one person in particular?"

"Not that I remember, no."

By now I was convinced Heather knew as little, or even less than I did.

"Do you mind if I take a look in her room?"

"Help yourself," she said, motioning toward the hallway. "Like I said, the cops left it in a mess."

Since I'm not a cop I didn't really know what to look for. Homicide would have taken any letters, diaries, notebooks or anything remotely personal and it was doubtful I'd find anything they might have overlooked.

The mattress and box springs were overturned and tossed across the bed frame. I pushed them back into place and sat down on the bed. The drawer from the nightstand was lying in the floor, empty except for some rubber bands, paper clips, and the working half of a Bic pen. In the bottom shelf of the nightstand sat a stack of *Cosmopolitan* and *Glamour* magazines, about the only thing I'd ever seen Cassidy read.

One night, when we'd both had a little to drink, she told me again about her dream of becoming Miss America, that it was all she had wanted to be ever since she could remember. The sad part is that she might well have done it, or at least come close, if she'd just had someone who believed in her, someone to help her and guide her when she was younger. I recalled what Heather had said about all little girls starting out with big dreams, and I remembered Walter Eskew and imagined what a man like himself would think of such ideas from his baby daughter.

Leafing through the magazines one by one, I began to feel closer to Cassidy with each turning page. But when I picked up the third one, a small, white envelope fell out. Bending down to retrieve it I could see the big blue letters in the upper left-hand corner. I opened the phone bill and began looking at the long-distance calls, all three pages of them. Except for a couple of calls to Ellijay, Georgia, most of them were to the same number in Atlanta, and all of them had been made within the last two or three weeks, beginning around the time she had broken things off with me.

So, there *was* someone else. It hurt a lot more than I wanted to admit, but at least it was a place to start.

I put the bill in my pocket, said goodbye to Heather and left.

By early evening I'd gone through four or five beers and twice as many cigarettes, the phone bill staring up at me from the coffee table the whole time, as if daring me to do something. I had my other guitar, a cheap Japanese job I kept around in case someone dropped by to pick. The strings were long dead, but I managed to get it somewhat in tune or, as we like to say, 'close enough for country.' I played some familiar chords, not conscious of where it was all going, just playing out of habit while my mind wandered around the room.

Without thinking, I dropped into a little finger-picking pattern and slowed it down to let myself get lost, then realized I'd been half-singing "No Place to Fall," an old Townes Van Zandt song that Cassidy dearly loved. The song had been part of our ritual on the nights she stayed over. Always, before turning in, she would take out one of my old Steve Young albums and play his soulful, mournful version of the song while we held each other and waltzed tenderly across the creaking plank floor.

Leaning back on the sofa, I played and sang to myself as more scenes of Cassidy and me spun through my head.

I remembered one of the last nights we'd spent together. We'd had dinner at Laurell's Oyster Bar, then spent the rest of the evening strolling the sidewalks past the shops, bars, and gaudy souvenir joints as we both lamented the impending demise of my cozy little neighborhood.

Cassidy hailed a horse and buggy, handed the driver a fifty and told him to drive until it ran out. The shiny black and gold carriage pulled us over the pavement as we settled into the back seat and drank in the humid, downtown summer night. Soon she was asleep in my arms and I promised him another fifty to ride us around for another hour while I held her and watched her sleep.

That night is my favorite memory of Cassidy. I got up to get another beer, then came back and purposely avoided looking at the phone bill, which by now was blinking at me like a cheap motel sign. I smoked a joint while fumbling for a legal pad and pen, although I knew the move was more posture than purpose and I probably wouldn't be writing anything, at least nothing worthwhile. I was too empty for words. Sometimes though, you just have to sit with your guitar in your lap and go through the motions, something I'd gotten very good at over the past few years.

Deep inside I knew that I hadn't been 'in love' with Cassidy, knew it just as surely as I knew that I did love her, the way you can only love someone when you know it won't be forever, when you can hear the clock ticking as you look at them, watch them walk, laugh, and live, every precious second you're together, tick-tick-tick. Pretty soon you get used to the ticking but it's never too far out of earshot, so that when the end finally comes you're almost as relieved as you are saddened, a state of acceptance by the doomed, like the condemned man walking the last mile who wants to sprint the last few yards to eternity.

I drank several more beers, took a few strong pulls from a fresh Jack Daniels bottle, and before long the guitar changed from an instrument to a crutch, eventually becoming an actual extension of my body. I leaned on it, clung to it, and in return it kept my tired and wounded soul from pouring out onto the floor like dirty mop water, the dawn and my heart both breaking as I nodded off.

CHAPTER 6

The sun was already high and hot when I came to the next morning, swearing as always to begin a serious search for new and healthier habits. I made coffee but took two Alka Seltzers, a handful of Advil and a cold shower before I had the first cup. By the middle of the second cup, I was steady enough to dial the Atlanta number.

It rang twice before a recording came on telling me the number had been disconnected. In all honesty, I was just as relieved as I was disappointed, so I poured more coffee, paced back and forth around the loft, and tried to figure my next move. That's when I thought of Faye.

Faye-What-City Weatherby was one of the regulars at

Mulligan's Pub and a couple other local joints on Second Avenue. She was an operator for BellSouth and could be found almost every afternoon between five and six at the end of the bar, having her two drafts before going home to a husband that, as far as I knew, no one had ever seen. She was a genuine southern Good-Ole-Girl, with a Tennessee drawl as thick as honey. A green-eyed beauty with absolutely no pretense, she wore her straw-colored hair long and straight, like an homage to the late sixties and early seventies, a time and place she held in devout reverence. She claimed to have attended over a hundred Grateful Dead concerts and I believed her.

With Faye, world history over the past thirty years was tabulated and earmarked by concert dates from around the country. If you asked her where she was the night John Lennon was shot, she might say, "Oh, I remember that, we were driving to a Lynyrd Skynyrd concert in Johnson City and heard about it on the radio. Man, they put on a helluva show that night, did "Free Bird" for forty-five minutes."

That's the way it was with Faye. Elvis' death was tied to a Jethro Tull show in Atlanta. B.B. King would forever be associated with the Berlin Wall. The Soviet Union crumbled as Clapton played "Layla" in Little Rock. Faye wasn't a groupie, it's just that she had somehow never left that place and time when all our lives revolved around musical events.

And because she was an operator, the Second Avenue crowd had affectionately nicknamed her Faye-What-City. She and I had knocked back a beer or two over the past few years and knew each other well enough to occasionally put the touch on one another for a joint when things were dry. A few months back I'd won some Allman Brothers tickets in a poker game and when I offered to trade them to her for a bit of smoke her eyes lit up as if I were handing her the keys to a new Trans Am. I was hoping she still remembered.

I started another pot of coffee and went downstairs to get a morning paper. The paper machine was only a few yards up the street but the humidity was so high I was already sweating by the time I got back upstairs. I unplugged the coffee and poured a huge glass of ice water instead, then sat down and started flipping through the *Tennessean*.

The front page was News-as-Usual, some obscure Third World republic taking the United States to task for refusing to dole out several billion in financial aid. Two field reports on the war on terrorism. A local bulletin announcing that political pundits were still touting Carter Robinson as the man to beat come primary time, and as expected, Robinson's "Thanks-but-no-thanks" disallowance on the inside page.

"While I am honored to be even considered by my party for such a distinction, I must decline for personal reasons, not the least of which is my pride in serving the people of Tennessee," he was quoted as saying. I took that as being a classy way of saying he was staying home to be near his ailing wife. Or maybe he was smart enough not to want the job in the first place.

Either way, I couldn't help but feel a little sorry for Robinson. Though he was jovial and could sometimes party as hard as any of the guys who came into Jezebel's, there always seemed to be an indefinable cloud of sadness lingering just behind the laughter in his eyes. At times his wide, toothy smile seemed overly practiced and contrived, an instrument for hiding some great suffering, though only he knew if it was the pain of his wife's illness, or of watching his chance at history slip away.

Finally, I found a small blurb in the Metro section, two short paragraphs that basically said the police were still investigating and that an arrest was expected any day now.

I had some time before Faye got off work, so I began to make a list of people to question. I put Heather's name down again, figuring she had to know more than she'd let on. Bear was next, then Aleta Thomas, though I knew she'd be hard to reach since she'd taken out a restraining order that kept me at least 500 feet from the club.

Afro-Dite still warranted serious consideration, regardless of whether Heather seemed to think so. I'd also need to find out the names of all the other girls working at Jezebel's and check them out one by one. Without entrance to the club and knowing that half of them lived in motels and crash pads, this would be particularly difficult, if not damn near impossible. Then I remembered something the drill instructors used to say when they were brainwashing us back at Parris Island: "The difficult we do at once, the impossible takes a little longer."

I couldn't help but laugh- you know times are really tough when you start quoting Marine Corps philosophy.

At quarter-to-five I walked up Broadway and hung a right on Third, heading for the BellSouth building, a post-modern structure right out of Gotham City. In fact, because of the two antennae-like towers at the top and thanks to some very creative lighting at night, this futuristic mass of glass and steel had come to be known as the Batman Building.

At 5:05 Faye walked out the door and turned left on Commerce, heading for Second Avenue where she made an abrupt right as if pulled by an invisible rope. I crossed the street and fell in behind her so that by the time we reached Mulligan's I was close enough to step around and open the door. She smiled when she recognized me.

"What's shakin', Jake?"

"Faye-What-City, you're as beautiful as ever. Let me buy you a beer."

"You can buy me a beer, Jake, but I ain't holdin' no smoke. Been dry as a popcorn fart for two weeks."

No one ever accused Faye of too much subtlety.

We sat at the far end of the bar, away from everyone, as I ordered drafts and citrus shooters for the both of us. Across from the bar, on the small stage in the corner, some poor misplaced picker was doing a bad impression of an Irish folk singer as he murdered "Danny Boy" and several other Irish dirges in order to get the twenty bucks the joint was willing to pay for a four-to-seven Happy Hour gig.

Faye raised her shooter for a toast.

"Here's to Good Rockin' and Good Friends."

We clinked glasses and tossed back the sweet, citrus flavored potion. It tasted like liquid sunshine, so I raised my hand and waved for two more.

"I need a favor, Faye."

"Let's hear it," she said, taking a slow pull on her draft.

"Do you have any phone company friends in Atlanta?"

She set her beer down on the bar and turned to me with a resigned look of apprehension.

"Maybe. Why do you want to know?"

"I've got an Atlanta phone number, recently disconnected, and I need to find out whose name it was listed in and possibly even an address."

Faye shifted in her seat, sipped her beer and said nothing

for what seemed like a long time. She stared straight ahead, as if she were reading something on the wall behind the bar, though it was more likely she was just time-traveling back to some memorable moment from a Marshall Tucker concert. I could almost hear "Can't You See" playing inside her lovely, innocent head. When the song was over, she came back to the present and turned to me.

"You know I can't do that, Jake," she shook her head. "I may not be getting rich at the phone company, but I've been there twelve years and I can stand it well enough that I don't want to go job hunting right now."

"I realize I'm asking a lot, Faye. But this is kind of a life-or-death situation. I wouldn't even ask but you're the only person I know who can help me."

We hadn't finished our shooters, but I ordered two more as she leaned over and looked at me with those beautiful, emerald eyes.

"You're a charmer, Jake, but the answer is still no. I ain't risking my job just to get you the address of some old girlfriend in Atlanta."

She obviously didn't know about the trouble I was in and I hadn't wanted to tell her. But without her help I might never know who the number belonged to and that was the only scrap of a lead I had. So I told her the story as she listened quietly, just sipping her beer and smoking, occasionally nodding but always looking straight ahead at that little spot behind the bar that seemed to have some kind of mystical pull on her vision. I hoped she was paying attention and not drifting away to another musical milestone on the road of her life. When I finished, she reached for her third shooter and drank it down.

"Jake, sounds to me like you're in deep shit."

"Absolutely. Will you help me, Faye?" I ordered more shooters but she waved the bartender off.

"No more for me. I gotta go home and get supper ready for my old man."

I tried to picture her in the kitchen frying pork chops, your basic flower child gone from Woodstock to Westinghouse. For a moment I wondered what they might talk about at dinner, though I knew that answer already.

"Thanks anyway, Faye. I know it's a lot to ask and I can't say I blame you."

She stood up and put a ten on the bar but I handed it back to her.

"This was my idea, remember? Besides, you're always good company."

She was standing close beside me and I could smell a faint trace of lilac. I looked at her face and saw again just how plainly beautiful she was, a classic from head to toe. I might never meet her old man, but I hoped he knew he was one lucky sonofabitch. She put her arms around my shoulders and hugged me, the sweet aroma of her delicate neck spiking my blood pressure off the meter. She must have sensed it too because she let go and took an abrupt half-step back, as if shaking off her own case of bad ideas.

"I'm not making any promises, Jake, but I'll look into it. Give me the number, just don't expect anything, okay?"

I handed her the piece of paper I'd written the number on and watched her carefully place it in her purse.

"By the way, Babe, thanks again for those Allman Brothers tickets. They were great seats and it was a cookin' show. They did, like, a fifteen-minute drum solo just like in the old days."

I nodded as she turned and walked out into the hot summer evening, dutifully on her way home to cook dinner for some guy who either did or didn't deserve her. For her sake, I wanted to think he did.

Common sense would seem to dictate that I pay the check and head home but, having never been blessed with a great abundance of that, I decided to sit at the bar awhile and enjoy the misty buzz.

I looked around the room for my old buddy Tony but didn't see him. Tony was a die-hard folkie who'd bought the pub eight or ten years ago just so he and his Celtic band would have a place to play. Except for weekends, when it was wall-to-wall tourists and Vandy kids, most of the locals still thought of it as our last neighborhood bar.

I was soaking in the middle of pleasant ruminations when I felt a broad, invasive hand squeeze my shoulder.

"Say, aren't you Django Jake Shepherd, world famous song-writer and all-around creative genius?"

The big, booming voice trashed my mellow buzz, sending a streak of white heat up the back of my neck as I turned slowly, then spoke into the face of Papa Joe Connors.

"You have exactly ten seconds to leave this bar, Old Man, or I swear I'll stick this longneck up your ass and turn you into the biggest corn dog this side of Coney Island."

For a moment he looked genuinely hurt, but the phony smile quickly returned to his huge, bearded face.

"Now hold on just a minute there, Jake. I've got some real business to talk about with you. I've got something going that'll make us both a lot of money if you'll just give me a minute. Let me buy you a beer, Lad."

He snapped his fingers at the bartender to get his attention. Now there were two people who wanted to kill him. I shook my head, declining the beer.

"Four-hundred and fifty bucks."

"Listen, Jake, I've got something--"

"*Four-Hundred and Fifty Bucks*," I repeated, louder.

The heat from the back of my neck had moved around to my face and was marching down my chest toward my stomach. A genuine rage was brewing and the anger it generated was not just for Papa Joe Connors. In fact, most of it was directed at myself.

Papa Joe was of the species who inhabited the lowest realm of life in the music business. He was an independent record producer who, of course, owned his own record label. He made his living off the dreams of others, usually ignorant saps with little or no talent and no shot of ever making it past anything but bottom-rung bar gigs.

But what these pitiful souls do have going for them is that they either have a few grand to blow on a demo session or single, or they've miraculously found a backer with several thousand who's willing to sink it all into an album-video- promotion package. The latter are usually women who've latched onto a husband or boyfriend with money to burn and see this as their big chance to finally become that Big Star they always knew they could be. The money man is usually a guy who thinks he knows a lot about music (and doesn't), has always wanted to be in show business (her manager), and sees this as a great opportunity to ride beside her up the great ladder of fame as she becomes the next Dolly Parton. And believe me, more than a few of them look like Dolly Parton.

Papa's scam worked like this: For X amount of dollars, he cuts two sides on you. You record these songs in the studio that he or one of his buddies own and then you get a CD pressed, usually anywhere from 500 to 1000 copies. In the old days, it was a 45 rpm record, which made for an even bigger profit. You took your box of 500 records back to Buttcrack, Missouri, gave one to your local radio station, gave twenty or thirty to friends, and the remaining 470 records went into your closet or garage and stayed there until either you died or your kids found them and turned them into Frisbees.

Nowadays things are much more sophisticated. After the CD is pressed, you'll get a few copies, and Papa Joe mails the rest to a bunch of 500 and 1000 watt radio stations around the country, little tiny stations that will play anything up to and including Norwegian shouting choruses, and then, miraculously, in a couple of weeks, maybe even while you're still in town, your song appears on the *Independent Record Chart*, a cheap, low-rent magazine that Papa Joe publishes and, (here comes the really good part), you look at the charts and, Lo and Behold, your record is at Number One, Garth Brooks is at Number Two, a couple of other suckers are at numbers Three and Four and climbing, George Strait is at Number Seven and- well, you get the picture.

Of course, you never make any money, but you can always take the chart and a copy of your record down to your local honky tonk back home and get yourself a solid weekend gig making twenty-five bucks a night for the next twelve years.

That is, unless you've still got a little money left and want to cash in on all this momentum by putting out another single. And you'd be surprised how many do just that, or even worse, spring for a video.

And what about the songs, you ask? Not a problem, because Papa buys them outright from whores like me.

Granted, my case is a little different. Because I've written a hit song that a few people have heard of, he'll call me in while he's still trying to close a deal, tell the mark who I am, and then tell them I'll be writing a song especially for them. Usually, that cinches the deal and I get an extra fifty or hundred bucks. I go home, go through a box of my songs that have been rejected by every decent producer this side of Bangkok, pick one out and drop it off the next day.

The problem with Papa is that, like most crooks, he doesn't always pay up. After the third time he stiffed me, I quit doing business with him and we parted ways in a less than amicable manner, with me promising to shove his head through his rectum the very next time I saw him on the street. It's bad enough being a whore but even worse when your pimp double-crosses you.

"Four-Hundred and Fifty Bucks," I demanded, rising from the bar stool.

"Okay, okay, I've got part of it," he stammered. "But first you've got to listen to me. Something big is going down and I really need your help."

"Something big is always going down with you, Papa, but I always seem to get in on the short end of the trick."

"But, Jake, this is dif-"

"You owe me Money," I growled, doing my best imitation of George C. Scott in *The Hustler*.

"All right, all right, like I said, I can let you have part of it. I'll pay you the rest in a couple of days. Hell, Jake, you know I'm always good for it."

As mad as I was, I couldn't help but laugh. Scumbag or not, it wouldn't do any good to smack some sixty-year-old geezer in front of my friends. Anyway, I tend to suffer fools a little more gladly when I'm slightly buzzed, though I knew I couldn't afford to soften up just yet if I wanted to get any serious money from the old coot.

"All right, Old Man, how much have you got?"

"A yard."

I slammed the beer bottle down on the bar, spilling more beer than I'd intended. The big bear of a fool jumped back and put his hands up over his face as if he expected me to dance on it.

"Not enough," I blurted. It felt nice to see the old fart squirm.

"All right then, two hundred," he said seriously.

"Half...and the rest in three days."

"Done."

He reached in the pocket of his embroidered denim shirt, the kind only tourists and peckerwoods wear, and brought out a wad of bills. He counted out eleven twenties and five ones and laid them on the bar.

"Thanks, Papa," I grinned. "I'll take that beer now."

He sat down beside me and told me the story I'd heard before, only this time, well, this time it was really different. He'd met a talented young girl, uh-huh, and this one had some serious money behind her and he'd managed to get some major-label interest going, enough to let him cut some sides on her. He needed some good material, no- make that great material, and he wanted to cut a song of mine called "Sheet Music," a tune I'd always believed in and even pitched a couple years back though nothing ever came of it. It wasn't exactly your typical country song, more an R&B feel, but when I'd played it for Toad he loved it, then learned it, then insisted on taking it to the streets for test marketing. A week later he was back with the results.

"To Hell with the charts," he proclaimed. "Any song that gets you laid is a hit in my book."

At least someone benefited from my prodigious talents.

Like I said, these old pipe dreams weren't anything new, just another verse and chorus of the TuneTown Shuffle. But I had to give Papa credit for not giving up. And while I hated to admit it, in a way we were a lot alike, both veterans of a vicious business and both of us still dumb enough or at least stubborn enough to think we still had a chance at the brass ring. When it came right down to it, we weren't really any different from the poor suckers who tripped over each other to sign on Papa's dotted line.

"I mean it, Jake," he insisted. "This one is gonna take off for both of us, you'll see. We're talking serious money here. You wait, Son, this time next year the name Yolanda Sweet will be a household word and you and me are gonna be fartin' through silk undies. Now, can we do bidness?"

"How much?" I asked, but he waved me off.

"Jake, I'm serious. This ain't no custom session. This is gonna be a real album and "Sheet Music" is probably the first single. All I want is the Publishing. You get all the Writer's share. Now, are you wit me or a-gin me?"

I turned and looked at him standing there sober as a judge and realized for the first time that he was damn serious. And that's when it hit me- My God, he was really going to cut a legitimate record on this chick and he was going to do it with one of my best songs. I could be back in business. Granted, I might get my royalty checks in care of Brushy Mountain State Prison, but I was back on the map just the same.

"Okay, Old Man, I'm in," I said. "But mark my word: If this turns out to be anything less than legit, I promise you I'll put a hollow point .38 right between your shifty, friggin' eyes. Are we clear on that?"

He nodded agreement and ordered two double-shots of Schnapps.

The poor fellow on stage was still wrestling with his imitation Irish brogue, though in truth no one was paying much attention. When he finished his song, Papa downed the Schnapps and slapped the bar with the palm of his thick hand. It sounded like a gunshot and the room went abruptly quiet as the singer froze in place.

"Say, Laddy," yelled Papa. "Do ya think ya could sing us an old Irish folk jig?"

The stunned boy leaned into the microphone. "Uh...such as?"

"How about, 'When Me Peter Goes to Dublin, I'll Be Comin' Back to Me.'"

It took a full beat before the room erupted into a simultaneous groan. I looked over at Papa, who was already gunning the second shot.

"What say we celebrate the turning of the worm with some shit-kickin' music?" I said.

He nodded and tossed a twenty on the bar.

"If you're waitin' on me, you're backin' up," he said, making for the door two steps ahead of me. I followed him out into the heavy night air, both of us pulled toward Broadway by the everlasting promise of dim lights, thick smoke, and loud country music.

CHAPTER 7

I n my amber-lit dream Cassidy and I are walking together past store windows, maybe in a shopping mall, maybe a city street. Her long slate hair falls across her shoulders and her tanned, faultless body is set off by a white cotton sundress and matching leather sandals.

Crowds of people pass us: men, women, couples, kids, and I watch them as they pass, no one goes by without looking at her. We walk close, brushing against each other only to bounce gently apart as Cassidy, oblivious to all the stares, alternates her gaze between the store windows and me. I feel like a king.

Suddenly, we're standing outside in the midst of a huge

crowd at a concert. The music is loud, mysterious and unrecognizable, a steady droning with hundreds or maybe thousands of people standing on the grass and swaying to the insistent melody in one mass, rhythmic dance. Cassidy is beside me, smiling as she moves suggestively to the music. As she dances, the crowd around us begins to pull back until finally she is dancing alone in the center of a grassy circle.

Cassidy begins to rise in the air, levitating, yet dancing all the while. When she reaches a point just above the heads of the crowd, she begins to float ethereally, drifting across the field toward the distant stage. The teeming crowd is larger now, clapping and cheering in unison as she hovers above them like a cloud, out of reach and hopelessly untouchable. As she takes the stage, the anonymous band recedes into the mist until finally there is just Cassidy, dancing alone onstage.

Back and forth she dances, from one end of the stage to the other as the maddening throng becomes louder and louder with their desperate chant, something I can't quite make out until I realize they are calling her name in syllables, "Ca-Sa-Dee! Ca-Sa-Dee! Ca-Sa-Dee!"

They begin moving toward the stage, slowly at first, then pushing, shoving, approaching pandemonium as everyone struggles to get closer. At that moment I notice that I, too, have been levitated above the crowd just enough to see within the threatening mass of bodies. I try to move toward Cassidy but I'm frozen in place, helpless to do anything but watch. Throughout the frenzied army I can see scattered pockets of violence erupt as the damp, copper smell of blood begins to fill the air. Here and there a knife blade flashes in the sunlight, a glinting mouth of teeth opens to scream but no sound can be heard above the deathly chant of "Ca-Sa-Dee! Ca-Sa-Dee!"

Cassidy peels the sundress up and over her head in one silvery motion, tossing the tiny frock into the mob. A young fool jumps to catch it and is immediately trounced by those surrounding him. I see his shiny black arm holding the dress as he goes under, his attackers smothering him like thick smoke and then, seconds later, they bring up his naked, bleeding body and hold him aloft before passing him over the top of the crowd until he comes to rest just inches beneath the spot where I'm hovering. Looking down at the ravaged body of the young black man, a scream catches in my throat as Benny Watts turns his head to look up at me, his face all but unrecognizable except for the familiar bloody smile. When he opens his mouth to speak, the noise stops for one cold moment.

"It's okay, Brother. What goes 'round comes 'round."

Then the mob washes over him, storming the stage and waving the bloodied sundress like a banner. I watch as Cassidy stands with arms open, welcoming the foaming legions who envelop her like a human ocean until she disappears from sight as the sea of lunatics pours across the field toward the horizon.

The dream shifts and I'm alone in a small room with no windows, only a door cut into two sections, upper and lower halves like you might find in the kitchen of some old farmhouse. The room is hot, humid, and I'm sitting in a chair sweating uncontrollably and wiping my face with my hands. The air keeps getting thicker with each breath as I stand and begin walking the few feet to the door. By the time I reach the top door the air is completely gone and I'm choking, gasping for the last bit of oxygen. At the point of blacking out, I grip the doorknob and pull with my last ounce of strength. It swings open as if spring-loaded and Cassidy's body tumbles out, her face and eyes still wearing that same expression of absolute surprise...

I woke up screaming and kicking but the noonday sun was all that heard me. I lay for a while on the damp, sweaty sheets and thought about the dream, though I knew too well the futility in trying to make sense of it. Benny Watts had been lurking in the dark recesses of my mind for years, prowling around with that simple, beatific smile lighting his way, an ongoing reminder of the long-term lease he'd taken on my subconscious.

I'd long ago reconciled myself to the fact that one day Benny and I would have a reckoning, and with that in mind I had declared a shaky moratorium on guilt and blame, for both myself and a senseless war that could never be forgotten nor understood. But Cassidy was a newcomer to the black territory of my thoughts, and I couldn't help thinking that she and Benny Watts would be moving in together now, sharing a mental condominium with property lines bordering on the edge of my sanity.

After a pot of coffee and a long shower, I dropped off my sheets at a same-day laundry on Fourth Avenue, then headed across Victory Bridge to check out the next name on my list of people to see.

Truck Bennett was a third-rate private detective straight out of central casting. He was as sleazy as they came so naturally our paths had crossed a few times. I'd done some work for him in the past, nothing serious, just some repos and simple surveillance, but every case always included some slime ball twist in the plot.

Once he hired me to repo a Cadillac but neglected to tell

me the Caddy belonged to a drug-dealing pimp who was not exactly a staunch advocate for gun control. Lucky for me the guy was a piss-poor shot and though he missed me with a hail of bullets, he still managed to put several holes in the Coupe DeVille. Truck, of course, had no sympathy for me but moaned endlessly about the fact that the bank might not pay him since the car was now damaged.

Another time, he sent me out to shadow this chippy who was supposedly fooling around on her boyfriend. Truck didn't tell me that her boyfriend ran one of the biggest numbers rackets in town, and what Truck didn't know was that the boyfriend had also sent two of his own goons to case her from a long, safe distance. Needless to say, on the afternoon I finally scored with some great pictures of her dry humping a bass player on the back steps of a recording studio on Eighteenth, the goons were waiting for me when I got back to the car.

"We'll take the camera," said the smaller of the two.

Bless his heart, the poor fella barely weighed two-twenty and at five-foot-three he looked like a small John Deere tractor, quietly idling and ready to plow.

The other gentleman looked the same, only bigger.

"Now," he demanded, holding out his large, thick hand.

"Sorry, Boys, but I'm with the CIA and this camera is U.S. Government property. You'll have to get your own dirty pictures."

The shorter one took a quick step forward and nailed me in the sternum with a piston-like jab that came out of nowhere and sent me careening down the side of my rental car. My ribs caught the side mirror as I fell, clipping it off at the fender before I landed on my face in the gravel with white steaks of pain tracing across my eyes. When I looked up the big one was standing over me holding my camera. Instinctively, I raised my left arm over my face and braced myself for a boot.

It never came. Instead, he slowly removed the film, then leaned over and placed the cheap, empty camera on the ground beside me.

"Here," he said. "I have a Mamiya at home."

Then they disappeared, as did my career as a snoop. Truck paid me but only after I showed him the hospital bill for getting my ribs taped and only after I convinced him that I could do the very same thing to him, if not right then, at least in the near future.

That had been a few years ago and I hadn't seen him until Jezebel's, where he'd come in every couple of weeks, always getting his first drink from me at the bar and whispering that he was on a case, then proceeding to get shit-faced while dropping money on every dancer in the house.

He'd go through two or three hundred bucks, then stumble out the door in search of whatever Sam Spade hustle he was running at the moment. As he shuffled away, I remember thinking that only a desperate fool would ever hire Truck Bennett for a case.

Be that as it may, Truck Bennett was still the closest thing I knew to a real private detective, and once over the bridge and into East Nashville I gunned the Eldorado up Gallatin Road as Eddy Arnold's celestial voice pleaded with his lover to "Make the World Go Away." I concurred.

I pulled into the potholed driveway of the dilapidated old house Truck used for an office, interrupting the antics of two mangy, cur dogs who'd chosen that spot for an impromptu love fest. He was behind his desk drinking coffee and reading the paper when I walked in.

"Jake," he smiled crookedly. "What a surprise, Come in. Want some coffee?" He poured a cup and set it in front of me before I could answer. Two flies immediately took up residence on the rim of the cup.

"I'm in a hurt locker," I said, foregoing any semblance of small talk. Truck and I had never pretended to be friends and so far, that was working out just fine. The coffee tasted like it had been reheated from yesterday.

"So I hear," he chuckled. "Word is, old Jake-the-Snake is soon to be married to the man with the most cigarettes. Got your Anal-Ease packed?"

Maybe I'd had too much coffee already and had a caffeine jag going. Maybe it was his shiny, stainless-steel front tooth grinning at me that set me off. Or maybe I just felt he'd had it coming for a long, long time. Whatever the reason, I reached across the desk and grabbed him by his dirty blue tie, pulling him upright just as I planted my fist squarely on his grinning mouth, trying my damndest to knock the crooked, metallic smile from his face. He went crashing back into his chair, rolled back into the wall and turned over, spilling his chubby butt onto the floor.

I sat down, took a sip of stale coffee and lit a cigarette as I waited for him to get up. It took a minute, but when he did, he was holding his bloody mouth with one hand and a nickel-plated, snub-nosed .38 with the other.

"You sonofabitch, what'd you do that for?" He had the gun pointed at me but it wasn't cocked.

"I guess I've just never been a fan of your humor."

He picked up his chair from the floor and sat down across

from me as he wiped his mouth with a dirty handkerchief, the gun resting on the desk by his coffee cup.

"What do you want from me?" he mumbled.

"Let's start with you telling me everything you've heard on the street."

He took a sip of the day-old coffee and winced.

"From what I hear the cops think it's an open-and-shut case," he began. "A domestic thing. Everybody knows you two were an item for a while, then for whatever reason, you split up. Jake wants his girl back but she says, 'no way.' They have a couple of arguments in the club in front of witnesses. Finally, Jake either strangles the girl or has someone else do it, then conveniently finds her body in the trash. End of story."

"What do you think?"

"I think it's none of my business and frankly I don't give a damn if they use you for a pin cushion. Personally though, I'll miss the girl because she had the best set of tits in the joint."

I came up out of the chair again, but he was waiting for me. He had the gun pointed at me again and this time it was cocked. The grin was back on his face, albeit a lot bloodier than before.

"Jake," he said calmly, "I know you don't think much of me, and I don't really give a shit. Now, I may not be John Wayne but trust me, even I can hit you from this distance."

I looked down the tiny barrel of the .38. It looked like a sewer pipe.

"Now sit down," he said, and I did.

He uncocked the gun but held it across his lap.

"I apologize for that last remark. I was just looking for some sort of reaction. A guy like me, he comes across some cold types in this line of work. Hell, you know, you've been there. It's a shitty job and that's why the business is filled with jerks like me. We're the only ones who can take it and not wind up screaming and tearing our hair out in some nuthouse. Even so, it still works on your head. You spend enough time doing this and eventually you reach the point where you don't even know or care which side you're on. You just do the work, take your pitiful money and try to stay alive. Now, tell me what you want, Jake."

"I need some help."

He opened the desk drawer and tossed in his gun, then took out a legal pad and pen.

"That's all you had to say, Jake. Let's get started."

I told him my tired story from start to finish, then told him about meeting the Eskews, but I didn't tell him about the twenty grand or the Atlanta phone number. I figured Truck had enough to go on and I didn't want his vision clouded with thoughts of a big payday. The less he knew, the harder he'd have to dig and while I might not be his biggest fan, I knew he was a lot better at scratching around than I was. When I finished, we sat looking at each other across the desk.

"I'll ask around, work the edges and angles," he said, "Frankly, it's not a hell of a lot to go on."

"Now you know how I feel."

"Are you sure you've told me everything, Jake?"

"Everything," I lied.

"Okay, I'll touch base with you in a couple of days."

I pulled ten hundred-dollar bills from my pocket and tossed them on his desk.

"This oughta get you started."

"Where'd you get this kind of money?" he asked, reaching for the bills.

"Bartending pays pretty good. Maybe you oughta look into it when your gumshoe days are over."

I got up to leave. "Sorry about your mouth."

"Don't flatter yourself," he said, the steel tooth shining like a bloody dime. "I've been hit harder by maître d's."

Outside, a blanket of dry heat had settled about the city and dust hung suspended in the yellowed, unmoving air. I drove back across the river and headed for the Hermitage Café, a little dive on Hermitage Avenue that was famous for home cooking and cheap whiskey. A ham-and-cheese omelet with a Bloody Mary that was two-to-one vodka and Tabasco sauce was just what I needed to put a collar on the caffeine.

My waitress was a tall, bent woman who looked about fifty but was probably in her late thirties, a victim of a life spent with two-timing boyfriends and cars with bad air conditioning. Her face had weathered into a resigned look of permanence, not necessarily a frown but rather a quiet acceptance to this, her lot in life. Her hands were leathery and strong and her light blue waitress uniform was squeaky clean. Her black-and-white name tag read *Phyllis*.

I knew she was new because I'd been coming here for years and had never seen her. The other two waitresses, Inez and Alma, didn't need name tags as they had only been working there for about a century and a half.

"How was your omelet?" she asked, as she picked up the empty plate I'd sopped clean with a biscuit.

"Hardly fit to eat," I smiled.

Phyllis shot back a surprisingly pretty smile.

"What's so funny?"

"You are," she blushed.

"And just why is that, Phyllis?" I grinned, thoroughly

enjoying her new-found happiness.

"Cause you're trying to be cool with egg all over your teeth, that's why."

At that, she laughed out loud, a genuine, throaty, good-ole-girl laugh, the kind heard every day in truck stops, Waffle Houses, and ramshackle beer joints all across the country. I liked her immediately.

"Well, in that case, bring me another Bloody Mary and maybe that'll wash it off."

She brought the drink and finished clearing my table while I poured over the morning's *Tennessean*, looking for any mention of Cassidy or the investigation. Not a word. I was in the middle of reading my horoscope when I was interrupted.

"Mind if I join you?" asked Sergeant Lyle, as he sat down across from me.

My stomach started a mild series of flips, but that could've been the vodka and Tabasco sauce going one-on-one.

"Not a bit, Sergeant. In fact, I was going to call and invite you, but then I figured you were probably out working, you know, doing your job?"

Lyle pointed at my Bloody Mary.

"Enjoy it while you can, Son. Where you're going they make hooch out of Sterno and potato skins."

"I like potatoes," I deadpanned, then immediately felt foolish, knowing Lyle could tell I was trying too hard to be glib.

He hadn't ordered anything but Phyllis brought a cup of coffee and set it in front of him. She might be new but she could still spot a cop. She walked away and glanced back at me but her smile had gone south.

Lyle pointed at the newspaper.

"I hope Jean Dixon is telling you not to take any sudden out-of-town trips. Might be bad for your future."

I folded the paper and set it on the table between us.

"I'm not going anywhere, Sergeant. I told you that the other night. Now cut the crap. Are you guys making any headway in this case?"

Lyle's fingertips drummed a steady beat on the Formica.

"Let's just say we're looking at all the possibilities, checking out every story and every lead that comes in and talking to everyone that'll talk to us. I have no doubt we'll nail whoever is responsible for killing that young lady.

"That's comforting," I said, lighting a cigarette.

Leaning forward, he reached across the table and pulled the pack of Marlboros out of my shirt pocket.

"Don't get too comfortable," he smiled. "As far as I'm concerned, you're still the lead bitch in this dog race."

He lit a cigarette and blew a cloud of smoke at me but I fanned it away. He'd like nothing better than for me to come across the table at him and I had no intention of giving him that pleasure. Besides, I always try to limit myself to one fracas per morning if possible.

I leaned in, affirmative body language and all that nonsense.

"Let me ask you something, Lyle. How long you been a cop- fifteen, twenty years?"

"Twenty-two. What's your point?"

"My point is this: you've been a cop, on the streets, for twenty-two years, and you want to sit there and tell me you don't have a gut feeling, better still, that you don't *know* that I didn't have anything to do with Cassidy's death? You know damn well it wasn't me and I can't, for the life of me, figure out why you're busting my shoes on this. Now tell me. Do you really, honestly think I killed her?"

He looked at me for a long moment without blinking, stubbing out his cigarette as Phyllis came over to pour more coffee. I was tired of playing games.

"Answer me, you sonofabitch." I guess the second drink had given me a case of big cajónes.

He reached for the newspaper but I knocked his hand away. Totally unfazed, he leaned back in his seat and crossed his legs.

"Son, all I know is, I've got a dead stripper, and all roads seem to lead straight to you. Tell me something, what would *you* think if you were sitting on this side of the table? Would you be likely to take the word of some guitar-slinging lowlife who had as much reason to kill her as anybody? I mean, Hell, Son, I see people every day wind up dead for a lot less than that."

"You still didn't answer my question. Do you think I did it?"

Lyle gazed across the table at me with the resigned look of an old mortician who dreams of Florida and retirement every minute of his waking life. He cut his eyes to the back corner where a cowboy was wrestling with an ancient pinball machine.

"At this point, I'm still turning over rocks. I mean, you knew her better than anyone else, so if you didn't do it, then you tell me where to start looking."

He motioned for a cigarette and I gave him the pack.

Then he waved Phyllis over for more coffee.

"Go on, Jake," he said, lighting the smoke. "I'm all ears."

"First off, I'm assuming you've checked out all the dancers at the club?"

"We're talking to everybody, but so far nothing has turned up."

"One girl in particular," I offered, "a tall mulatto, dances under the name Afro-Dite. I know for a fact she had a beef with Cassidy and she's no stranger to the system."

"We know about her," he nodded, "but we checked her out and she's got a tight alibi. She was at the hospital with her kid that night. Even the nurses vouch for her. Anything else?"

Why was I the only one who felt that Afro-Dite's story deserved some serious scrutiny? Both Lyle and Heather had dismissed her with a wave of the hand. I hadn't intended to, but I went ahead and told him about the phone bill and the calls to Atlanta. As I talked, he sipped coffee and smoked, nodding occasionally. When I finished, his expression was the same as when I'd started.

"Is that it?"

"That's all I know, yeah."

"Well, to tell you the truth, Jake, that's not much. And as far as the Atlanta business, we've known about that from day one."

I sat there dumbfounded and felt the color drain from my face. How stupid could anybody be? Here I was, running around like I had this incredible piece of the puzzle, getting Faye involved at great risk, when all Lyle had to do was pick up the phone and call for a printout of her call record, which was exactly what he had done.

"So, what did you find out?" I said, as nonchalantly as I could fake.

If he knew I was rattled he didn't let on.

"Not much, really. Some computer nerd in Atlanta. Said he'd been talking to the girl and her roommate about doing some kind of soft-porn website on the Internet. Seems to be a lot of money in that nowadays. Guys run up their credit cards paying to see chicks do the same thing on a computer that you can see in any strip club. Some of it's a little harder though, and pretty sophisticated.

"Near as I can tell, your girl was about to make a move up and take a shot at some big money. And my sources say the computer guy is legit."

"Have you talked to him?" For some reason, I wasn't buying it. Maybe I was looking through rose-colored glasses but I couldn't picture Cassidy as the porn princess of cyberspace. Not exactly a stepping stone to Miss America.

Lyle shook his head. "I haven't, but the boys in Atlanta have and they say he's cool. The phone calls were just business. He ain't a player."

"Who is he? Tell me his name. If he's so legit, then why was his phone number disconnected?"

"Who he is doesn't matter. Like I said, he's been checked out. And let's not forget who's the police officer here. How do I know you didn't find out about the girl's plans and go ballistic? Like I said, everywhere I look the finger keeps pointing back at you."

"Christ, Lyle, I watched her strip every night. I saw her shake her booty in front of any guy who had a dollar to stick between her tits. Why should I get upset if she wanted to go on the Internet?"

"I don't know, Shepherd, I really don't. Maybe it's one thing to have your old lady strip in a club but something else entirely when it comes to guys looking at her and yanking off all over the world. Hell, I *still* think there're some things you're not telling me. But I promise you one thing, Son, I *will* find out the truth."

My guts were burning, and it wasn't from the Tabasco sauce.

I slammed the table with my fists, spilling coffee and sending spoons dancing across the Formica top.

"Lyle, Goddammit, listen-"

"No, *you* listen, Shepherd," he ordered. "Like I told you, we're checking out every possibility, every dead end, every lie, every smoke-filled pipe dream. If you're clean, you got nothing to worry about, but until we know for sure that you are, you keep your sorry ass right where we can find you at any given hour of the day or night. Do you understand me, Son?"

I nodded slowly as he got up from the table.

"And one more thing: if you're gonna put somebody on the street, you need to do better than Truck Bennett. That dead-beat sonofabitch couldn't shake a story out of my grandmother."

He threw a dollar bill on the table and walked out, taking my pack of cigarettes with him.

Phyllis came over and quietly set my check in front of me.

I paid it with a hundred-dollar bill.

CHAPTER 8

A fine vodka mist lit my face as I spent the rest of the morning and early part of the afternoon driving around and thinking about what Lyle had said. Maybe Cassidy had bigger fish to fry all along. Or maybe she'd kept me hanging on for convenience, or worse, out of sheer boredom, a way station along the superhighway to bigger and better things. I didn't want to think so, but I knew just how much of a blind fool I could be in situations like that.

One thing was certain- Heather had lied to me or at least hadn't told me everything. Either way, it was time for some straight answers.

Traveling south on Twelfth Avenue until it turned into

Granny White Pike, then on across Woodmont Boulevard, trying my level best not to gawk at two leggy co-eds jogging along the sidewalk in front of Lipscomb University, I pulled into Heather's driveway and found it empty. She'd probably landed somewhere else the night before. I'd give her a couple of hours and try again.

I drove home and parked behind the feed store and was almost to the stairs when I spotted the faded black limousine idling noisily at the far end of the parking lot. A broad smile swept across my face as I turned and walked over to the waiting, smoking limo.

Angie LeFevre belonged to another place and time. Years ago, when I first rolled into town as a green, snot-nosed kid, Waylon was clean cut, Willie hadn't gone back to Texas, and Kristofferson and Mickey Newbury were redefining country songwriting. Johnny Cash was King and the reigning country Queens were Loretta and Tammy.

A couple of younger talents were also making a lot of noise at the time: One, a sweet, buxom blonde named Dolly, and the other, a fiery redhead from El Paso named Angie LeFevre. She could down-home twang with the best of them, but what set her apart was her bluesy style that always managed to take a simple three-chord country tune and elevate it to another level.

The Music Row bigwigs tried to keep her pigeon-holed and within the bounds of what they thought country music ought to be, but Angie had been fortunate enough to grow up in Texas, where country music was like gumbo, with a little bit of everything thrown in: blues, jazz, Cajun, polkas, Tex-Mex, pepper with a dash of wailing steel guitar and stir with twin fiddles til done.

Angie stayed true to her music, and although she was constantly butting heads with producers and record labels, she eventually established a strong fan base and started selling records, which was, of course, the bottom line. At that point Nashville welcomed her with open arms, not because she'd made it in spite of them but because the one thing Nashville will always accept is success.

And then, in true Music City fashion, all the record companies rushed to create their own Angie LeFevre clone. Of course, no one even came close, but it did mirror the ongoing theme of the music business, which is that very few are willing to take the risks to be Number One, while almost everyone is content to follow a proven trend and join the mad scramble for Number Two. There's a metaphor there.

I remember walking down Music Row wide-eyed, a guitar slung over my shoulder, knocking on doors and trying to get someone, anyone, to listen to my precious songs. Back then you could walk the entire area in an hour or so and behind every numbered door on those streets lay the glimmering, elusive promise of fame and fortune. I was too broke to afford a demo tape so I just played my songs for whomever would listen and, more often than not, people would listen, at least for a verse or chorus before holding up their hand and saying, "What else have you got?" and then you quickly moved on to another song.

I have to credit all those years of rejection for giving me a thick skin. I guess it's true what they say about songwriters in Nashville— you need the heart of a poet and the skin of an alligator just to survive, much less make it.

It was on Music Row that I first met Angie LeFevre. I was walking west one afternoon when a glistening black limousine slowed to a crawl beside me. I was full of myself in those days, ninety percent ego and ten percent talent, a paper tiger held together by equal amounts of stubborn pride and naiveté. I kept walking and pretended not to notice, as if a long black limo creeping along the curb beside me was something that happened all the time. Finally, I stopped and the front window slid down as the driver, a young kid about my age, leaned over in his blue chauffer's uniform and motioned toward the back seat.

"Let's take a ride, Chief."

I hesitated a moment, then opened the door and peered inside. There sat Angie LeFevre, a goddess in red hair and rhinestones, a martini in her hand and looking every bit as classy as Catherine Deneuve. She smiled and I almost slapped myself to make sure I wasn't dreaming.

"C'mon, Cowboy, get in and sing me a song."

We rode around for fifteen or twenty minutes as Angie sipped her martini while I played and sang to her my rudimentary but nonetheless heartfelt songs of love and betrayal, bad luck and lost dreams, old dogs, outlaws, repossessed pickups and failed gold mines. In other words, a lot of things I knew little or nothing about. Of course, I wasn't ready for the big time and Angie knew it. But she listened politely to three or four songs before the driver pulled over to the curb at almost the same spot he'd picked me up. I hadn't noticed but we'd been circling Music Row the whole time.

"You've got some talent, Cowboy. You just need to keep working on it. Don't give up."

"Thanks," was all I could say, as the limo drove away and I went back to my shuffle down Music Row, completely unaware that my entire life could've changed in that very moment if only I'd been ready.

After all, 'being ready' is really what it's all about in this town. In spite of all the generalized horror stories about how hard it is to make it in the music business, the fact is, if you just keep plugging away relentlessly, knocking on doors and staying single-minded about your dream, sooner or later you'll get a shot. And when that time comes, you'd better be ready to deliver.

Looking back, maybe it was a little easier in the old days because the business was full of a lot of veteran music people who were capable of spotting raw talent and knew how to nurture and mold that talent into something good, something genuine and true. Nowadays, the pace is breakneck and you'd damn well better be fully developed and loaded for bear when that big golden finger points at you because it might be the only chance you get. A great statesman, I forget just who, maybe Disraeli or Tom T. Hall, once said "the secret of success in life is for a man to be ready for his opportunity when it comes." So much for career advice from a time-worn veteran.

As the years went by, and country music began crossing over into pop, it seemed Angie's star had begun to wane just about the time mine was ascending. By the time I was an A-list writer she'd been relegated to small independent record labels with little or no distribution and, in the natural order of all things musical, she soon vanished from the airwaves.

But I'll never forget that afternoon on Music Row. As far as I'm concerned, she was and still is, one of the greatest to ever step in front of a mic. We became friends and over the years she recorded several of my songs, all on various independent labels, and none of which ever made me a dime. That was fine by me. Angie could take one of my songs and turn it into some-thing I could never imagine, overcoming in the process the poor production and sparse arrangements she was afforded. I said it then and I'll say it now- "Sub-Urban Cowboy" put me on the charts, but it was Angie LeFevre who first made me feel like a poet.

And then, when my flame burned out about as quickly as it was lit, when I was given a swift kick back to the end of the line and lost my heart and soul to a deadly love affair with pills, booze, and cocaine, it was Angie LeFevre who pulled me out of a living grave and took me home to her little cottage in Leiper's Fork and locked me in the basement with the faint hope of keeping me alive. She spent a month talking me out of suicide, another two months nursing me back to health and getting me clean, and several weeks after that just trying to build up my courage enough for me to walk out the front door and face the sunlight without running for the shadows. That's not the kind of thing you forget, and it's certainly not the kind of debt you ever get paid off, though Angie never asked for anything in return except for my friendship, which she had in spades.

I opened the back door and sat down on the cracked and worn leather jump seat across from her. She looked the picture of health in starched jeans and white silk blouse, and her eyes shone with a twinkle that would make a shooting star envious.

"Hello, Stud," she purred, in that wet, sultry voice that always sent my blood pressure whistling.

"You're ten years too late, Sugar. The stud was put out to pasture a long time ago."

We reached across the aisle for a hug and the smell of her perfume was pure honeysuckle.

"Don't kid me, Jake. If I know you, you've probably got a couple of cheerleaders up there practicing somersaults."

We both laughed and then she spoke just in time to head off the oncoming silence.

"Really, Jake, are you okay?"

"Yeah, I'm all right," I answered. "Still kicking. How about you, how's my favorite Lone Star Lady?"

"I'm fine, Jake, but don't dance the mess around. I'm worried about you. I...I heard about your situation. Is there anything I can do? I mean...I guess I don't really know what to say but you know that if you need anything, anything at all, I'm here to help."

"Thanks, Angie, I know that. And I really appreciate it. It means a lot to know I still have some good friends left in this world. But really, you shouldn't worry. It'll all work out. You'll see."

"Okay, but you know where I am if you need me any time of the day or night. Promise you'll call me if you do."

"I promise."

She slid over in the seat and took one of my hands, holding it tight in both of hers.

"Enough of the bad stuff," she smiled. "This is not entirely a social call."

"What do you mean?"

"You're not going to believe this, Jake, but I've got a deal with Warner Brothers." The sound of her voice told me this was serious and I could tell she was trying her best to hold back the excitement.

"Well, it's not an album, really it's only two songs. No, actually it *is* an album but my part of it is two songs. Warners is putting out an album called "Classic Country Ladies," and it features me and four other gals who had hits in the Seventies. I know it's not a big deal, Jake, but I'm just excited to be able to go into a real studio again."

"Don't kid yourself, Angie, it is a big deal, a very big deal. It sounds like a terrific concept. When do you start?"

"In a couple of weeks, I think." The excitement was all over her face as she shifted in her seat like a little girl. "I know it won't get much airplay here in the states, but the people at Warners think it'll do well overseas. They're even talking about a possible tour."

"That's wonderful, Angie. If anybody deserves a chance to record again, it's you, Babe."

"Better get that tux out of mothballs, Sweetie, because you just may be escorting me to the CMAs next year."

"It would be my pleasure, Angie. And you know me, I never turn down the chance to be seen with a beautiful lady."

Angie might be pushing sixty, but she could still turn heads from half a block. Three cheers for modern medical science.

"Thanks, Jake," she said. "But I haven't told you the best part: We all get to do two songs each, one of our old hits and one new song. Jake...I want to cut 'Sheet Music.'"

I felt my face go ash white as a long, exasperated sigh rolled off my lips onto the floor of the aged limo. Angie sat back, a bewildered look replacing the smile that had been there just seconds before.

"What's the matter? I thought you'd be happy. What's wrong? Dammit, Jake, talk to me."

For once I was at a loss for words as I sat there wondering just what the odds could be, that I could go years- no, make that decades without a cut, become a complete has-been, and then have *two* people tell me they want to cut one of my songs, both within a twenty-four-hour period. It was overwhelming, incomprehensible, and absolutely fucked up.

The bottom line, and yes, there's always that ever-present bottom line, was one of pure economics. Although this would undoubtedly be Angie's last chance at a big recording session, even she knew the album would be virtually ignored by country radio. And while European sales could sometimes be substantial, overseas royalties were notoriously hard to collect or very slow at best. Whereas, Papa's little Bimbo was major-label material and poised for her launch as the Next Big Thing, which meant I could be rolling in dough this time next year, even if all that rolling took place in a six-by-eight room at the Cross Bar Hotel.

And there was one other thing. I'd given my word to Papa, no matter that he'd screwed me on just about every deal we'd been involved in- it was still my word. I thought about the scene in *The Wild Bunch* where William Holden and Ernest Borgnine are arguing about leaving the Mexican village and stiffing the corrupt Mexican General. Holden argues that they've given him their word, but Borgnine looks him in the eye and says, "Bullshit! It's not your word, it's *who* you give it *to*."

So, as Yogi Berra once said, "When you come to a fork in the road, take it." There was no way I was going to turn my back on Angie when I had this chance to help her with something that meant so much. And I wasn't about to walk away from Papa's deal either. Chances were good that Angie's record would die a silent death or, most likely, not even get released. Papa would never even know. And when his little cupcake had my song all over the radio, well, I could deal with Angie then. But for now, I had no intention of throwing water on her long-deserved opportunity.

"Jake, are you going to tell me what's wrong or do I need to slap the plu-perfect shit out of you?"

"Huh, Oh,...I'm sorry, Angie. I guess it's just been so long since anyone wanted one of my songs that it kind of stunned me, that's all."

"You *do* want me to cut the song don't you, Jake?"

"You bet I do, Sweetheart, and I want to thank you for raising me from the dead as a songwriter. It's like I still don't believe it, you know?"

"Well, you can believe it, Sugar. The way I see it, this couldn't happen at a better time for either of us. We both deserve a break."

"Yeah," I nodded. "Timing is everything."

"That and good lighting," she winked. "Listen, Jake, I've got to run but I'll keep you posted. And don't forget about what I said earlier. If you need anything, even if it's just someone to talk to, you call me anytime."

"Will do, Angie."

"Now cheer up, Cowboy. You're a player again."

I got out and watched the old limo pull away, smoking and sputtering as it made its way up Second Avenue, wondering if the next time I saw it she'd be trying to run me over for pulling the plug on her recording session at the last minute.

CHAPTER 9

After picking up my laundry, I made another pass by Heather's apartment with no luck. I headed back downtown with no destination in mind, wondering where to look next and who to look for as the stereo played and David Houston sang "Almost Persuaded" in that searing, plaintive tenor. In another life he would've been an opera singer.

Easing up Eighth Avenue past the massage parlors, some with pink neon signs and others with no signs at all, just large numbers on the doors of nondescript houses, I wondered how places like that could operate openly here in the Buckle of the Bible Belt, but I'd long ago quit trying to figure out the logic of

City Hall. As I drove past Kiki's Health Club, a few of the girls were sunning outside in lounge chairs and it was not a pretty sight. Big hair, tattoos, heavy makeup and cigarettes in hand, I tried to picture them in the morning, packing lunches and getting kids and husbands out the door before donning heavy pantyhose, a Lycra mini-skirt and tube top, then heading out for another day in their own particular service industry. I managed to smile for only a brief moment before a tired sadness came over me.

Farther up Eighth, past the missions and shelters where the homeless wandered the sidewalks with no agenda other than a safe, shady spot, a meal, or the promise of a drink, I sat at the red light at Demonbreun and watched as a dozen men moved aimlessly, their eyes clouded with the same thousand-yard stare I'd seen so often during the war.

The light changed and I was about to drive on when something caught my attention in the rear-view mirror: the old wino- the one that crawled out of Bear's truck that night in the alley. I blinked twice and watched him turn and shuffle down a side street beside the bus station. I sped away but had to drive two blocks before I could make a right turn to circle back. By then, he was gone. Easing through the alleys connecting Seventh and Eighth Avenues, tight little gray passageways littered with empty wine bottles, discarded clothing and sleeping drunks, I drove all the way over to Lafayette Street and back several times but the wino had disappeared.

I cursed my own ineptitude for not thinking of him before. It was possible he'd seen something that night though I knew the chances were slim. Still, it was a shot, and I wasn't exactly being overrun with possibilities.

Crisscrossing through the alleys several more times with no luck, I motored back down Demonbreun past the smaller shelters but there was no sign of him, just the same weary, hollowed faces that were becoming a little too familiar now. My best bet was to come back early in the morning around five or five-thirty when the shelters kicked them back out onto the streets. If he'd spent the night inside, there was a chance I'd see him. If not, then I'd have to look under every bridge and cardboard box from here to the Farmer's Market. There was an even chance I'd find the old guy but it might take a couple of days, assuming of course that I *had* a couple of days.

The phone was ringing when I opened the door of the muggy apartment. Faye wanted to have a drink when she got off work.

"It's okay," I said. "I already know about the website guy. But believe me, Faye, I appreciate all the trouble you went to for me."

"Are you saying you don't want it?" Her tone was less than happy.

"Of course I want it," I recovered, not wanting to appear ungrateful. "I'll meet you at the Pub at five."

"You owe me for this one, Jake," she said, and hung up.

It was only three o'clock so I took a quick shower before heading up the street to Mulligan's Pub. By the time she arrived I was already two beers ahead of her. I ordered one for her as she slid onto the stool beside me.

"Man, I've been waiting for this beer since two o'clock," she sighed.

She smiled but it was a tired smile, the same expression anyone would wear after spending all day staring at a computer screen and talking to idiots. She took a slow sip while I sat there and let her breathe out the day.

"So, what you're telling me, Jake, is after I've gone to all this trouble and risked my ass for you, now you don't need the poop after all, is that right?"

"I'm sorry, Faye. I thought it might be a lead but it turns out it was just some nerd she'd been talking to about the Internet. I think Cassidy was in the early stages of putting together an adult website."

"Since when do you need a website to strip?"

"Well, from what I hear, the Internet can be pretty lucrative. You get ten thousand guys paying ten bucks a month to see you shake your booty, that's a hundred thousand dollars a month. Pretty good money, if you ask me."

"You're damn right it is," she said, then added, "*A Hundred Thousand Dollars?* Man, I'd take my clothes off and stuff 'em up my own ass for that kind of money."

I laughed out loud and nearly choked on a swallow of beer.

"Please...," I coughed, wiping the tears out of my eyes.

Looking at her then, this natural, unspoiled beauty, I tried to imagine what she'd look like on stage, driving men to mayhem as she peeled off layer after layer until she was as naked and pure as Venus Rising from the Sea. She must have known what I was thinking because she jabbed me in the ribs with her elbow.

"Rein 'em in, Big Boy, cause it ain't happening, at least not in your lifetime."

I came back to earth with a dull thud.

"Anyway," she went on, "I may be wrong about this, but I cross-checked the number several times and it never came up as an internet company. And if what you're saying is true, it looks like someone is taking public relations to a whole new level."

She handed me a slip of paper with a small computer print-out. I looked at the name and address: *Bodiford, Garmon & Foxe-Public Relations,* with an address on West Paces Ferry Road in Atlanta.

"Are you sure this is from the number I gave you? The number I called had a recording that said it was disconnected."

"It was," she answered, "but it was originally taken out as a private number from this company at this address. Seems weird, but really it happens all the time. Some big shot wants a direct line for his wife or his mistress or some other deal that he wants to keep secret."

I looked at the piece of paper again. I didn't know a lot about Atlanta, but I did know that West Paces Ferry was where the money was: a beautiful, tree-lined street filled with multi-million-dollar homes that ran straight into the heart of Buckhead. Even the Georgia Governor's mansion was located there. You'd have to be one big-time computer nerd to have an office in that neighborhood. I folded the paper and put it in my shirt pocket.

"Thanks, Faye. Who knows, maybe your time wasn't wasted after all."

After she left, I stayed for one more beer, smoking and think-ing, now and then taking the folded paper from my pocket and staring at the name and address, wondering what it all meant. I did know one thing- I wasn't going to get any answers by sitting in a bar, at least not a bar in Nashville. I paid the tab and started for the door but stopped a full ten feet before I got there. It was still daylight outside and even through the dark green tint of the window glass I could see Brundidge, the rookie cop, standing in a doorway across the street, holding up a copy of the Nashville

Scene with one eye on Mulligan's Pub, trying his neophyte best not to look suspicious. Instead, he stood out like a rented suit.

Out the door to the sidewalk, I turned left, heading up the street to see if he'd follow, which he did from a safe distance and seemingly unaware that I was on to him. I decided to let Brundidge play his game, knowing I could lose him easily enough when the time came. Besides, if I busted him, Lyle might replace him with someone who knew what they were doing. At least this way I'd always know exactly where he was.

I made a lap up and down Second Avenue before going home, giving Brundidge a good opportunity to walk off some baby fat. Closing the apartment door behind me, I left the kid to the humid night air and his own dimpled visions of Rockford. I was watching the Braves on the tube and planning my next move when the phone rang.

"Mr. Shepherd?"

"Mr. Shepherd was my father. I'd feel a lot younger if you'd call me Jake, Charlotte.

"Then Jake it is. I just wanted to touch base and see how your investigation is going."

"I don't know, Charlotte, I'm not sure I'd call it an investigation, but I am running down a few leads and up a few blind alleys. At this point I'm afraid I don't have anything of significance to report. I've got some people helping me but nothing's turned up yet and to tell you the truth, I'm not sure it will. As far as the police are concerned, the list of suspects is very short and my name is still at the top."

"Well, I just want you to know that my parents and I appreciate everything you're doing. I have faith that sooner or later something will turn up. But please, promise me you'll keep me informed of anything you find out. No matter how slight or inconsequential, I want to know."

"I will," I lied, wondering what Charlotte might think of her sister's internet project.

"I have no doubt you're doing everything you possibly can. Listen, Mr. Shep- I mean Jake, I'm in town for a couple of days to take care of Margaret Ellen's affairs. I was wondering if we might get together this evening over dinner, that is, if you don't already have plans?"

For the last hour I'd been going over a scheme in my head to sneak off to Atlanta and check out the address Faye had given me. I didn't want to be rude, but I certainly didn't need to waste two hours with Charlotte repeating what I'd already told her in thirty seconds. Still, it was her money that was keeping me in the ballgame.

"Actually, I do have plans a little later, but I suppose we could get together for a quick bite. I can be at the Music City Motel in an hour if that's all right."

"That's fine, Jake, but I'm at the Renaissance, downtown on Commerce. I'll meet you downstairs in the lobby."

The Renaissance? Jeez, that was only about fifty steps up the tourist ladder from Nolensville Road. Either Charlotte knew a little something about traveling first class or she was smart enough not to stay alone at the Music City Motel. Thinking back to that first meeting with her and her parents, I remembered how she had looked so out of place sitting in the greasy diner.

"See you in an hour," I said, then hung up the phone and took my third shower of the day. I put on fresh jeans and a clean shirt, then grabbed a linen sport coat as I locked the door and bounded down the stairs.

Pulling out of the parking lot, in the rear-view mirror I saw Brundidge scrambling across the street toward an unmarked police car, but I was through the light and headed up Broadway before he ever made it. I slowed down and stopped for the light at Fourth to give him time to catch up, then drove to the Renaissance and valet parked. From the glass front of the hotel entrance, I saw him pull in across the street and cut his lights.

"Get good and comfortable, Fat Boy. You're in for a long night," I said out loud.

CHAPTER 10

Charlotte was waiting in the lobby, a vision of tall beauty in a black silk pant suit. She offered a slender, perfectly manicured hand as I approached.

"Thank you for coming, Jake."

"It's good to see you, Charlotte," I said, taking her hand. "You look elegant."

"You mean for a girl from the hills of Georgia?"

"No, I mean from Park Avenue, Palm Beach or anywhere else."

"That's very sweet. Are you hungry? I understand the restaurant here has an excellent menu."

"Maybe later," I said. "I was hoping you might be up for a drive?"

A quizzical smile fanned across her lips.

"A drive? I thought you said you had plans later."

"I do have plans. But I just at this moment decided to include you in them. What do you say, want to go for a little spin?"

She paused a moment before conceding, "Alright then."

"Great. Let's go upstairs so you can change into something a little more comfortable. Lead the way."

"Aye, Aye, Sir," she saluted, as I followed her down the hall to the elevators. I stood at the back of the glass booth hoping Brundidge could see me from the street below, watching his car grow smaller as the elevator made its silent climb. At the fifteenth floor we got off and Charlotte led me down the hall and opened the door to a suite that must have cost five hundred bucks a night. I was a little overwhelmed, to say the least.

"Do you mind if I ask a question?" I said, glancing around at the opulent surroundings.

"I'll save you the trouble," she answered. "My parents would not be comfortable staying in a hotel such as this, so I chose a place where they might feel more at ease. The Music City Motel suited them just fine and, of course, that was fine with me as well."

"You're lucky you didn't get knocked in the head there, especially with the money you were carrying."

"I've always been able to take care of myself," she said, opening her purse to reveal a small .25 caliber revolver. "Besides, I'm never afraid when my father is around. He's a man who should not be underestimated."

"Well, I hate to preach," I said, "but preachers get knocked in the head too. There're some rough folks in that part of town."

"Like I said, don't underestimate him. Fix yourself a drink

while I change clothes," she added, motioning toward the wet bar. "By the way, where are we going?"

"Atlanta."

She stopped in her tracks and turned around, her face suddenly blank.

"You're joking, right?"

"Not a bit. Wear something comfortable."

"But...why?"

"I need to see a man about a horse."

The joke went past her but she cocked an eyebrow anyway. "What about dinner?"

"We'll eat in the car. Nothing like burgers and fries at seventy miles an hour for creating ambiance."

Her mouth opened again in protest, but the words lingered in her throat until finally, she turned and closed the door to the bedroom. She came out a few minutes later in a short denim skirt and breezy white cotton blouse. Her long, tanned legs were silky smooth as I watched her sit on the small sofa and put on a pair of expensive leather sandals. In that moment I realized she was every bit as beautiful as Cassidy, maybe even more so.

She listened as I laid out the plan. After putting her hair up under a ball cap, she was to take the stairs down four flights to the eleventh floor, then take the elevator to the lobby where the valet would have her car waiting at the front door. I'd take the stairs down the back and be waiting for her on the Seventh Avenue side of the hotel. With a little luck, Brundidge would be zeroed in on the fifteenth floor and waiting for my return to the glass elevator.

It worked. I was standing on the Seventh Avenue sidewalk smoking a cigarette when Charlotte pulled up in a shiny, black Volvo Turbo.

"Teachers are so underpaid," I quipped, as she slid over and gave me the wheel.

"Funny," she said. "Actually, it was a gift from an old boyfriend."

I took that admission as a nice way of letting me know I was way out of her league.

I drove over to Fifth and up a couple of blocks to see if Brundidge was still in place, which he was. I cut over to Fourth and went south across Broadway, then up the hill to the Interstate as Charlotte and I lit out for the home of the Braves.

Driving east on I-24, we made small talk as she relaxed and began to tell me more about Cassidy and herself.

"I was never as adventurous as Margaret Ellen," she confided. "Even when we were little girls, nine or ten years old, she was the one who wanted to be a movie star. My dreams were always smaller, even back then. I remember looking around the bedroom we shared, at the bare wooden walls that held just one picture, a small print of 'Jesus in the Garden.' I swore that someday I'd have a house with wallpaper and thick carpet in every room, with expensive paintings hanging throughout, while at the same time Margaret Ellen would be talking about growing up and marrying the President and moving to Hollywood to live in Marilyn Monroe's house. My God, that girl could dream."

Her voice caught and she turned her face toward the window. I drove on as the silence said everything for her. In a moment she reached into her purse and pulled out a small plastic bottle, leaned her head back, and dropped two drops of liquid into each eye.

"Allergies?" I asked. But she shook her head.

"I had laser surgery three weeks ago. I have to keep my eyes moist for the next few months, but it feels so wonderful not to wear glasses anymore." She took out a foil packet of pale blue tissues and drew one, dabbing at the corners of her eyes.

"Doesn't that feel good?" she said, placing the soft, damp towelette against my forehead.

"It does," I said, resisting the urge to close my eyes against the cool, silky fabric.

"I found them on the internet. They're made by the same French company that sells spring water. They're expensive, but totally organic. You can't buy them in the states."

She said it as though she were claiming membership to an exclusive club, one still undiscovered by the unwashed masses. Charlotte Eskew had come a long way from Ellijay, Georgia, I thought to myself.

Nearing Monteagle mountain the night had lost its muggy humidity so I killed the air conditioner in favor of rolling down the windows for a breath of cool air. Charlotte let back her seat and was reclining with her gorgeous legs resting on the dashboard as the wind rushed through the window, lifting the bottom of her denim skirt just slightly, then finally blowing it back across the top of her thighs. The moon roof was open, and the full moon lit up the inside of the car with soft blue light.

"We were such silly little girls," she said finally. "So full of big ideas and so afraid of everything that lay outside our little room. We were terrified of our father and yet completely aware of this great big love that he had for us. Our mother was always the intermediary, running interference between us and him, especially after we became teenagers. He was just so strict. We couldn't even wear shorts, for God's sake. Our dresses always had to be at least half-way between our knees and ankles. High school was just unbearable. Looking back, I'm surprised we didn't run away earlier than we did."

"Being a preacher's kid isn't easy," I said. "I was raised by my grandfather and he was a preacher, like your dad, only he travelled a circuit and dragged me with him all over the back roads of West Virginia and Kentucky. Soon as I had my size, I bolted too. Headed straight for all the wrong places and things until I finally wound up in front of a judge who was understanding enough to give me a choice between jail or the Marine Corps-"

"-And I'll bet you had no trouble making the right choice," she interrupted, laughing.

"I'm not so sure about that. But at the time, I was headed down a hard road. When you're a kid it's easy to get turned off by religion, and having it forced on you just pushes you farther away. I guess the Devil is always pulling at you from one side or the other, and when all that energy starts rolling in the same direction it's only natural to roll with it."

"Well now, aren't you the philosopher," she teased. "Wake me up when you start quoting Nietzsche." She turned her beautiful head toward me and closed her eyes.

I've never been one to resist the opportunity to impress a beautiful lady. Besides, how often in life does a shitkicker like me get the chance to quote Fred Nietzsche?

"Our destiny exercises its influence over us even when, as yet, we have not learned its nature: it is our future that lays down the law of our today."

"You're quite the enigma, Jake Shepherd," she said, then reached over and gently squeezed my thigh, sending a rush of adrenalin all the way down my leg and out to the gas pedal. The speedometer read eighty-five and climbing.

By the time we reached Chattanooga, Charlotte was sound asleep, so much so that I turned on the radio for company. I found an oldies station in Ringold, Georgia and half-listened as the Fifth Dimension sang about having "One Less Bell to Answer."

Driving on into the Georgia night I tried to imagine Charlotte and Cassidy as little girls, full of innocent dreams and fantasies, the whole wide world just one huge infinite possibility. I wondered at what point in our lives do we finally become aware that everything isn't really possible, that all dreams don't ultimately come true and not everyone lives happily ever after. Like so many of Life's sneaky little disappointments, I guess it happens gradually rather than suddenly, and by the time you realize it, capitulation is already wrapped tightly around your shoulders like a Mexican serape.

Charlotte's story had struck a familiar chord, and I wondered briefly why I hadn't felt the same kindred response with Cassidy, until I realized Charlotte had told me more about their childhood in thirty minutes than Cassidy revealed in the entire month we were together.

The whole conversation had me thinking about my own family tree, my father and grandfather Floyd in particular.

My father, who died in a mining accident when I was twelve years old, was the first songwriter I ever knew. He taught me chords on an old Sears Silvertone guitar that came with an amplifier built into the guitar case.

Dad wrote beautiful songs about the West Virginia hills and the coal miner's life, and he finger-picked that old Silvertone just like Merle Travis. But he could just as easily whip out a jazz standard like that of his other hero, the French/Turkish guitarist, Django Reinhardt. When I was born I was christened Django Travis Shepherd, though it became apparent early on that I would never live up to that moniker. But some pick the strings and some pick the words. Dad, however, could do both.

I still have a batch of his songs tucked away in a safe place. My favorite is a mining song called "Thunder in the Hole."

"It's the most frightening thing you can imagine," he said, fear resonating in his eyes as he spoke of being underground and hearing the chilling, thunderous sound the earth makes as it moves and shifts about, reacting to the invasion of something as severe as a mine shaft. "The kind of thing that'll make you get religion real fast," he added, then sang:

"I heard thunder, thunder, rumble and roll

There ain't no non-believers when it thunders in the hole."

I didn't doubt it was true. But the hole he worked and died in was nowhere near as deep as the one he left in my life.

After his death my mother went crazy. I went to live with my grandfather, and she was sent to the state hospital in Charlottesville, where she stayed for two years before dying of pneumonia.

As for my Granddaddy Floyd, he worked thirty years in those same coal mines, and found God the night he raced a cave-in all the way to the mouth of the mine, claiming later that he saw Christ standing in the entrance with arms outstretched as he ran blindly and furiously through the belching smoke and fumes, the only survivor in a catastrophe that claimed eighteen men.

It changed him forever, not just spiritually but physically as well. His coal-black hair turned snow-white overnight and the worn, beaten expression in his weathered eyes and face disappeared, and in its place, a wild-eyed look of joy and salvation. He felt 'called' to preach and did so at every opportunity, whether it be at a church service, fish fry, election, or coon hunt. Since he had no church of his own, we travelled a lot: he, my Aunt Ruby and me, first into the nearby hollers around West Virginia, and then eventually into Maryland and back down into Kentucky with Granddaddy Floyd preaching, Aunt Ruby on the piano and singing, and me, playing guitar and passing the hat for a Love Offering.

I served four long years in that army of the Lord before running away one night during a prayer meeting in Cumberland, Maryland. I flagged a trucker in Ridgely, then rode my thumb all the way to Sarasota, Florida. Eventually I hooked up with a traveling carnival show, landing work first as a lot boy, then with the flat stores and grinds, and finally working my way up to the exalted position of bandleader with the Hoochie Coochie show. It was there I met and fell in love with my first stripper, a rough, salty redhead by the name of Ivory Dale Blevens, better known around the midway as Slingshot. But that's a whole 'nother story.

Charlotte had been napping peacefully beside me until I stopped in Dalton, Georgia, the carpet capital of the world, for black coffee and a stretch.

"Perfect timing," she yawned, as she got out and headed for the ladies' room. A tank of gas and a fresh pack of cigarettes and we were back on the road as I smoked and sipped coffee while Charlotte purred like a prom queen on her way to Daytona for Spring break.

The Georgia State Patrol almost invented radar so I kept the Volvo dead on seventy as we took our time on I-75, past

Calhoun, Cartersville, Marietta, until we hit the Atlanta city limits and the West Paces Ferry Road exit not too far beyond. I turned east toward Buckhead, searching for street numbers as I drove. The last time I was on this street I was headed for a party at the Governor's Mansion with Jimmy Carter and the Allman Brothers. Wild days then, long gone now.

It took about two minutes to find it. I don't know what I had expected, maybe I'd imagined it being closer to Peachtree Street and in the heart of Buckhead. Maybe I was expecting an imposing four or five-story office building with lots of glass and steel. In any case what I found was definitely not what I'd imagined.

The address on West Paces Ferry was a house, or rather a mansion of red brick with white marble columns sitting squarely on several acres of perfectly manicured lawn and surrounded by a sturdy brick and wrought iron fence that I judged to be somewhere around nine feet tall. At the entrance was a heavy steel security gate, complete with a small brick guard house containing one serious-looking guard in a summer service uniform.

I drove on up the street and out of sight before turning around, then cut the lights as I headed back for another look. About a hundred yards down the street, I found an opening in a line of parked cars, slipped in and cut the engine. My first notion was to get out for a closer look but decided against it. This was certainly not an area of town to be walking casually down the street at two a.m. without attracting attention. Too many guard dogs, security cameras and patrol cars cruising by to risk getting stopped. I'd have to do all my recon from the driver's seat, at least on this trip. I glanced over at Charlotte sleeping like a baby on the reclined seat.

Slowly my eyes studied the huge fence from the gate to the corner of the property and down the back side. I counted three security cameras perched on the brick posts and presumed that was just the tip of the iceberg.

In a few minutes the guard came out of his perch and began walking in our direction. For a moment I thought he'd spotted us, but then he stopped abruptly at the corner of the property, turned and looked down the fence line. Reaching up, he hit a switch on the fence column and the entire section of the fence lit up along the bottom as it ran for a couple hundred yards toward the rear of the property.

The guard sighted down the fence line for a few seconds, then switched off the lights and headed back for the gate. As he was walking back, the rear section of the fence lit up the same way, indicating a second guard. Whoever lived in that big mass of brick and marble was either very paranoid or owned something that required very tight security.

Passing the gate, the guard walked to the other corner and repeated the lighting procedure. This time he spoke briefly into a walkie-talkie, then killed the lights and walked back to the guard shack to resume his post. My watch read 2:05 a.m. I waited in the dark car as both guards repeated the drill at 2:30 and again at 3 o'clock.

I'd been so busy watching the guards I hadn't noticed the pair of headlights moving slowly down the long driveway until the car was almost to the gate. The guard snapped to attention as a white limousine eased through the open gate, turning up the street in our direction. Caught momentarily in the headlights, I froze like a deer as it approached, slowing considerably until it inched alongside us at a dead crawl. I knew we were being checked out so I turned to look at the car. All the windows were heavily blackened, and all I could see was a reflection of me sitting in the Volvo as the limo came to a complete stop for a brief moment before speeding off.

I looked over in the seat at Charlotte, still asleep, but she had somehow slid off the reclined seat almost to the floor, her face pressed against the door and out of sight. I hadn't even heard her move.

As three or four cars drove past us, I started the Volvo and pulled out into the traffic. Driving by the gate, I slowed just enough to glance through the steel bars toward the imposing mansion. No guards were visible inside the grounds but there had to be more somewhere.

A few blocks down the street I stopped and pulled Charlotte back into the seat, then hit the ramp to I-75 North and headed back, stopping only for coffee in Marietta and then again in Chattanooga. We made Twangtown in a little over three and a half hours with Charlotte sleeping soundly all the way.

CHAPTER 11

The next morning I called Charlotte for the lunch date I'd promised and by two o'clock we were sitting on the deck at La Paz, a Southwestern restaurant in Green Hills, eating spinach quesadillas with goat cheese and drinking margaritas.

"Thanks again for the company last night," I toasted, raising my glass. "You were a real trooper."

"I'm afraid I wasn't all that much company," she smiled. "But I enjoyed the ride and the conversation. I'm just sorry I fell asleep and left you to do all the work. Did you find whatever it was you were looking for?"

"I'm not sure. I found the address, but I still don't know who or what lives there. I'll be a lot better prepared when I go back for another look, although my guess is that drop-in visitors aren't necessarily welcome."

She took a short sip from the straw in her margarita and nodded.

"You know, Jake, no one would blame you if you decided to let this go. It doesn't seem right for you to put yourself in danger, and I'm not sure anything you find out will help that much at this point. To tell you the truth, I think my parents have started to reach some sort of acceptance with it all."

"I appreciate that, Charlotte, but I'm really doing this as much for myself as for anyone else. I'm not tossing in the towel just yet."

Charlotte leaned across the table, her eyes already misty with a warm tequila glaze. "Whatever it is you find there, you will tell me about it, won't you?"

"Of course I will," I nodded. "After all, I work for you now, remember?"

She smiled and tossed back her lustrous auburn hair and if I hadn't known better I would have sworn she was in the early stages of flirting. Probably just a little encouragement from José Cuervo, but that was okay- José had been helping me out for years. I thought back to the night before and the soft squeeze on my thigh that almost sent me careening off Monteagle Mountain.

"How long are you going to be in town?"

"Just a couple days. Long enough to take care of Margaret Ellen's affairs and go through her things, decide what to keep and what not to. It's not something I'm looking forward to."

As she spoke, the corners of her mouth turned down with a resignation we both understood. I knew she was still hurting and I almost felt guilty for not being more visibly remorseful. I was beginning to accept Cassidy's death just as I had ultimately accepted the breakup of our brief relationship.

"If you like, I can go with you to the apartment," I offered. "That is, if you think it would make things easier."

"Thank you, Jake, that's very sweet of you, but I'm afraid this is something I need to do alone. You understand, don't you?"

"Of course I do. Just be prepared for a mess because the police really tore the place up."

"Well," she said, "I'm sure they'll return everything when they finish their investigation. But as far as the mess, I spoke with Margaret Ellen's roommate and she told me she'd straightened up the room and even boxed up some things for me to go through. She sounded very sweet. That was a very nice thing for her to do, don't you think?"

I nodded agreement, although sweet wasn't normally the word I would've used to describe Heather. And it did seem odd that she had overcome her fear of entering Cassidy's room so soon, even for a little housecleaning.

"I'll write down the directions for you when we get back to the hotel. It's not really that hard to find from downtown. Just get on Twelfth Avenue and keep going until it becomes Granny White Pike. You'd be surprised how many streets in Nashville have more than one name."

"You're telling me," she said, "I almost went crazy last summer trying to find my way around."

"Last summer?"

"Yes, I was here as an advisor to the Student Political Caucus from our school. That's how Margaret Ellen discovered the town, on a weekend visit with me. We both fell in love with Nashville and swore that we were going to move here permanently. And of course, as was her style, Margaret Ellen did exactly what she said she was going to, only she did it way ahead of me. I just wish for once she'd waited a while before running off up here by herself."

"You can't blame yourself for that, Charlotte. She was a grown woman capable of making her own decisions. Don't do that to yourself. It's not fair."

She looked away for a moment, out across the deck, past the rushing traffic on Cleghorn Avenue to another time, another summer. I knew she was hurting but she turned back to me and shook her head before mounting the bravest of smiles.

"Please forgive me, Jake, but I absolutely refuse to ruin this incredibly beautiful afternoon." She raised her glass and I joined her in a long, slow drink as the chilled tequila washed the blues from the air between us.

Even though it was late August, the afternoon breeze was easy, with just the slightest whiff from the west combing through Charlotte's reddish-brown curls. At the other end of the deck a singer was warbling "Desperado," a song I'd always believed to be a shoo-in for the Top Ten on Hell's jukebox.

Charlotte leaned closer across the table, pinning me with those misty, hazel eyes, a dash of salt rimming the edge of her bottom lip, waiting for the sweet lick of her moist tongue.

"Tell me something, Jake. Why did you quit?"

"Quit what?" I answered, without taking my eyes off her mouth.

"Music. I don't know, I...I guess I don't understand how someone just walks away from something like that. I've always thought being a writer or musician was almost like a...a 'calling' for lack of a better word. Am I making sense?"

I nodded, remembering how my grandfather had been 'called' to preach.

"I don't know," I shrugged. "It's hard to pinpoint a specific moment or event. I just know that somewhere along the road of my life, I fell into a ditch and stayed there. One minute I had everything and the next minute I had zip. But I'll tell you something, I never made excuses for what happened. I always accepted responsibility for everything and readily admit it was my fault."

"Was it booze and drugs?"

I couldn't help but wince at the banality, even though her question was sincere.

"It would be simple enough to blame it all on booze and drugs, Charlotte. But the fact is, they were just a small part of it. The real problem is that I woke up one morning and realized I no longer believed in myself: I was a fraud, a phony. I'd come close, but no cigar. I had the distinct honor of being a has-been and a never-was all at the same time. I wish I could tell you there's some sort of symbolic poetry in all of that, but the truth is, sometimes things are just what they seem. When the Muse or Bitch Goddess of Art or whatever else you want to call her, when she hops a train, then Baby, you're left with a mule to ride and everything else comes to a grinding halt. And then you wait, which is what I've been doing these last few years."

Charlotte sat back in her chair and I realized I'd been steadily raising my voice. What the hell, she wanted straight answers, by God she got 'em. Talking about myself always made me edgy, especially when the conversation centered on the sad un-fulfillment of my once great and promising talent. When you're facing a murder rap, as I appeared to be, you have to figure the future holds plenty of time for woeful reflection and regret, in my case twenty to thirty years' worth.

"Do you think you'll ever write again?"

"I write all the time, Lady, it's just that none of it is ever worth a damn. Now, if you don't mind my asking, why all the interest in the long-dead career of a one-hit wonder whose only claim to fame was a silly novelty tune years ago?"

"Because I've always been fascinated by the creative process," she smiled, cooling me instantly with just the faintest flash of white teeth.

"Now it's all clear," I nodded, suddenly aware of her motive. "I feel like an idiot for not putting two-and-two together in the first place: English teacher. Aspiring writer, obviously. Probably have a notebook full of poems and short stories tucked away in your desk drawer, right? Maybe even a novel. No, it's even worse- you want to chuck your brilliant educational career to write songs, is that it?"

If my intention was to embarrass her it fell short.

Her smile widened, then blossomed into a laugh.

"You couldn't be farther from the truth, Jake. And I teach International Marketing, by the way. I admit to being a serious fan of the written word but I honestly haven't harbored any desires to be a writer, at least not since I was a little girl. But I do like to surround myself with greatness, so maybe that's why I chose teaching."

"Why not take some of that International Marketing know-how and go make some money with it?" I asked. "Let someone else teach for chicken feed." I regretted the words as soon as they came out of my mouth.

"Because teaching is an honorable profession," she said.

"And I've been fortunate to make some good investments."

She winked at me, but I was well aware that she had once again put me in my place. She leaned back and applied her eye drops, then dabbed at her eyes with her chic blue towelette.

"Ever know any real writers?"

I might as well have smacked her across the face with a cold halibut. The playful smile vanished and in its place a stoic resonance.

"Just one, ...a long time ago." Her expression indicated it was something she didn't want to talk about and yet I could tell she was dying to tell me.

"Go on," I coaxed, although I had the feeling I could probably tell the story myself or at least lay down a good outline.

"There's really not much to tell," she began, as if all along the entire conversation had been directed to this very moment.

"I was in college, at Emory, and he came to town for a reading. Looking back now I can see that I was just a dizzy schoolgirl and I'm sure he must have thought so as well but, anyway, after his reading I waited in line to get an autograph. I'd read his book at a particularly volatile time in my life and felt I'd received some important answers and perhaps even a strange sense of direction. I know that sounds silly, but in retrospect I think we're all like that in our early twenties, don't you? We're just so open and optimistic and so very eager to find some sort of meaning in all the madness."

She took a sip of her drink and shifted in her seat to cross her legs, her soft thighs making the damp whisper of flesh against flesh.

"Anyway," she continued, "I waited in line for over an hour as he signed books and smiled at each person in line. But when my turn came, he didn't smile at me, not in the least. He just stared at me for the longest time before writing inside the cover of the book. When he finished, he closed it with a quick snap and handed it to me without saying a word, no smile, just a simple nod of his head.

"But in that moment, that small instant, it was as if he was looking inside me, not just into my heart but all the way down into the depths of my soul. That simple nod of his head had communicated so much more than all the blank smiles in our lives. Do you want me to tell you what he wrote?"

I nodded as she blew a small breath and went on.

"It said: 'Dear Charlotte, I am blinded by the brilliance of your beauty. I would give my last breath to spend just a few moments with you. Please call me at the Peachtree Plaza Hotel tonight after nine.' And then he signed his name with a flourish."

She had my attention, even though I could see the end coming a mile away. I let her run with it.

"Did you call him?"

"Oh yes. I called him at 9:05 that evening from the lobby of his hotel. He said he was finishing up a meeting and that I should take the elevator to the sixteenth floor and knock on his door at precisely 9:30."

"And you did exactly as he asked."

"Exactly."

"Let me guess," I interrupted. "You went to his room, he made you a drink, and then he took you to bed."

"No, not really. He made me a drink and we talked for a while. He talked about his life, his work, and his family. He told me that he and his wife had not been intimate for years. The sadness in his heart was palpable, and at some point he began to cry inconsolably, railing at his lonely and barren life."

"And that's when he took you to bed," I injected, at the same time trying to catch the waitress' attention. I wanted to be fortified just in case Charlotte began to get graphic in her storytelling.

"I held him as he wept, and when it was over he apologized profusely. He was ashamed for behaving like that in front of a stranger, even though it seemed as if we'd known each other forever. He kissed me and said he was sure I'd been sent from Heaven to save him from the misery and isolation of a lonely life. We'd been embracing on the sofa, when suddenly he fell to his knees on the floor in front of me and began to pray loudly."

Charlotte was wrong about her talent. She had me 'tore up from the floor up' and I fidgeted in the seat as she took a slow, seductive pull at her drink and went on talking.

"Needless to say, I was so moved by such a display of emotion that I hardly noticed that during his prayer he'd maneuvered himself into a position of supplication directly between my knees."

"I love this story," I said, drawing a quick breath.

Charlotte was beginning to subtly rock back and forth in her chair, almost in rhythmic cadence to her sultry, yet mannered speech.

"And then he finished praying with a loud 'Amen' and without so much as a 'by your leave,' he lifted my skirt and buried his face in my lap. Believe me, it was all very emotional," she sighed, as she slumped back in her chair, quivering and spent from the memory of it all.

I sat there enthralled, tequila drunk and so aroused I could have taken her right there on the patio of the restaurant. This beautiful woman, this goddess, this seductive, wild, exquisitely vulgar and yet so very proper lady who had just told me her greatest and most precious secret, a soft and vulnerable woman who was looking to me for strength and answers but was right now slouched in her seat across the table laughing breathily while trying to focus her dreamy, slitted eyes.

"Is that a true story?" I asked.

"Does it matter?"

I leaned over and half whispered, "No, but tell it to me again, a little slower this time, and don't leave anything out."

She made a shivering motion as she bit her bottom lip and sucked on it for a long moment, all of which only helped turn my knees into guacamole.

"As you can obvioushly see," she slurred, "I've quite reashed my limit. Can I depend on you to see me safely back to my hotel?"

"Absolutely," I replied, knowing full well at that moment she could have depended on me to do just about anything she asked- fight the Hundred Years War, join the Billy Graham Crusade, shave my head and eat crackers, you name it.

I paid the tab and helped her to the car, then drove up Hillsboro Road against the rush hour traffic while the dust and humid August air drew the sweat out of us both like some ancient Indian ritual. By the time we reached the Renaissance she was almost asleep, but she managed to walk to the elevator where, once inside, she threw her arms around me and kissed me deeply before passing completely out. I carried her to her suite and laid her on the bed, then stood and watched her as she sailed away into the salty, lime-colored sea of tequila dreams.

As I removed her sandals, her breathing turned into a soft purr as she rolled onto her side, the short linen skirt climbing above her smooth thigh and exposing her pale white panties. I covered her with a light blanket and, closing the bedroom door, went into the living area and slept on the sofa until after midnight, then quietly got up and went home.

CHAPTER 12

"**W**ake up, Knucklehead. Nobody naps on my payroll."

Truck Bennett was sound asleep in his car, parked in front of the old house on Gallatin Road and obviously still crashed from the night before. I banged on the window of the battered Plymouth to wake him up.

Truck had bought the Plymouth, a worn-out former police patrol car, at an auction for nearly nothing. And, in a genuine show of good breeding or lack thereof, instead of painting the whole car a new color, any color besides patrol car white, Truck just spray painted over all the police insignias and stripes until he had a genuine, white-trash blues mobile.

"How can you tail anyone in that gaudy piece of crap?" I once asked him.

"At a distance," was all he'd said.

It took a few knocks but I finally roused him awake. His face was bloated, and he looked like an English bulldog with a toothache.

"I like your new digs, Chubby, except in this neighborhood you could wake up with your bedroom on blocks and your throat cut."

"Screw you, Shepherd. What are you, the neighborhood watch?"

"Just looking out for you, Truck. I need you safe and sound until you earn your thousand bucks."

"Don't worry about me," he groused. "I pass out here a lot of nights just so's I can be at work early the next morning. Gives me a jump on the day."

He staggered a little as he went up the steps of the old brick building that, like the both of us, was way past its prime. Once inside I made coffee while he fumbled around for Alka Seltzer and aspirin. He took off his rumpled, filthy shirt and exchanged it for one only slightly less dirty from a closet in the hall. In a few minutes we settled down to a breakfast of coffee and cigarettes as I told him about the phone number and my trip to Atlanta.

"Whatever the heck it is, it sounds like a big operation," he mused, lighting another Pall Mall from his first one before stubbing it out. "Any joint with a walking patrol front and back has obviously got something inside that's mighty important. Something either very valuable or else something they don't want anybody to see."

"You'd think it was Fort Knox," I said.

"Well, you never know, it might be the Atlanta version of Fort Knox. Give me the address again and let me do some checking around. I've got a couple buddies down there working security for all the movie stars that come through. Let me give 'em a call and ask 'em to check it out."

"Go ahead," I said. "But something tells me the only way to find out anything about that joint is from the inside. I'm going back for a closer look."

"Really? And whose army are you taking with you? You go running off down there half-cocked and I can promise you'll wind up in deep shit or worse."

"What have I got to lose?"

Truck shook his head wearily. "Look, Jake, do you want answers, or do you just want to throw a firecracker in the out-house? In this business, a lack of patience will get you big-time killed. Now, give me some time and let me check this out."

I thought about it for a moment. He was right.

"Fine by me," I nodded. "All I know is that Bodiford, Garmon & Foxe is supposedly a PR company located some-where in the building. But I'm thinking it all has to fit together. You just don't throw up that kind of security and then start subletting offices to outsiders."

"Well, like I said, I'll make some calls and get back to you," he promised, then absently-mindedly began shuffling papers on his desk. I took that as a hint that I could leave. I knew he hurt too bad to start drinking again so maybe he was actually going to do some work. If that was the case, I didn't want to get in his way.

"I'm out of here. Call me if you find out anything."

"You bet," was all he said, as he poured another cup of

coffee, then grabbed an old newspaper and headed down the hall toward the bathroom.

I walked out into the hot, humid morning, a late-blooming dullness beginning to form in the back of my head from yesterday's margaritas. Pointing the Eldorado back across the bridge with the stereo on low volume, I daydreamed as Billy Walker sang about crossing the Brazos at Waco.

A vision of Charlotte Eskew floated cloud-like and foggy through the Cuervo leftovers in my brain. I thought about how she looked at lunch the day before: her hair, her eyes, her perfect full lips with just a crust of margarita salt begging to be licked off.

Heading south on Third Avenue I almost hung a right on Commerce to the Renaissance but didn't. Charlotte was probably up and gone by now anyway. I couldn't think of many things worse than going through the personal effects of your recently deceased kid sister.

Once, in another lifetime, when I'd been in Vietnam about a week, one of the first details I caught was loading duffel bags onto a truck. I was still in the rear, getting processed and acclimated before being shipped north to spend the rest of my tour hiding in elephant grass and tromping around in water buffalo shit.

It was choking hot, well over a hundred degrees and perfectly matched with that swell Asian humidity, and we were sweating and cursing as we loaded these countless bags onto a stake-bed truck. It took about an hour before it dawned on me what we were doing- we were sending home the personal effects of dead Marines. All those olive-green bags were on their way back to Camp Pendleton or Camp LeJeune to sit in a warehouse until some Colonel felt enough time had passed before shipping them home so some poor Marine's family could sift through their child's last possessions.

I can remember, even in that angry oven heat, the frigid chill that went up my back when I thought about some disinterested Marine tossing *my* duffel bag up on that same truck a few weeks or months down the road. And with that thought, the icy chill became frozen to my tailbone, obliterating the Asian heat and cold-welding itself to the core of my psyche. It went with me to the bush, on recon patrols, through firefights, even went with me on R&R. It flew back to the world with me too, and only after a long and lethal bombardment of alcohol and drugs did it finally begin to thaw. Eventually it melted away but it left a small shadow that I still carry around like a tattoo on my ass- I forget it's there until something or somebody reminds me of it, like Benny Watts staring down in one of my dark, rainy nightmares, smiling and reassuring me that everything is going to be okay, grinning with that bloody mouthful of glistening white teeth and pointing to the cool shadow sleeping next to my soul.

I desperately needed something a little more cheerful to occupy my mind and, as luck would have it, at that moment Billy Joe Shaver's voice came ringing out of the speakers and before I knew it, I was singing right along with him to "Georgia on a Fast Train." By the time I reached Music Row the black cloud had lifted.

Papa's Range Rover was parked behind the studio, along with several other trucks and 4X4's and a shiny red BMW with Florida plates. I parked the Caddy under a shady tree and went in the back door and down the stairs to the studio.

Several musicians were milling about, setting up equipment, going over charts. Behind the glass wall of the control room Papa was talking animatedly to a petite, tanned blonde beauty who couldn't have been a day over seventeen. At the console sat Stewart, the engineer, fiddling with knobs and slides and paying absolutely no attention to the precious young thing standing within inches of his face.

As I made my way to the control room, I tried to remember the last time I was in a studio, probably two or three years. After a minute's thought I realized, somewhat sadly, it had been almost six years since I'd been inside a real studio, or at least anything with more than sixteen tracks.

Papa was in full character when I walked in.

"Jake, come in m'boy- Jake Shepherd, I want you to meet next year's CMA Horizon Award winner- Miss Yolanda Sweet." He motioned to the girl who turned and smiled at me with the innocent face of a sun-tanned angel. She held out her little hand for me to shake.

"How do you do, Mr. Shepherd," she cooed, in a damp voice. "I'm really down with recording your song."

I didn't know if she could sing, but she looked like a movie star and she had a voice that was made for midnight phone calls. If there was a country version of Lolita, she was it. I struggled and finally spoke.

"Nice to meet you," was all I could get out.

Luckily, with Papa around, talking wouldn't be necessary.

"Jake, isn't she just the purtiest thing you've ever seen? And she sings every bit as good as she looks."

I glanced at Yolanda Sweet for the requisite blush, but she looked as if she was used to hearing that stuff all the time. My question was, how in God's name did Papa land her? A lot of bigger players than him would have given her a deal on looks alone, just to have her around.

Sometimes you can just look at someone and tell they have everything it takes to go all the way. By God, Yolanda Sweet had it. The very sight of her made my ears ring with the sound of cash registers.

"Are you nervous, Yolanda?"

"I guess," she shrugged, then blew a huge pink bubble of gum.

Okay, so maybe this wasn't her first rodeo after all. Fine by me, she could be as big a brat as she wanted if she was going to cut my song and make me rich.

I thought for a moment about what it would be like to be back on top again. Money, respect, reputation- all the things three minutes on the radio can bring. Then I remembered Angie LeFevre, who would most likely be devastated when Yolanda's version hit the charts ahead of her, backed with tons of promotional wallop. At first she'd want to kill me but I knew she'd eventually get over it. Besides, I kept telling myself, it was all just the nature of the music business. All sins and shortcomings can be forgiven in just three minutes here in TuneTown. If all that was coming my way again, then a little sucking up to Yolanda Sweet was a small price to pay.

"Yolanda," I said, summoning up my very best sincere voice, "I just want you to know how grateful I am that you chose to record "Sheet Music." I've always believed in that song and felt it could be a hit if the right person ever cut it.

"Right now, it's just words on a piece of paper, but the moment you pick it up, Yolanda, the moment you take it into your heart and hold it and mold it into something greater...when you take the air from your own mouth and breathe life into it so that it becomes yours...in that moment this song becomes a living, breathing thing. I just want you to know how much I...I appreciate your taking my little words and turning them into a...Song."

With those last few words my voice caught in my throat as if I were trying to choke back a tear. A famous Opry singer taught me how to do that and it worked damn near every time.

And it must have worked with Yolanda Sweet. I stood there holding her little hand in both of mine as I watched the crystal, watery trail start down her smooth, bronze cheek. She sniffed a couple of times, then finally threw her arms around me like some long-lost uncle she was welcoming back from the war. She hugged me tight and kissed me on the cheek like a proud niece before whispering "Opryland Hotel, Room 1422," in my ear and darting her tongue in once to make sure I got the message. Then she turned and walked out into the studio to survey the goings on, hands on her hips like a little general.

I felt my heart stop, so I waited to see if it was going to start again or if I would just die right where I stood. It kicked in when Papa slapped me on the back.

"Goddangit, ain't she just the hottest thing you've ever seen? If I was you, I'd go home and start writing her next hit today. When she hits with this one, it's only natural to turn right back to you for the next one. If you're smart, Son, you'll take advantage of it."

I put my finger in my ear to wipe away the dampness and couldn't help laughing. I knew she was jailbait but what-the-hell, I was already heading in that direction anyway.

"Is she putting down my song today?"

"Oh no, not for at least a day or two. I want to get her used to the studio first. We may take a dry run at it sometime this week, but I've got a couple of throwaway sides I want to do first until I think she's ready."

Translated, that meant he was getting ready to milk someone for more money. Same old Papa. Give him a golden goose and he couldn't resist squeezing that neck just a little bit.

"Well, call me when you're ready to do the mix," I said. "I'd like to be here for that."

I went through the studio, weaving around the amps and microphone stands as I made my way toward the stairs. Off in the corner, Yolanda Sweet was whispering something to the drummer.

CHAPTER 13

The old Caddy almost drove itself to Cassidy's apartment as I rode along with the window slightly cracked, smoking a cigarette and breathing in the misty, late-summer rain that had begun falling, listening to the tires hum a damp music on the slick neighborhood streets.

I knew that, emotionally, I still hadn't dealt with Cassidy's death and would eventually have to. Grieving for the loss of her was not the same as searching my heart for a place to lay the guilt, or blame, or even a sense of responsibility. I've always had a tendency to be hard on myself, sometimes too hard. But try as I might, this time I seemed to be having trouble putting on the hair shirt. Cassidy was a grown woman who made her own decisions.

Being a dancer was her choice, even as she dreamed of bigger and better things just as all of us do. And it was her decision to break it off with me, which she had done as best she knew how. Still, I couldn't help thinking there was something she wanted to tell me, or at least talk to me about and wouldn't, or maybe couldn't.

When I reached the apartment Heather's rust bucket was gone and Charlotte's Volvo was parked in the driveway. The front door was unlocked, so I called out "Hello" before letting myself in. Charlotte didn't answer but I could hear her moving about in the back bedroom.

"Charlotte, it's me."

"Back here, Jake," she finally answered.

I walked back to the bedroom that no longer seemed familiar, a stark room stacked with boxes and clutter, the last material imprint of Margaret Ellen Eskew on this world. Her death had left a legacy of old magazines, some clothes and hats on the closet floor, a few CD's on the dresser, a radio/ alarm clock, and a huge, purple stuffed elephant standing in the corner waiting patiently for her return.

Charlotte was going through the dresser, tossing Cassidy's T-shirts and underwear over her shoulder onto the bed. When she looked up at me she smiled weakly, took a step towards me, and then collapsed into my arms sobbing. I stood and held her to let her get it all out, and at some point I noticed I was crying right along with her, unashamed and uninhibited, both of us seeming to draw the black grief from deep within each other.

With her arms still tight around my neck, Charlotte took a step back, pulling me with her as we tumbled onto the bed now covered in Cassidy's discarded underclothes, a great pile of T-shirts, panties, bras and stockings that seemed to swallow us up and cover us with Cassidy's scent as we lay holding on to each other, as if through this sad and strange union we were somehow holding on to Cassidy as well.

After a few minutes the tears stopped but we still held on, breathing against each other as we fought for strength to overcome the powerful, unforgivable urge that had slowly begun to surface. Charlotte pulled back, and for a moment I thought we were saved, but then I saw her eyes were open, just inches from mine, and I wondered if the surrender I saw there was hers or just a reflection of my own. She kissed me then, and I knew I was damned but I didn't care.

We tore at each other in a way that was scarcely human: torrid but tender, desperate but deserving, and as we came together I remember thinking how ashamed I should feel when, in truth, all I felt was this great, overwhelming sense of need, a physical, emotional, and spiritual longing that one must surely feel when the promise of home seems like a distant memory that fades with every step in that direction.

Once inside her I let go as Charlotte took me to this new world, a place of soft murmurs and breathless sighs, a land of damp, musky smells and sweet, warm honey, a country of shared souls where all things were forgiven and promise was absolute. She kissed and bit at my neck, clutching my hair with the fingers of one hand and pushing with the other at the small of my back, drawing me deeper and deeper as I fought to prolong the release that burst suddenly and loud, like the thunder resonating outside the little cottage.

When it was over we lay together, holding each other without speaking as the rain fell softly against the windows and the room darkened into evening. Finally, my mouth formed the only word in my new vocabulary.

"Charlotte..."

"Shhh...," she whispered, placing a finger on my lips.

"I'm not sorry," I breathed.

"I know," she sighed, and snuggled closer against me.

We fell asleep and when we awoke it was almost ten o'clock. After getting dressed in silence I helped her load a few boxes into her car. She was going back to Atlanta the next day so I suggested dinner, but she was tired and I understood.

After she finally agreed to meet me for breakfast the next morning, I went home and had the best night's sleep I'd had since I was a little boy back in West Virginia, when I would lie in that wrought-iron bed under a pile of quilts and drift off to sleep, the rain tapping out its own gentle Morse code on the tin roof, the stale cloud of Prince Albert smoke hovering near the ceiling, assuring me of quiet slumber.

At nine the next morning I rang Charlotte's room from a house phone in the lobby of the Renaissance but got no answer. Thinking she might be in the shower, I took a table in the coffee shop and read the paper as I waited.

Cassidy's murder was old news by now so there was no mention of her or the investigation. The front page detailed the upcoming buyout of several small music publishing companies by a huge conglomerate, as well as a bulletin about a young Hollywood actress who'd been missing for several days.

Sounded like a cheap publicity stunt to me, either that or a cover-up for a rehab visit.

There was the annual August profile of the Vanderbilt

football team, with the usual lame prediction that this could very well be the year for the Commodores. All this as well as the recurring update on Carter Robinson, who still insisted he had no interest in the oval office. I paid scant attention to the story, but I did chuckle at the thought that Robinson had to be losing just a little sleep, wondering when the ever- inquisitive media would start snooping around the family tree and find Aleta Thomas and her strip clubs hanging from a low branch.

After calling Charlotte's room again and getting no answer, I took the elevator to her floor but my heart fell when I turned the corner and saw the housekeeping cart parked just outside the open door of her room. I stood in the doorway as a young Laotian girl was putting the finishing touches on the freshly made bed.

"Where did she go?"

The young maid looked at me with a surprised but blank expression.

"Check Out," was all she said, as she tightened the bedspread around the pillows.

I was disappointed and angry and she was the closest victim. I walked over and grabbed her arm and spun her around.

"When did she leave? How long ago?"

Startled, the tiny brown maid jerked away, her eyes wide and her little mouth open in surprise.

"Check Out! Check Out!" she snapped, the fear in her eyes quickly turning to hostility. Then she motioned toward the door with her little arms. "You go now. You go."

For a split second a vicious, carnal thought flashed across my mind like a tracer bullet and I flinched, stumbling out the door in shock and nauseous disbelief.

At the front desk they told me Charlotte had indeed checked out early but left something addressed to my attention. I took the letter-sized envelope back to the coffee shop and plopped down at my table, hurt, disgusted, and feeling more than a little sorry for myself. Inside the envelope was a note, handwritten by Charlotte on hotel stationery. I ordered more coffee and read her words repeatedly, as though I were trying to memorize them:

Dear Jake,

Please forgive me for leaving like this but there have been far too many goodbyes lately. Yesterday was wonderful, although I lay awake most of the night wondering if it was real or just something I had dreamed. As far as timing goes, I think we both know that ours couldn't possibly be any worse. I realize it's not much but please know that you will never be far from my thoughts.

One more thing- I want you to promise me you'll try to find that thing within yourself that you've lost, or perhaps buried. I'm talking about your passion, the thing that drives you and gives you purpose, the thing that makes you who you are. No one will ever make you happy until you do, Jake.

My classes start next week and I must get back and pack as I am moving north of Atlanta to Dahlonega to teach at a small college in the mountains. I'm not all that well-traveled, but I do know there is no place on Earth like the North Georgia mountains in the fall. Take care of yourself, Jake, but most of all, be good to yourself, and know that you are always in my heart.

Love, Charlotte

When I finished reading the letter, I folded it back into the envelope and stuck it in my shirt pocket just as the waitress came by with a fresh pot of coffee. She reached for my cup but I waved her away.

"What time does the bar open?"

CHAPTER 14

Just like cops, there's never a bartender around when you need one. With two hours til pouring time in the hotel bar, I decided that, rather than a drink, a long drive was what I really needed to shake off the caffeine and try to sort out some of the confusion, guilt, and emotional mess left over from Charlotte's thorough trashing of my psyche.

Heading up Broadway, I caught the westbound ramp to Interstate 40, easing into the sparse, late-morning traffic. Twenty minutes later I got off at the Kingston Springs exit and followed the Harpeth River for several miles down the winding highway, past the little town of Pegram, until I found the first dirt road that looked inviting.

I shifted the Eldorado into low and lunged up the narrow lane and into the woods, climbing hills and plowing through gullies until I came to an old logging road that looked like it hadn't been used in fifty years. Straddling the ruts, which were about a foot deep, I let the front-wheel drive pull the car straight up the path for what seemed like half a mile. It was a steep climb but the Caddy was sure-footed, and she never slipped or wavered until we reached the top of the hill, which opened into a huge field that held the decaying remnants of a corn crop several years old.

Cutting the engine, I got out of the car and looked around. I was at the top of something, the world maybe, standing still and listening for something other than the sound of birds. At first there was nothing, but then, after a minute or so, I began to pick up a soft, steady thrumming coming from my left, about fifty yards from the end of the dead cornfield. There was no trail and the weeds were waist high, so I walked between the last two rows of dried corn stalks toward the sound I barely heard.

At the end of the rows the weeds thinned, but still I stepped lightly, keeping an eye out for some stray copperhead that might have wandered out beyond the tree line. When the weeds played out I found myself looking not ahead but down, straight down, a couple hundred feet to the Harpeth River which was rolling lazily over the sleeping rocks below. As I looked down over the rocks, I saw I was at a bend of the river, on top of a cliff, and at that moment I knew exactly where I was.

I'd taken leisurely canoe trips down the Harpeth a few times, not white-water by any means, just a Sunday afternoon float with a beautiful lady, a six-pack, and a picnic lunch. And every time we came around this particular bend in the river, I'd never fail to stop and stare in amazement at the majesty of this towering granite cliff, imagining what it would be like to look down on the river from there, the very same cliff that I was standing on now. I realized I was in the most peaceful place I'd been in a while, and I didn't so much sit down but rather collapsed into a sitting position, slumping forward and breathing in long, deep gulps of fresh air.

Once again I tried letting it all go: Cassidy, Charlotte, Lyle, the Eskews, everything. I focused on the soft, slow movement of the river as it wound around the shaved rocks and into the bend where it fell over flat granite sheets before dropping easily and hurrying off downstream. Across the river, cows and horses were grazing in a sparsely wooded pasture that bordered the far bank, and the earthy smell of damp grass and fresh manure wafted over the water.

I let the cool peace wash over me like soft summer rain that falls for just a few minutes, taking the steam out of the hot afternoon and giving you a second wind to finish up the last few rows before heading back to the barn.

As my breathing slowed and became steady, I could feel the weight lift from my shoulders as a new, clean field of energy began to surround me. It felt pure, invigorating, and I must have sat there meditating for the better part of an hour without moving. I was alone at the top of the world. Or at least I thought so.

"Helluva sight ain't it?"

I jerked up at the sound of the voice, whipping around to see a man standing less than twenty feet from me. How did he get so close without making a sound? One thing for sure- he was no farmer. Dressed in camouflage fatigues, jungle boots and rain hat, except for the mobile phone holstered at his side he looked like he'd just stepped out of the Mekong. A cold fear gripped at my throat and I felt my stomach tighten. Seeing *Deliverance* two or three times will do that to you.

He must have read the alarm in my eyes because he immediately began to put me at ease.

"I didn't mean to scare you," he smiled. "I couldn't tell if you were sick or drunk or getting ready to do yourself in."

He pointed to the edge of the cliff.

"Who are you?" I managed to ask without my teeth chattering.

"Name's Pat," he said, still not moving. "Question is, who are you? This here's private property and it's my business to know who comes up here and what they do."

I told him my name and that I was just trying to get away from everything for a little while.

"I apologize for trespassing," I went on. "Once I got on the logging road I didn't want to stop until I got to the top of the hill. I didn't see any houses around so I just kept climbing."

"This is part of the old Belcher place," he said, motioning out across the dry cornfield. "Old Man Belcher died a few years ago, so I lease a couple hundred acres from his widow."

"What do you do here?" I asked.

"I live here about six months of the year, off and on. Got a camp back in the woods and I just sort of look after the place. I like being outdoors, keeps my mind sharp."

I didn't feel threatened anymore, so I pointed at his clothes. "Military?"

"Retired," he answered, "Special Forces, twenty-six years. I come here to re-group. It's great therapy and it keeps me off the golf course."

He was shorter than me, maybe five-eight, five-nine. Even in his fatigues I could tell he was in good shape for a man his age, which I figured to be within a few years of myself. His eyes were steel gray, flat and cool, and his face was tanned and smooth except for a thin horizontal scar that ran across the bridge of his nose from the inside of one cheek across to the other. I guessed it to be the track of a bayonet.

We walked over to my car and stood for a while smoking cigarettes, the old military way of establishing brotherhood. As we talked, we found we'd been within a few klicks of each other in and around Khe Sanh during the biggest Tet Offensive of the Vietnam War.

"Seventy-seven days of Hell," he said softly, his eyes glazing over as we both remembered the death and horror of those long weeks. There was no need for war stories, so we smoked like buddies, brothers now because we'd been to the hard place together. We'd both hit the wall and both managed to come home. Any faults or mistakes were mutually forgiven.

Pat finished his cigarette and field stripped it, sprinkling the remaining bits of tobacco over the dry ground and putting the filter in his shirt pocket. I reached in and stubbed mine out in the ashtray of the car.

"Let's take a walk," he said, then headed into the dead cornfield without waiting for an answer. I followed a few feet behind, one eye on Pat and the other scanning back and forth across the weeds for snakes. About a hundred yards into the field Pat made an abrupt left turn as we walked a faint trail leading to the woods at the other side.

The cornfield had been easy travelling but on pine needles the leather soles of my cowboy boots proved to be less than

worthy. Even with a path to follow I still spent more time slipping and sliding than walking. Pat was patient though, and if I
got too far behind he slowed the pace until I caught up. It was a
struggle, but I managed to stay with him until we finally reached
a small clearing with a circular stone fireplace about two feet
high standing in the middle. The clearing was bordered on two
sides by a thick blanket of heavy underbrush, with the far end
facing the river, offering a glimpse of the cliffs on the other side.

Pat walked over to a hickory tree, reached up to a branch
about head-high and grabbed the end of a rope that had been
tied just out of sight. He began pulling on the rope, and as he
did so part of the blanket of underbrush lifted, revealing a modern-day campsite that would have made Daniel Boone proud.

"A little trick I learned from the VC," he smiled, as the tent
like netting lifted and folded back through an elaborate system
of ropes and pulleys.

"I'll be damned," was all I could say, shaking my head in
wonder at the homemade double bunk with straw mattresses,
a picnic table, and a couple of storage lockers. He'd even made
a sink that drained and a curing box for meat. A small generator
peeked out from under a canvas.

"What's in there?" I asked, pointing to the rest of the bush
that was still covered, although at that point I wouldn't have
been surprised if he'd had mortars and heavy artillery stashed
in there.

"Just more of the same," he said. "Once or twice a year I have
a little get-together with some of the boys from the old outfit,
a little reverse R&R for a bunch of fat, balding businessmen.
They fly in for a weekend, we drink a little and bullshit a lot,
then they go back to their mini-vans and subdivisions."

He opened one of the lockers and pulled out a bottle of Jameson's Irish Whiskey and two plastic cups.

"Let's drink to good friends who didn't come back," he toasted.

"Amen," I said, closing my eyes and picturing Benny Watts' smiling face as the smooth whiskey slid down my throat. We drank another but I covered my cup before he could pour a third shot.

"Sorry," I said, "but I still have to navigate that land barge back down the hill. And I've a feeling it's gonna be a lot trickier going down than it was coming up."

He laughed and put the bottle back in the locker.

"I'll walk back with you. I need to make the rounds anyway. This time of the year, with all the kids canoeing down the river, I try to keep an eye out for trouble. The water is too low to give 'em much of a ride so most of 'em just get drunk and have a good time. Now and then though, one of 'em will start a fire, then go off and leave it and that can be dangerous when it's this dry. And every once in a while the local redneck boys will four-wheel it up to the top of the cliff and have a drunk party."

"And what do you do when that happens?"

"I just hang back in the woods and let 'em roar. As long as they don't make too big of a mess I keep quiet. They're just kids letting off steam."

"What about hunters in the winter?"

"There's no hunting here. And I don't tolerate a bunch of gun-toting rednecks. I run 'em off before they ever get started up the hill."

I didn't doubt for a minute he could do it.

We made our way back to the car, shook hands and said

goodbye, two brothers who met in the middle of life's journey and whose paths would likely never cross again.

"Thanks for the hospitality," I said.

"Good luck," he nodded, then turned and headed back into the cornfield.

I caught a glimpse of him watching me as I turned the big boat around and began easing down the steep hill in low gear. Approaching the first switchback, I glanced in the mirror but he was gone. I took it easy going down the long winding trail, and by the time I reached the paved road it was almost dark.

CHAPTER 15

The night air felt cool on my face as I drove with the windows down, the breeze fanning the lingering spark of Pat's whiskey on my tongue. There was just the faintest hint of a chill, a whisper really, a soft feather of air reminding you that summer is almost over and fall is just around the corner.

I got off at the Broadway and Demonbreun exit and drove two blocks to a little club called Baby Dolls. Some of the girls working there had also worked with Cassidy at Jezebel's and I thought I might do some digging around at Baby Dolls without attracting a lot of attention. Pulling into the parking lot, I did a double-take when I saw Heather's beat-up Dodge Omni parked about three spaces down from the front door, along with about a dozen Harleys.

Unlocking the trunk, I retrieved the half-pint of Beam I keep for emergencies, or as my Uncle Homer used to say, "I keep a little whiskey in case of snakebite, and I also keep a snake," then paid the cover and ordered a cup of ice from the waitress as I made my way to a table in the back. There was a small crowd, maybe thirty or forty guys, not all that bad for a weeknight. It was Amateur Night and that explained all the bikes outside. The bikers were there with their old ladies (the ones who didn't strip full-time) to go after the two-hundred-dollar prize money.

Two college girls sat at a table to my left, chain smoking and nervously watching the door to make sure none of their classmates wandered in. I doubted if they really understood what a pivotal moment this could be for both of them. A lot of girls get started in the business just like they were doing, on a dare or just some crazy idea with a girlfriend, thinking they'll giggle about it a few years down the road. They win a few bucks and decide to try again next week and before you know it, they're working three nights a week and taking home a grand or more and pretty soon it's, "Goodbye English Lit- Hello, Two-for-One-Couch-Dance," dropping out for one semester that eventually stretches into years.

I felt like walking over and telling them to run like hell, but I'd long ago given up trying to save the world. They were all grown up and haired-over and it was their choice to make. Besides, the taller of the two looked like someone you'd see in a Victoria's Secret catalogue and any other night I might have moved closer down front myself when it came her turn to dance.

Onstage a small girl named Sabrina was riding the wood to Delbert McClinton's "Never Been Rocked Enough." To say she was short wouldn't begin to describe her. She was, in fact, only slightly tall enough not to be considered a dwarf. Her figure was certainly dwarf-like: short legs, thick thighs, a small waist and a somewhat longer abdomen with small, firm breasts and totally shaved. She wore her dark hair long so as not to attract attention to her rather large head. The guys loved her and she was one of the top money-makers in town. She'd worked every club in Nashville over the past several years, moving on to another joint if some manager busted her chops for the wrong thing. She could write her own ticket and did.

Sabrina stepped down from the semi-circular stage onto the small walkway that separated the edge of the stage from the long counter surrounding it. As she danced, she would stop in front of each man sitting at the 'Breakfast Bar' just long enough to make eye contact, then turn and bend over as she waited for him to stick a dollar bill in the white garter she wore mid-thigh. She worked her way around and back up to the stage where she finished the song on her belly, hunching her thick, round butt in the air as every swinging dick on the front row stood up and applauded, each of them trying to imagine what it would be like to spend just a few glorious, sweaty minutes with her.

Unfortunately, I knew what it was like. We'd shared a desperate bump-and-run a few years back during one of the darker nights of my soul, and Sabrina turned out to be even crazier than I expected. It was a tequila-fueled marathon that ended in a blackout, and when I came to the next morning, I was wearing a studded dog collar and my pubes were braided in corn rows. But she taught me one thing: I'm nowhere near as kinky as I thought.

I sat there and watched the front row of screaming goof-balls, as they stood and frothed at the mouth for this young, tender, Botticelli-like nymphet who, at that moment, could ask no price they would not pay.

"Five-fifty," said the waitress as she set the cup of ice in front of me.

I paid her and then joined in the applause as Sabrina scooped up her clothes and exited the stage, completely ignoring the ovation.

They can have her, I thought. It's a dog's life.

"What are you doing here?"

Heather had finally made her way to my table.

"I could almost ask you the same thing," I countered, as she stared down at me through a haze of cigarette smoke.

"I couldn't go back to Jezebel's," she said, taking a seat in the chair next to mine. "It's too spooky around there. Bad vibes. Several of the other girls left because business went south." She pointed to the other side of the room where a couple of familiar faces were doing table dances.

Heather was wearing a black nightie jacket with black panties and black thigh-highs, and the club lights made her hair seem more silver than blonde. Her smooth skin glistened like a damp, dirty thought.

"Would you like to buy the lady a drink?" the waitress asked, appearing like clockwork within seconds after Heather sat down.

She started to wave the waitress off, but I handed her ten bucks and ordered a club cocktail, which was nothing more than Seven Up with a splash of grenadine. Dancers were expected to hustle drinks, and I wanted to keep Heather there for a while.

I decided to play dumb and not mention anything Lyle had spoken of, particularly about Atlanta.

"Have you heard anything more from the Eskews?" I began.

"Cassidy's sister came by yesterday to get some of her things, but I was on my way out the door as she came in. I boxed up a lot of stuff for her but when I came back last night I couldn't tell she'd taken much of anything. Most of the boxes were still there. She did leave a note saying someone from Goodwill would be coming by to pick up the clothes."

"Any of the girls working here I should talk to?"

Heather looked around the club for a moment, then shook her head.

"I don't see any," she said. "Besides Afro-Dite, there were only a couple that didn't like her, and they were trouble to start with. Yvonne and Sheila, a couple of Harley whores who'd just as soon cut you as look at you. But I think they're still at Jezebel's. Both of 'em been dancing there forever."

The waitress brought her drink as Heather and I sat looking at each other in silence. Onstage a black girl was doing splits in a skimpy cheerleader outfit as Koko Taylor shouted about pitching a "Wang Dang Doodle." I could say one thing for Baby Dolls- they had damn good music. Four or five college boys were tossing money at the black cheerleader who was now on her knees, hunching and slapping her ass in time to the music.

Playing dumb only works when someone else is talking, and Heather wasn't having much to say. I decided to cut to the chase.

"Tell me about Atlanta, Heather."

She jerked back as though I'd just tossed a drink in her lap.

"I know all about it," I lied. "I just want to hear your side of it."

"How do you-?" she gasped, grabbing my forearm and digging her long, red nails into it until I could almost feel the skin break. "Cassidy would never have told- she even made me promise...you don't know..."

"It's okay," I said. "I just want you to tell me about it. I want to hear your side of it because I'm a lot more likely to believe you than the cops. Now come on."

She eased up on my arm and sat back, turning her head from me to the stage and back to me, except when she turned back the surprise was gone from her face and in its place, a smile about as genuine as the five-thousand-dollar breasts that were straining against her black lace bra. They were heaving nervously, belying any illusion of the poise she was trying to project.

"It was really just a lot of bullshit," she began. "A lot of big talk and very little action. This dude came into the club awhile back and started talking to Cassidy and she introduced me to him. He was always telling us how much money we could make on the internet just posing and doing some real light girl/girl stuff. I thought he was blowing smoke, but he did give us a grand apiece to let him take some pictures of us in his room.

"Anyway, the deal was that we would get the upfront money and then he'd send us checks every month as more people joined the website. The plan was to come up here every month or so and shoot pictures, and in about a year Cassidy and I would be stars on the Web. At least that's what he told us."

"And you believed him."

"Hey, Man, a thousand bucks for fifteen minutes work would make a believer out of a lot of people. He seemed okay, didn't try any funny shit or anything, and once he and Cassidy settled their differences, he just shot the pictures and paid us and let us go."

"What differences?" I asked.

"Cassidy wouldn't do it unless he let her wear this wild-ass aluminum-looking wig. She looked like something out of *Blade Runner*. Plus, she changed her make-up so you really couldn't tell it was her. At first the guy wouldn't go for it, and he even got a little pissed, but Cassidy held out til finally he had no choice; it was her way or the highway. And he really wanted those pictures."

"How many times did you see him after that?"

"None," she said, shaking her head. "He went back to Atlanta and was supposed to come back in a month but he never did."

"Did he call her? Did she call him?" I asked.

"I don't know. They may have talked a couple times after that, but like I said, nothing ever came of it."

I shook my head as if I believed her. "What's the guy's name, Heather?"

"Why?"

"Because I want to know," I demanded, my patience long gone. "Because I'm a suspect- no, let me rephrase that- because I'm the *prime* suspect in a murder case and I want some God-damn answers *now*. So quit screwing around and tell me his name."

She recoiled, a hand rose to cover her lips, then molted into a fist.

"All right," she blurted. "His name is Mark."

"Mark who?"

"I swear, Jake, I don't know. He talked with Cassidy more than me. I just knew him as Mark. I swear, if I knew his last name I'd tell you. Jesus, Man, ease up!"

But I was just getting started.

"What was the name of his company? Did he give you a business card?"

"He didn't," she nodded. "And he was always vague about his business. He just said he worked in computers. Hell, I don't even know if Mark was his real name."

"How long ago did you meet him?"

"A while back, maybe six weeks or so. Like I said, he mostly came in to see Cassidy. He never said so directly, but I always got the feeling he had something to do with Aleta's club in Atlanta. He mentioned it a couple of times, said the girls there were all just knock-outs and that he was helping them make some serious money on the web. But I always got the feeling he was working for someone else."

Her words made about three laps around the inside of my head until the Stupid meter finally rang like a fire alarm. I'd completely overlooked the fact that Aleta had a club in Atlanta. Here I was, looking for a link between Cassidy and the Atlanta phone number, and it had been right under my nose the whole time. When it came to strip clubs, Aleta had the Midas touch, and with three joints to draw talent from, it was only natural that she cash in on the fresh internet money out there. The only problem was, Jezebel's didn't have a website. That seemed odd, and somehow it didn't add up, though I had a feeling Aleta could do the math.

"Heather, that whole scenario seems to have Aleta's thumbprint all over it. Did the guy ever mention her name?"

"Not that I recall. And I think I would've remembered if he did."

"What did he look like?"

She shifted in her seat and took a sip of her Seven Up.

"I don't know," she began. "He wasn't as tall as you, thin, maybe late twenties. He wore glasses, sorta geeky, if you know what I mean."

"What color hair?"

"Dark brown, and trimmed real short."

"Moustache or beard?"

"No, like I said, just nerdy."

I sat there searching through my memory bank, but I knew there was little chance I'd remember anyone who'd only come into the club a couple of times. Besides, I was usually too busy to pay any attention to the crowd unless there was trouble on the floor, not to mention the fact that if you work in a roomful of naked women, even a grizzled old fart like me will spend more time looking at flesh than the clientele.

The waitress came by and I ordered more drinks.

"Heather, I can't help but think there's something you're not telling me."

"Jake, don't you think if I could help you in any way that I would? I know what a jam you're in, Man, and I know you didn't kill Cassidy."

"Then who did?"

"How the Hell do I know? Christ, Jake, I just went through all this once today, I damn sure don't feel like doing it again."

She started to get up but I rose and put my arm around her and she went soft against me.

"I'm sorry, Heather. Please, sit back down." Then, in the next breath, "Who did you talk to at the police station?"

"The big guy, Detective Lyle, only he came over, woke me up in fact, around ten. Gave me the third degree, just like you're trying to do. I told him just like I'm telling you, that I don't know nothin.'"

At least Lyle and I were on the same track. "What did he ask you?"

"He was just asking me about Cassidy, and about...," she paused and looked off toward the DJ booth.

"About what, Heather?"

She reached into her little clutch purse, pulled out a Virginia Slims menthol and waited for me to light it.

"What else?" I insisted, touching a flame to the end of her cigarette.

"He asked me about you, Jake," she said, inhaling and then blowing the smoke casually back across her shoulder. "He wanted to know about you and Cassidy."

"What did you tell him?"

"I told him the same thing I told him the first time. That it was history and that you were both okay with it."

"Did you tell Lyle about the website deal?" She shook her head slowly.

"He asked me about it but I played simple. Sorry, Jake, but you already know how I feel about talking to cops."

I wasn't sure if she'd told me everything or even if what she had told me was the truth. But I couldn't think of any reason why Heather would burn me. One thing I *was* sure of- if Lyle thought she was lying, he'd be coming down hard on her very soon.

Heather took a deep drag from her cigarette, tilted her head back as smoke rose deftly from her open mouth in little soft clouds.

"Listen, Heather, sooner or later, you're going to have to tell them about the website guy. I can promise you Lyle will be back for another visit. You're not doing anyone any favors by not telling him, understand?"

"Except maybe myself. Look, Jake, I gotta go, I'm up next and these assholes fine you if you miss your cue. I promise I'll think about it, okay?"

She got up to leave as I glanced out across the roomful of feverish men cheering on the gymnastics of the college girl I'd noticed when I came in. Even from this distance I could tell she was eating it up. A star was being born right before our eyes. God help her.

"I'll talk to you tomorrow, Heather," I said, but she was already heading for the wings.

I went out into the late-night summer air, the faint chill a little more noticeable than before. Easing the Eldorado out of the parking lot, it dawned on me that I had a serious buzz working. Plenty of time to catch some music, maybe even figure out a way to get in front of Aleta.

CHAPTER 16

I drove Downtown and parked in the lot behind the feed store, then walked the five blocks back up Broadway to Ghost Town, a dingy little honky tonk that was generally overlooked by the tourists and Music Row hipsters who sometimes came slumming in search of slick retro acts who played pitch-perfect oldies with tight arrangements but had more in common with Slim Jim Phantom than Slim Whitman.

Ghost Town was my kind of place, nothing fancy, just dollar beer and good music, meaning that instead of Garth Brooks you were more likely to hear songs by Charley Pride, Lefty Frizzell, Ernest Tubb, Johnny Horton, Carl Smith or tons of other legendary tunes, even if they were sung by a cast of folks who admittedly possessed more desire than talent.

A thin, almost gaunt, middle-aged singer was finishing up the last few bars of Webb Pierce's "Wondering" when I walked in. There were about ten people sitting around at tables talking, and a couple of them applauded as the frail troubadour on the tiny stage hit his last chord.

I took a seat at the bar and ordered a beer.

"Thank you...Here's a Ray Price song..."

I sat there listening as he sang "Crazy Arms," the way it was meant to be sung, plaintively, from the heart in a dim lit bar with cinder block walls and a low, Celotex ceiling that keeps the cigarette smoke hanging just above your head like a favorite old hat.

I sipped my beer and listened. This guy wasn't half bad. He finished the song to scattered applause and rather boisterous cheering from some fool at the bar who I recognized as myself.

He nodded his thanks but never smiled as he looked across the room in my direction.

"Any requests?"

A young girl called out the name of a current singer but the man on stage pretended not to hear.

"Hank Thompson," I yelled without thinking.

He struck a B-flat on his Japanese guitar and executed a rousing rendition of "Six Pack to Go."

When he finished, I clapped like a kid and wanted more. "Faron Young," I shouted.

He sang two verses and a chorus of "Wine Me Up," then segued into "Hello Walls."

I was in hog heaven. I ordered another beer for myself and

one for him, then carried it over to the small stage and set it in front of him.

"Thanks, friend," he said, as a frail, weathered hand reached out for the longneck. His dark eyes were sunk deep in their sockets, and his pinched face bore witness to the fact that, even though he might not be George Jones, he damn sure had the right to sing about hard times.

As I turned to go back to the bar he did a four-note D run into "Sweet Dreams," a song made famous by Patsy Cline and several others including its author, Don Gibson, one of the greatest songwriters of all time. Legend has it Don recorded "I Can't Stop Loving You" and "Oh, Lonesome Me" the same day. Not a bad day's work if you ask me.

I kept downing beer after beer, calling out song titles or artists as soon as he finished each tune. This guy seemed to know everything in the book.

"Dorsey Burnette," I challenged.

He looked down from the stage and half-smiled as he leaned into the microphone and sang "Tall Oak Tree."

Every time his beer would get half-empty, I'd send another one up to the stage. It seemed the more he drank, the better he played. He was eating it up now, glad to be playing for someone who appreciated his efforts and his seemingly unlimited repertoire of classics. Even some of the other customers were starting to come alive.

"Hawkshaw Hawkins," I called out.

He did a note-perfect version of "Lonesome 7-7-203."

"Johnny and Jack," I yelled.

He only nodded and took a long drink of his beer before playing "Ashes of Love."

The small crowd was really starting to pay attention. No one dared to make another request. As soon as he'd hit the last chord of a song, all eyes would turn to me in anticipation of whatever I might call out next. It was like a strange duel between me and the ghostly figure on the shadowy stage. And no matter what I tossed out, he sang it note-for-note, word-for-word, as damn-near perfect as you could ask for.

"Leroy Van Dyke."

"Too easy," he snarled, then nailed "Walk On By," and went right into "The Auctioneer."

I was pretty loaded and it was getting close to take-it-on-home time. As solid as he was though, I wasn't about to let him beat me. I'd been waiting for the chance to throw him a slider. I rose from my stool, took a twenty-dollar bill out of my pocket, and held it up so he could see it.

The tiny honky tonk was dead quiet as we stood facing each other across the room, me at the bar and the rail-thin singer on stage. Only now he was standing erect, the smile gone, almost daring me to take my best shot. Every eye in the room was on me, waiting for me to make my move.

I finished off my beer in one long swig and dropped the bottle to the floor, where it bounced twice and rolled away without breaking. Nobody moved, not even the bartender.

"Rex Griffin," I challenged, almost catching a breeze from all the heads turning quickly to the singer.

He squinted his eyes for a second or two, then took off his worn cowboy hat and scratched his gray, balding head. When he reached down for his beer I knew I had him so I put the sawbuck in my pocket and stumbled toward the door, drunk, proud and full of myself. Passing the stage I dropped a dollar bill into his tip jar and flashed him my best winner's smile as he looked down at me with no expression. He might be good but he was no match for the Kid, I said to myself.

I was almost to the sidewalk when his voice stopped me in my tracks. The tiny crowd went nuts as the old gypsy sang "The Last Letter" as if it were the only song he knew and he'd been singing it every night for the last forty years. I leaned against the door jam and listened to more soul, more pain, more heartfelt emotion than anyone has heard since radios went transistor. When he finished, I walked over to the little plywood stage and lay the twenty-dollar bill at his feet, then reached for my wallet and pulled out four more twenties, placing them on top of the first one.

"Thank you very much, friend," he whispered as he reached down with a translucent hand corded with thin, blue veins. I closed my hand around his and looked up into those sunken eyes.

"You're freakin' great," I blathered. "What's your name?"

He gave my hand a firm, friendly squeeze but his eyes seemed to look through me into some dark, private place only he was heir to.

"Names don't matter, friend," he said. "The music's all that counts. Thanks again though."

He picked up the money, stuffed it into his faded jeans and turned to face his small group of newly won fans.

"How about some George Jones?" he asked.

Everyone nodded and applauded.

I hit the sidewalk as he began rocking the house with "The Race is On." I managed to stumble the five blocks home without getting mugged or arrested and made my way upstairs with considerable effort, falling into bed with my clothes still on.

➤ ➤ ➤

The monsoon rain was coming down so hard the trees and foliage were no help against it. Every step was a struggle, and it was impossible to see more than a few feet in front of me. I could smell the mildew and feel my toes rotting in my wet boots.

Benny Watts was walking point, although the rain kept us close enough together that he was only a few short yards ahead. At brief intervals he'd stop and try to listen through the deafening downpour, his eyes straining to see beyond the wet thickness as he waited for me to catch up. When I did, he'd turn to me and our eyes would say silently the thing we spoke aloud so often it had almost become a mantra.

"You got my back ain'tcha, Brother, 'cause I sho nuff got yours."

"Right On," I nodded. "Wrapped tight."

Benny moved out again as I waited until he was almost out of sight before following. But in the wet darkness, I got tangled in the underbrush and lost my footing, the jungle so thick I didn't fall, just sank deeper into the maze of limbs and bush. I dropped my M-16 as I battled against the choking vines, struggling frantically and then, just when it seemed I'd be eaten alive by the twisting labyrinth, the rain suddenly stopped and Benny appeared directly in front of me, his face the perfect picture of peace as the damp jungle let loose its grip, returning me to my feet.

Benny stood with his arms raised and palms down, Christ-like, and I tried not to look at the raw bloody welts that circled his neck. He opened his mouth to speak and I waited for him to repeat his part of our incantation, but no words came out. Instead, blood poured forth onto his chest and down the front of his fatigues, turning to steam as the crimson droplets touched the jungle floor. His eyes were wide and radiant, and I felt myself welling up with shame and self-loathing, even as he tried to put me at ease when he finally spoke.

"It's all right, Brother," he smiled. "It all comes back around."

I wanted to ask him what he meant, but then he began to rise up from the jungle, his hands flapping like odd little wings as he hovered in the air in front of me like some black, beatific hummingbird. A wave of terror wrapped itself around my chest like a python, pushing the air from my lungs and dragging me back into the dark abyss while I bucked and fought for breath. The jungle closed around me, and as I fell away my choking scream filled the mildewed air.

The scream woke me up and I found myself on the floor beside my bed, my feet tangled in the twisted sheet. I lay there taking air in deep gulps, sobbing uncontrollably and praying out loud to all the Gods for help in pushing Benny Watts back into that jungle forever, back into the dark graveyard of my memory where he'd been waiting soundless as a sniper all these many years.

CHAPTER 17

Katherine Robinson was dead. Though she'd been out of the public eye for years, as a member of a prominent Nashville family and the wife of Carter Robinson, her death made the front page of the *Tennessean*.

Truck and I sat in his office drinking coffee and smoking, reflecting on the headline staring up from the newspaper on his desk.

"That's too bad," he said, shaking his head. "I remember her from years ago. She was an elegant lady, always volunteering for one cause or another. She and Robinson were the beautiful couple about town and not too many Sundays went by that you wouldn't find their picture somewhere in the society pages."

"I know," I said. "She'd been sick for a while."

"From what I hear she'd been in bad shape for the past several years," he added. "Had a series of strokes, couldn't talk, bedridden, a pretty sad way to end an otherwise storybook life."

"Everybody dies sooner or later," I said. "Some folks just take longer than others."

"True enough," he agreed. "But when my time comes I damn sure hope it's quick. I don't relish the thought of some bored stranger having to feed me and wipe my ass."

I let the remark pass without comment.

"It says here the body's already been cremated and a memorial service is planned for tomorrow at noon. Do you think Aleta Thomas will be there?"

"So what if she is," he frowned, almost taken aback by what he knew I was thinking. "Jake, you can't confront her at her sister's funeral, for God's sake- Katherine Robinson was a Senator's wife. There'll be politicians there from all over the country, not to mention a shitload of media. You won't be able to get within fifty feet of Aleta."

"I'm not so sure about that, Truck. Most of the media will be covering Robinson and the other bigwigs. Even though Aleta was the black sheep of the family, I doubt she'll draw a lot of attention in that crowd."

"Doesn't sound like a very bright idea to me," he argued. "If I was a suspect in a murder case, the last thing I'd want to do is create a scene with a bunch of tv cameras around. You may think you have a nod-and-a-wink acquaintance with Carter Robinson but trust me, you cause a stir at his wife's funeral and you just might find yourself put so far away you won't see daylight til your grandkids are on social security. The guy has more clout than God."

"I've got no beef with Robinson," I countered. "I just want to talk to Aleta. I know it's a callous move, but I'm fast running out of options."

"Believe me, he won't see it that way. And if I were you, I'd come up with another plan."

"Well, I've got about twenty-four hours to do just that," I said, folding the paper and heading for the door.

But I didn't. By ten-thirty the next morning, security had already sealed off a four-block area around the First Presbyterian Church on West End Avenue, near Vanderbilt University. I left the Caddy behind a fast-food joint, then hoofed it six blocks up the opposite side of the street to join the burgeoning crowd and television news crews gathered to watch the arriving notables.

At eleven the limos began lining up, an Honor Guard of Nashville police escorting them to the drop-off point in front of the church. One by one they unloaded their dignified cargo: politicians and wives, scattered celebrities, country singers and Hollywood types, public figures, even several obvious but unfamiliar foreigners who came to pay their respects to the wife of Carter Robinson. It was a fitting testimony to the power of the man and even I felt a little overwhelmed at the spectacle.

By noon the church was packed and waiting for the arrival of the family. Robinson was first, followed by Katherine's elderly parents and her brothers. Minutes later Aleta arrived and entered the church alone as the sound of organ music drifted across the street.

The temperature was above 90 degrees, but the close-knit crowd and the steaming sidewalk made it feel even hotter. I took off my sport coat and slung it over my shoulder, then began making my way toward Aleta's limousine parked down the street just beyond the church. Easing under the branches of a big magnolia tree a few yards from her limo, I lit a cigarette and waited in the shade, trying to be as inconspicuous as possible.

I wasn't at all proud of what I was about to do. As I smoked I tried talking myself out of it, telling myself there would be other opportunities for confronting Aleta. But I knew that wasn't true. And I doubted she'd been back to the club since Cassidy's death. There was simply no other way.

"I hope you're not planning on doing what I think you're planning on doing."

The hair on my neck stood straight up. It was Bear's voice, coming from the back seat of the limo with the window down. I took a second to calm myself, then crushed out the cigarette and stepped out into the sunlight.

"I just need to talk to her, Bear, that's all. I'm not here to make trouble, I promise."

"That's good, 'cause in case you haven't noticed, Ms. Thomas has other things on her mind today. Why don't you show a little respect. You want to talk to her, you come by the club and talk to her like a gentleman." His face was in the window, the dark red knot of his tie slightly visible above the door.

"You know good and well I can't go near the club. I thought we were friends, Man? I'm being set up and I can't believe you're just gonna stand by and let it happen, especially after all the crap you and I have gone through. The least you can do is let me talk to her for a couple minutes."

"Not today, Jake. Look, I like you, always have. You're the best at watchin' my back when the shit hits the rim. But Ms. Aleta pay me a good wage to take care of things and long as she sign my check, that's what I'm gon' be doin', ya know what I'm sayin'?" He placed his huge hand over the bottom of the window, his fingers like thick, black sausages.

I'd always been mildly amused at Bear's ability to vacillate between proper English and street vernacular.

"Give her a few days, then come by the club. I'll see that you get in to see her," he promised.

"Dammit, Bear, I don't have a few days."

"Sorry, My Man, but that's the best I can do today."

"You know damn well you won't let me in to see her. She'll have me arrested if I so much as knock on the door."

"I ever lie to you, Jake?"

"You mean, not counting right now?"

His eyes went very still and serious as he looked at me for several moments without saying anything. I felt my legs get a tad weak and I shifted my feet so he wouldn't see my knees shake. In the distance I could hear the music from the church start up again.

"I'm gon' give you that one, Jake," he finally said. "It's on the house. Now you listen to me- you may be on my short list of friends, but if I have to get out of this car you gon' be a blank page. Come by the club in a few days like I told you. But right now you best be shuffling yo' self down the sidewalk."

"I'm gonna hold you to your word, Bear," I said, walking away. Behind me, I could hear the music get suddenly louder, which meant the doors of the church had opened and the crowd was filing out. I hung a right at the corner and kept going, glancing over my shoulder until the limo was out of sight, hidden by a row of hedges.

When I came to a break in the hedge I slipped through, then ran from tree to tree across a grassy lawn next to one of the Vanderbilt buildings. I waited, watching the crowd, until I finally spotted Aleta heading down the sidewalk in the direction of the limo. Without thinking, I tore out running across the grass, hoping to reach her before she got close enough to the limo for Bear to intervene. I managed to catch her halfway between the church and the car. When she saw me she jerked to a halt, dropping her purse.

"Aleta,...I know about Atlanta," I said, out of breath but still coherent enough to pick up her purse and hand it to her.

"Please...," she whispered, taking the purse from my hand. Her eyes were red and wet with tears.

"Aleta, you're going to have to talk to me or the cops sooner or later," I said.

"Not now...please," she begged, then began hurrying toward the car.

I fell in beside her just as Bear exited the limo down the street and started walking rapidly in our direction.

"I know you're in this, Aleta, I just can't prove it yet. But I swear, if you don't-"

"-Hush your mouth and keep walking or I'll shoot you right here on the sidewalk." I felt something hard against my back as the voice behind the threat became recognizable: Brundidge.

"Move away from the lady and keep walking with me, Shepherd," he said, nudging me with the gun to the other side of the walkway. By now Bear had reached the scene and had Aleta by the arm, leading her to the car.

"You blew it, Jake," he said, as he closed the limo door behind her. "You just screwed yourself big time, My Man."

I said nothing, just kept walking with Brundidge's gun poking against my ribs, turning the corner as he herded me up the hedge-lined street to his car.

"Get in the front seat and keep your mouth shut," he ordered.

He slammed the door behind me as I slid into the passenger seat, waiting as he walked around to the driver's side and got in.

"Okay, Shepherd, you have to make a quick decision here," he said, starting the car. "Do I take you straight to jail or do we drive off and, assuming you've got some good answers, maybe I let you out somewhere downtown? What's it going to be?"

"Up yours, Brundidge," I said, turning my head to the window.

"Okay, suit yourself, Bad Ass," he replied. "But don't say no one ever gave you a chance. And whether or not you want to admit it, I just saved your bacon back there."

"My apologies, Officer. I'm forever in your debt."

Brundidge shook his head and blew a long breath.

"That's right, Shepherd, keep playing that role for all its worth. You're heading for a place where the bad guys will bone your ass for a biscuit."

"What do you want from me, Brundidge?" I blurted.

He hung a right at the light and headed down Broadway in the slow-moving funeral traffic.

"First off, I want to know what you hoped to accomplish back there? Ten more seconds and you'd have wound up on the evening news. Pretty stupid move, if you ask me."

"I don't have any moves left, Brundidge. People do crazy

things when they're desperate. I just wanted to let her know that I knew what was going on, that's all."

"And just what do you think is going on?"

"Beats the hell outta me," I sighed. "But I do think Aleta has something to do with it all. I just wanted her to know that I was on to her."

"Tell me what you know, Shepherd." We were heading downtown, to what I assumed would be another round with Sgt. Lyle.

"Are you taking me to jail, Brundidge?"

"I'm listening," was all he said.

I told him about the Atlanta connection, the phone number, the possible link to Aleta's club there, all the things I figured he knew already. And since I had nothing to lose, I went ahead and told him about my trip down there and how it all seemed to add up to something a lot bigger than I could figure out, given my lack of ways and means. He listened without interrupting, until I was through with the tale and back at square one.

"How did you know I'd be there today?" I asked, even though I already knew the answer.

"What makes you think I was there to watch *you*, Shepherd? Could be you have an exaggerated opinion of yourself."

"Oh hell, Brundidge, you think I don't know you've been shadowing me for days? Christ, I can't even take a dump without feeling you looking over my shoulder."

He made a right by the Federal Courthouse and turned into a parking garage, going up three levels until he reached an empty floor, then pulled over and cut the engine.

"You got a problem with me doing my job, Shepherd?"

Poor kid, he wanted so bad to be hard. He just didn't have it in his gene pool.

"If your job is walking in my footsteps day and night, then you bet your ass I've got a problem with it," I retorted, looking out at the empty concrete floor of the parking deck. "And if you've got the balls to leave that badge and gun in the car, I'll be more than happy to get out and continue this debate one-on-one."

He rolled his window down and looked straight ahead, as if he were thinking about taking me up on the offer.

"Well, I hate to be the bearer of bad news, Shepherd, but I'm a problem you'll have to learn to live with. As of right now, I *own* your ass- understand? And you know what else? Right now, this very minute, I'm on vacation. I'm spending my whole vacation babysitting your dumb butt just so's I can be there when you screw up again, which you will sooner or later, I'm sure. You want to quit playing games, then fine- no more games. Just take it for granted for the next week I'll be right behind you everywhere you go. Just like your frigging aura, I'm right outside your skin. No need to call the Psychic Hotline, because the only future you have is with me, dead on your ass every minute. Are we clear on that?"

I looked at the little squirt and started laughing, not from his Hollywood spiel but because there was nothing else I *could* do.

"Brundidge, do you mean to tell me you're so dedicated you're following me around on your own time? You're really spending your hard-earned vacation doing this?

"That's right, Shepherd. What's so funny about it?"

"Nothing," I coughed. "It's just that you're an even bigger

pissant than I thought." Then for added insult, I got out of the car and lit a smoke, half-hoping he'd come after me and get western.

"So you think I'm a pissant, is that it?"

He got out of the car and tossed his gun in the front seat, then began walking around to my side.

"I damn sure do," I laughed, tossing the cigarette and getting ready to plant one on him, cop or no cop.

"Then let me ask you something, Shepherd. Something real serious." He was standing within a foot of me and I could've easily kicked him in the balls but I still needed him to throw the first punch.

"Go ahead," I invited.

"Why do you think I didn't take you straight to jail?"

"Maybe because I haven't broken any laws today," I smirked.

"Wrong, Sport. You're a suspected felon and you just broke a restraining order." He was leaning into me, almost as if he wanted me to throw down on him.

"That restraining order is for the club, Brundidge. As long as I'm 500 feet away, Aleta has no grounds."

"Maybe not," he nodded. "But how much do you want to bet I can't keep your tail on ice for a week until your lawyer can argue that?"

He was right and I knew it. All of a sudden I felt beat, as a bone-tired languor began to wrap itself around my entire being. My legs went heavy and numb.

"All right, Brundidge, I give up," I sighed, slumping against the fender for support. "Just tell me what this is all about. I'm tired of trying to fight the whole fucking world."

I took a couple of deep, labored breaths as I waited for him to speak, watching as the heated glare in his eyes began to melt away. He backed off a step and relaxed his posture.

"To begin with, Shepherd, I don't think you killed that girl."

Absolute surprise would not come close to describing how I felt upon hearing that.

"I've been watching you for a week, and you don't act like a guy who's trying to beat a murder rap. Plus, there's some other things I can't talk about right now."

My mouth still wouldn't move, so I just stood there shaking my head in wonder as he went on.

"I don't know where all this is heading, Shepherd, but I aim to stay glued to you until I find out. Now get in the car and I'll take you home."

"I don't want to go home just yet," I said.

"Then where do you want to go?"

"Truck Bennett's. It's off Gallatin Road."

"I know where it is," he muttered. "Get in."

Crossing Victory Bridge a few minutes later, I looked down at the turd-colored Cumberland River and wondered again at the unexplained mess of my life.

"What's happening to me, Brundidge? Why is all this happening to me, of all people? Have I accidentally crossed the wrong person without knowing it? Pissed off some gangster who wants me sent up the river? This is all just so...so crazy."

"To tell you the truth, Shepherd, I really don't understand it myself. But if you ask me, there seems to be a lot of things going on that neither of us knows about. I'm just trying to figure out how you managed to end up right-smack-dab in the middle of it all."

"Well, let me know when you find out," I said, looking down again at the nasty, brown water and thinking how peaceful it looked from up here.

CHAPTER 18

Truck was on the phone when we went through the door and it shocked me to see him sitting there in a fresh, starched shirt and tie, clean shaven and alert, as if for the first time in years he'd gone to bed sober the night before. He hung up the phone and took a pull off his coffee cup before nodding at Brundidge and speaking to me.

"You get a pet?"

"Truck Bennett, allow me to introduce my backside for the next few days. This proud specimen of Nashville's finest is Patrolman- Hey, what's your first name Brundidge?"

"Brundidge will do just fine," replied the little mound of ham.

"Yeah, well, nice to meet you, Brundidge," Truck greeted. "Now get the hell out of my office."

"Ah, c'mon Truck. Let me keep him, please. He's just so cute, and I promise to take care of him, really I will."

I ran my palm over the top of the kid's head before he could slap my hand away.

"Fuck both of you," he snapped, almost to the point of tears.

"Some vocabulary you got there, Son. They teach you that at the academy?" Truck could see Brundidge was relatively harmless, so he shrugged his shoulders and looked at me in a way that suggested if I didn't care then he certainly didn't.

"If he stays he has to be useful," he added, motioning toward the empty coffee pot. "Fill it from the sink in the bathroom."

Brundidge opened his mouth to say something, then thought better of it. He took the coffee pot from its nest on top of the file cabinet and headed down the hall. Once Truck heard the water running, he leaned over and whispered.

"Is he for real?"

"Worse," I said. "He's not but he doesn't know it.

I gave Truck a quick synopsis of my run-in with Aleta.

He listened but didn't seem at all surprised.

"Don't worry," I said, motioning toward the bathroom. "He's not hard to lose."

"Well, before we lose him, maybe we should use him," he grinned, just as Brundidge walked back into the room.

"What's so funny?" Brundidge asked, as he poured the water into the moldy coffeemaker.

"Oh, nothing," Truck smirked. "Jake and I were just trying to guess your first name. He thinks it's probably some kind of pussy name like Francis, but me, I think it's probably something a little more sophisticated, like Tutwiler or Gladstone."

Brundidge set the yellowed coffee pot in its cradle and stepped back to watch it brew.

"It's Alvin."

"You mean like the chipmunk?" Truck hooted.

"No, not like the chipmunk, not at all. Just Alvin."

"Okay, Just Alvin," Truck said, as he held up his hands in a show of acquiescence. "But if you're so doggedly determined to tag along after Jake here, why don't the two of you get out and start turning over some rocks."

"Meaning what?" retorted Brundidge.

"Well, since Aleta Thomas is off limits for the time being, why don't you see if you can't dig up this phantom wino Jake keeps talking about. Maybe he knows something."

Brundidge pursed his lips in thought, weighing the possibilities, then filled a Styrofoam cup with half-brewed coffee.

"Okay, but keep in mind I'm still a police officer. I'm not doing anything illegal."

"Let's go," I said to Brundidge, and we started for the door. "By the way, Truck, a couple of names you need to check out-Yvonne and Sheila, two dancers who weren't in Cassidy's fan club. As far as I know they're still at Jezebel's."

"I'll see what I can come up with," he nodded, scribbling the names on a pad.

Once in the car, Brundidge headed his Ford down Gallatin Road toward the Interstate.

"Go through town," I directed. "Let's check out Eighth Avenue."

"Who's driving, Asshole?" he snapped.

I've always believed the best working relationships are grounded in a firm foundation of mutual respect. With that in mind, I drew back my left hand and smacked the back of Brundidge's head with my open palm, just hard enough to send his face smashing into the steering wheel. The big Ford lurched and ran off the side of the road, narrowly missing a parked car and a bus bench.

"Jesus," he winced, blinking his eyes to regain his focus. "What'd you do that for?"

It felt even better than I expected, but I resisted the urge to slap him again.

"Like I said, go through town. I want to take the long way down Eighth Avenue."

"Okay, Shepherd, but I swear to God- you hit me one more time and I'll put a round right through both your friggin' ankles, and that's a promise," he threatened, as he rubbed the back of his head but nevertheless wound his way through downtown until he could make a left on Eighth.

Riding slowly down the street, I glanced right and left along the sidewalks and alleyways trying to catch a glimpse of the wino, wondering at the same time if I was putting too much stock in the old man. Chances were good he'd drifted on to another town and there was an even better chance that if we did find him, he wouldn't remember seeing anything that night. Still, he was a faint ray of hope, and I'd always believed that a long shot was better than no shot at all.

I hadn't noticed the paperback book almost hidden between us, stuffed between the cushion and the back of the front seat. I pulled it out and held it up, reading the title aloud: *Maximizing Your Potential for Success in an Ever-Changing World: How to Harness the Leadership Skills You've Always Thought You Have*

Even if No One Else Does.

"Geez, Brundidge, you planning on becoming a car salesman or something?"

"In your neck," he snorted. "If you'd ever read a book in your life you'd know there's some good stuff in there. I'm still young, not old and washed up like you. Who knows how long I'll be on the Force. There's a lot of big money to be made on the outside."

"Maybe so," I shrugged. "But it might help you become a little more well-rounded if you'd read some good authors every once in a while."

"Such as?"

"Well, for starters, Faulkner, Joyce, Thomas Wolfe. Maybe some contemporary guys like Garcia-Marquez and Cormac McCarthy."

"Oh, yeah? What do they sell?"

"Just words," I answered, then tossed the book in the back seat. Not everyone wants to be enlightened.

We hit the missions and shelters along Eighth Avenue and Lafayette with no luck. A description of the wino wasn't any help either, since most of them really do look pretty much alike. Hundreds of homeless men could fill that bill.

After driving east for several miles on Lafayette, we doubled back and again took the long, slow route down Eighth Avenue, keeping our eyes peeled for the wino. As I studied the right-hand side of the road Brundidge checked the left, sometimes calling my attention to street characters that fit the description I'd given him. The radio was tuned to a soft rock station and we rode along without saying much, scanning the sidewalks and doorways as Air Supply sang about being "Lost in Love" and not knowing why. I couldn't say much for Brundidge's taste in music but then, not everyone gets all torn up over Narvel Felts like I do.

I was just about to make that comment to Brundidge when I spotted the wino stumbling down my side of the street. He was drunk as a lord, taking three steps forward and two steps back, smiling like a politician, his glassy eyes having lost their focus hours ago.

"Right there," I pointed. "That's him."

Brundidge eased the car to the side of the street as the bum staggered toward us. Just as he passed my door I jumped out, grabbed the old coot by the back of his nasty shirt collar, opened the back door with my free hand and tossed him into the back seat, all in one motion.

"Whu-," was all he said before his head hit the other side door, though he likely didn't feel it.

"Let's go," I said, jumping in.

"Great. Now I'm involved in a kidnapping," Brundidge whined as we sped away.

"Relax, we're just taking him for a ride." I turned back to the wino, who had managed to pull himself up and into a sitting position, his dirty old head bobbing up, down and around like one of those little toy dogs you see in the back windows of lowriders.

It took about thirty seconds for the entire car to start smelling like a broken toilet. Brundidge turned to me with big wet tears in his eyes.

"I'll never get the smell out of here."

"Of course you will," I said. "Hell, I smell like that half the time and my car doesn't stink. A little Clorox and some Simple Green and she'll be good as new."

Even so, we drove to Truck's office with the windows down, running a red light or two along the way.

"Get that nasty sonofabitch outside," yelled Truck, as we led the wino through the front door and eased him into a metal chair.

"Sorry, Truck," I said. "But I don't believe in making my friends wait on the porch. Bad manners and all that."

Truck stared at the barely human pile of rags for a long minute before speaking again.

"And you think this poor fool knows something?"

"I don't know, but I have to find out. Christ, it's just about the only chance I've got. I figure we can pour coffee down him until he's sober and then ask him. In the meantime, pray that he can even remember that night."

The old wino's chin rested soundly on his chest as a long stream of drool worked its way from his bottom lip down the front of his filthy shirt that looked like it might have once been orange.

"Looks like he's a UT man," chuckled Truck, pointing at the semi-orange shirt. "I'll tell you one thing- it's gonna take a whole lot more than a pot of coffee to sober this guy up. Hell, it could take days. I doubt if he's been straight since Reagan was in office, which, come to think of it, may have been what started him drinking."

"You got any Lysol?" asked Brundidge.

"Jesus Christ, Boy, you can't wash a man with Lysol. You'll kill him."

I could tell Truck was a little uneasy with the wino being there. It made him nervous, just as it did me. Maybe it was because somewhere deep down we both suspected we had more in common with the old guy than we had differences. It was just a matter of where we were positioned in the race.

"I need to clean up the car," said Brundidge. "He stunk it up."

"Under the bathroom sink," snapped Truck, motioning toward the hall. Over in the corner in the metal chair, the wino sat motionless, snoring softly.

"Did you find out anything about Atlanta?" I asked.

"Not much, I'm afraid. My buddy looked into it but couldn't find anything out of the ordinary. He says it's a legitimate PR company, and they handle a few minor celebrities. There's also a computer company listed there. I can't remember the name but I've got it written down. He thinks the joint might be some kind of front for something. Believe me, if he can't uncover anything, it really is clandestine because he's one of the best in the business."

Once again, I was more than a little confused.

"It just doesn't sound like the kind of thing Cassidy would be involved with," I said. "I'm trying to be objective, but I can't seem to make a connection."

"Well, Jake," he said carefully, "I hate to bring it up but maybe she was carrying on with someone that worked there. I mean, it's logical if you think about it. A guy comes through town, stops in the club, tosses around a lot of dough, makes a bunch of promises, gives her his work number and goes back home. Next thing you know they're talking every day, making plans. Hell, Jake, you know how that scene plays."

"I know," I agreed, "and I know I've said it before, but Cassidy wasn't like that. She heard more bullshit every night than most people hear in a lifetime. And as far as the PR thing goes,

I don't know too many flacks that represent strippers. I'm sorry but it just doesn't tally."

Truck nodded as if to imply that he understood. But I knew better.

"I have to make a court date in three days," he said. "If you're determined to go back down there we need to do it right away so I can get back."

"Fine," I said. "Let's go."

"What about your friend there?" he asked, pointing at the sleeping wino.

"Either he goes with us or we sober him up right here," I answered. "I can't take a chance on losing him again. He might know something or he might not but I aim to find out either way."

Truck shook his head with a resigned weariness, then reached in his bottom desk drawer and pulled out a fresh quart of Evan Williams.

"If that's the case, then I need a drink," he said, breaking the seal.

"Me too fershur," said the wino, the twist of the bottle cap bringing him to life like a friendly alarm clock.

We spent the rest of the afternoon and evening taking turns with the wino, tossing him in and out of cold showers and pouring pot after pot of black coffee down him until he was at least wide awake, if not sober. Truck called an ex-girlfriend to come over and shampoo the old man's nasty, matted hair and beard, then gave him a shave and haircut. He even donated an old suit, which was a good thing because we'd thrown the wino's fungoid rags out the back door. By midnight we had him sitting upright in the metal chair looking like he was waiting for his next serving of potato pie at Thanksgiving dinner. He was clean and freshly shaved, but the gaunt and haunted look would never wash away.

He sobered up just enough to tell us his name was Burt and he was from Kentucky, but the lethal combination of street life and cheap wine stretched out over a period of years had taken such a toll that he had almost lost the language. We kept pouring coffee down him anyway, until it became apparent that old Burt had more problems than just drink. The lost, faraway look in his eyes had probably been there for decades, and he, like so many un-institutionalized mentally ill, had most likely wandered away one day from a family secretly relieved to find him gone.

"Burt, remember the night behind Jezebel's?"

"Yessir," he said, with a blank look and absolutely no conviction.

"Remember, something happened before the police came?"

"Po-leece? I ain't done nuthin'."

"It's okay, Burt, nobody's gonna hurt you. Remember what happened to the girl, before the police came? Remember in the alley that night, you were sleeping in the bed of Bear's pickup."

He blinked his eyes and for a moment I thought maybe he was digging around through the dusty closets and cob-webbed corners of his fragile memory. Twisting his mouth and scratching at his new, close-cropped haircut, he seemed to be trying, in his own feeble way, to pull something out of there.

It was well after midnight. Brundidge had sacked out on the sofa but Truck, to his credit, was hanging in there with me, making coffee and helping me tug on what was left of Burt's memory.

"Dammit, Burt, try and remember," Truck implored. "Something happened to the girl that night in the alley. Did you see what happened? Did you see anything? Try to remember the girl, Burt. Did you see the girl?"

It went on for another hour before Truck finally threw up his hands and shook his head.

"I'm sorry, Jake, but the old fart can't even remember this morning, much less something that happened two weeks ago."

He was right and I knew it. It looked like Burt was about to take his place right alongside the rest of the lost causes of my life.

"Nekkid," Burt muttered.

The poor fool hadn't even noticed his new clean clothes. "You're not naked," laughed Truck. "Hell, that's a forty-dollar shirt you're wearing."

"Nekkid gurl."

That got our attention. We ran to the old man and knelt before him like deacons.

"What about the naked girl, Burt? Tell us about her. What happened to her?"

"Tank..." He was trying, bless his sodden heart.

"Tank...tank...trew her..."

"What the hell does that mean?" asked Truck, more to me than to Burt.

"I don't know. Burt, try hard to remember. What tank? What do you mean?"

"Tank...trew her...away," he said, certain of himself and proud for having remembered it. For a half-second his eyes had almost seemed to go clear.

Then it dawned on me. Tank. The dumpster. He meant the body in the dumpster had been thrown away. Which, of course, we already knew.

"Can you remember anything else, Burt?" I pleaded.

"Tank trew her away," he said again, as I watched the clarity in his eyes fade and the yellow, smoky fog roll back in. He nodded his head a couple of times, then looked up at Truck as if he'd just met him on the street.

"Drink?"

Tank threw her away. He never saw anything after all. I felt the air ease out of my lungs as I fell back on the floor dejected and disappointed, disgusted with myself for banking so hard on such a long shot.

"I'm sorry, Jake," Truck said, "but it's not over yet. We've still got a few angles to work. Let's let the old fellow go."

"Tank trew her away," Burt demanded, as if maybe I hadn't heard him the first time.

"Yeah, I know," I said, then echoed, "Tank threw her away." I flashed on a mental picture of Cassidy's body hanging from the door of the dumpster, then shook my head hard to lose the image.

After we helped him to his feet and out the front door, Truck gave Burt twenty bucks and led him to the sidewalk.

The poor guy looked up and down the street, searching the night for the neon glow of the only landmark he cared about- a liquor store. Folding and refolding the twenty in his hands, he was at least lucid enough to realize that all the liquor stores were closed at this hour and that it would be a long night unless he could find some compatriot to share a bottle.

He turned back to us, still folding and refolding the bill, until finally Truck went inside and came back with the bottle of whiskey and handed it to the old man, whose eyes brightened, even in the dark, like a kid at Christmas. Clutching the bottle with both hands, he sauntered off down the sidewalk in the direction of the interstate, the whine of the big trucks pulling him like a fishing line to the dark shelter of a waiting bridge underpass.

Back in the office we pondered our next move as Brundidge lay snoring on the sofa.

"What do you want to do?" Truck asked.

"I'm too tired to sleep," I said, surprised at the absurdity of that statement. "Let's ride."

"Not so fast, Jake. If we're going down there, and if that place is as tight as you say, then we need to get a little better prepared. Take my car and go back to your place. Get a couple hours sleep, and pack a grip in the morning. You got a gun?"

"Thankfully, no," I said.

"Then you can use one of mine," he offered, reaching into his desk drawer and pulling out an old military issue .45 automatic that looked like it had last been used on Normandy Beach. I'd carried one myself for a while escorting prisoners for the Marine Corps when I got back in the States. Those old pistols were famous for two things: being terribly inaccurate but also very dependable. You might not hit anything with one, but you could rest assured it wouldn't jam on you.

"You keep it 'til I need it," I said. "I don't need to add a gun rap to my growing list of charges, especially for some piece of scrap iron that wouldn't hit the water if you threw it out of a boat."

"Suit yourself," he shrugged, then motioned at Brundidge sleeping on the sofa before whispering, "What'll we do about him?"

"You two assholes aren't going anywhere without me," said Brundidge, his eyes still closed.

CHAPTER 19

By four o'clock the next afternoon we were outside Marietta, chowing down to a late lunch of pulled pork barbeque at a little joint on Highway 41, just a few miles from the Atlanta city limits and West Paces Ferry Road. Afterwards, I sprang for three rooms at a nearby Days Inn and we all crashed for the afternoon, napping and waiting for dark.

A sound not unlike a dynamite explosion jolted me awake and I stumbled to the window to see the beginnings of a torrential thunderstorm, shuddering blasts of thunder followed by streaks of electric lightning with the rain pelting down in sheets. I thought about Charlotte, remembered the musky taste of her damp skin on that rainy afternoon that now seemed years ago, but then the thought was gone with the next pink bolt flashing across the summer sky. I started a mini pot of coffee before taking a hot shower, then dressed in a black jogging suit and kicked back on the bed, sipping from a Styrofoam cup as I surfed the TV channels and waited for midnight.

At twelve Brundidge and Truck showed up similarly dressed in dark sweats and ready for recon. Brundidge was even wearing black camo paint under his eyes and God only knows where or how he came up with it.

"Let me guess," I said. "You're either a deep CIA operative or Lou Reed dressed for a big night on the Boulevard."

"In your neck," was his snappy reply.

"I still think this is a bad idea, Jake," Truck said, "my gut is telling me to stay home."

"I'm wishing we'd done more than just circle the block today," Brundidge added. "One of us should've gone over there and snooped around. Maybe a delivery scam or something, anything to get a closer look."

"No way," I said. "If that place is tied to Cassidy you can bet they're all on alert as it is. Something like that would be like sending up a flare."

Outside, the rain continued to beat a driving, machine-gun rhythm on the asphalt.

Brundidge saw the weighted leather sap I'd brought along. He picked it up from the bed and began tossing it in the air.

"If you get close enough to anyone to actually use this," he quipped, "that'll be the point at which we're all officially fucked."

"All right, listen up," Truck said, suddenly the self-appointed squad leader. "We take no identification with us, no wallets, no car registration, nothing."

"What if we get stopped?" said Brundidge.

"You'd better hope we don't. For one thing, they'll take one look at your Rambo getup and figure we're not on our way to the Farmer's Market at this hour."

Brundidge glanced over at the mirror as Truck went on.

"I borrowed a Georgia license plate earlier from one of our motel neighbors so we won't stick out like a bunch of tourists. I want to make two passes by the place to check it out before we decide how or even *if* we're going in. With luck, the rain might give us a little cover. We may not have time for a lot of talk once we get there so let's go over as many things as we can right now. Remember, the idea is to get in and get out as quickly as possible, ten minutes max, preferably five. Any questions so far?"

"Just one," asked Brundidge. "What are we looking for?"

Truck shot me a look that made the question all the more credible.

"To tell you the truth, I really don't know, Hoss," he answered. "Jake?"

"Look for anything that might link Cassidy to that place. She'd made a lot of phone calls to that building and I want to know why. Look for a name, hell, look for her name on something, a file, a letter, anything."

"Well, I hate to throw a damper on this," said Brundidge, "but chances are, if this place is as high-tech as you say, then there won't be any files. Everything will be on disc and drives with passwords out the wazoo. Ten minutes isn't a lot of time in a situation like that."

"I understand," I said. "But we have to try. Now that we know the wino didn't see anything, this place is the only shred of hope I have left."

"Duly noted," said Brundidge, "and let's not forget my entire career is on the line as well. If I get caught with you two losers I'll be lucky to get a job with Pinkerton guarding the Walmart warehouse, and that's if I don't go to jail for aiding and abetting."

"Okay, if you girls are through bitching, I think maybe we oughta move out before the rain slacks up," Truck said. "Jake, you drive.

"One more thing," I said, "anybody gets caught, you're on your own. By that I mean you're just a burglar with a bad crack monkey and you broke in to see what kind of electronic shit you could boost. Whatever you do, don't give up the other guys. Are we sync on that?"

Brundidge opened the door and looked out into the stormy black night.

"Christ," he grumbled, "It's raining like a cow pissing on a flat rock."

Once on West Paces Ferry Road, we drove past the guard shack as slowly as we could without being obvious, which wasn't much of a stretch with the pelting rain. The guard was inside and appeared to be reading something or at least not overly interested in the traffic on the rainy street. We drove around the block, a huge block, with even larger fenced mansions on the other side assuring us there was little hope of any kind of rear entrance.

I made one more circle for Truck's benefit, letting him take it all in while I repeated the bit about the fence and the light check on the half-hour. After the second lap I pulled over and parked on the tree-lined street as we waited for the guard to make his appointed rounds.

We hadn't been there five minutes before two sets of blinking headlights burst into view from the far end of the street. By the time the two white limousines reached the entrance, the guard was already outside with the gate opened, waving them in. The limos turned and passed through, then proceeded down the long driveway and disappeared behind the building.

"Oh well, so much for the best laid plans," said Brundidge.

"You're right about that," Truck said. "Let's get the hell out of here. There'll be other nights."

"No way," I countered. "I'm going in."

"Don't be stupid, Shepherd," said Brundidge. "There are at least two carloads of people in there. They may be having a freakin' party for all you know. I say let's beat feet."

But I had no intention of making a third trip.

"I think that could work in our favor, Brundidge. If nothing else, it'll create a distraction."

"You may have a point," agreed Truck, "but it's awfully risky."

"Breaking and entering usually is," I said.

Instead of slacking up, the rain was coming down harder and the thunder seemed to be getting closer again. At one o'clock the guard came out of his shack wrapped in a poncho, ran to the corner and flicked the light switch for just a split second, then scurried back to the dry safety of his cover. We watched the rear for the same thing and sure enough, in a moment a wash of light illuminated the back side of the property for a few seconds and then went out as if extinguished by the rain.

But then something unexpected happened. The front door of the mansion opened, and another poncho-clad figure came out and started running down the steps and across the lawn toward the guard shack.

"They made us," Brundidge said.

We sat in chilled silence as the man approached the sentry post and stepped inside, speaking briefly with the other guard, who then hooded up and ran back toward the house and through the front door, which he appeared to open without a key.

"Looks like somebody's getting a break," I observed.

"Yeah," Truck whispered, "and it just might be us."

It took about thirty seconds to put the plan together. I popped the bulb out of the dome light so the doors would open unnoticed, then slipped out onto the rainy sidewalk and began a slow crawl back toward the guard shack, staying low against the cars on the opposite side of the street. When I reached a halfway point between the sentry post and the corner of the fence, I huddled against the fender of a big Mercedes and waited.

At half-past, with the rain still coming down in buckets, the guard threw on his wet poncho and began a hurried dash to the corner of the fence. I crossed the street and fell in about ten yards behind him. As expected, he threw the light switch and sighted down the fence for a brief moment, then cut the light and lowered his head for the run back to his post.

On his second step I caught him across the bridge of his nose with the weighted sap and even through the pounding rain I could hear the crunch of bone as he fell in a moaning pile onto the sidewalk. I pulled his limp body between two parked cars and relieved him of his pants and poncho, then put them on over my clothes as Truck appeared with duct tape for his mouth, wrists and feet. I ran for the guard shack as Truck heaved the guard onto his shoulder and made a clumsy dash for the car, where Brundidge was waiting with the trunk open.

Once inside the shack I had only seconds to look around at the bank of video monitors on the console, one of which could easily have been playing the scene that happened moments before. But then all the screens changed to other camera angles and I knew our chances had at least improved a bit, if not a whole lot.

"Don't leave 'til the other guard comes back," yelled Truck, as he and Brundidge ran inside and out the back door of the shack, each taking a different route toward the big house. I watched until they were out of sight and breathed a silent prayer.

A few minutes later, one of the front doors opened and a figure ran out and headed in my direction, hopefully the first guard returning to his station. As far as I could see, Truck and Brundidge were clear, and as the guard came nearer, I let him get within a few feet before lowering my head in the poncho and taking off, mumbling audibly as we passed in the downpour.

"Later."

"Fuckin' rain," he grunted, as he jogged past me.

Once on the large porch I ducked to the side of a big white column to catch my breath momentarily before going in. There was no sign of Truck or Brundidge, still I walked directly to one of the doors, turned the knob, and was surprised to see it open effortlessly as I stepped into a long, almost cavernous foyer with four closed doors, two on each side, near the middle of the long hallway. The muffled thumping of dance music reverberated from another part of the house.

I tossed the wet poncho in the corner and slowly began to make my way down the hall. No mounted cameras were visible, although that meant nothing. With the foyer marginally lit there was no use trying to appear covert, so I tip-toed down the long hallway until I came to the first door on my right, tried the knob, and once again found it unlocked. Taking a slow deep breath, I opened the door and stepped inside.

Two figures dressed in wet, dark sweat suits were sitting in chairs directly in front of me, both their heads covered by heavy black hoods and their arms tied behind the chairs: Truck and Brundidge.

"What took you so long?" was all I heard before a sharp crack sent a blinding flash of white light streaking across my eyes, giving me a momentary soft feeling in the back of my head. I don't even remember falling....

I came to slowly, in short blinks, in and out of consciousness until my eyes finally focused on the blackness. It took a moment to realize I was hooded, but when I heard Truck scream out in pain I came wide awake real quick. Sitting in a chair with my arms tied behind me and the back of my head throbbing like a John Phillip Sousa march, it sounded like Truck was only a few feet away and someone appeared to be working him over pretty good.

I wasn't sure if Brundidge was still in the room and for a moment I almost called his name, but then stifled myself as a new series of cries filled the air and I knew he was having his turn. I heard Brundidge faintly begging "Please...please...," between sobs, then a high-pitched scream that must have come from somewhere deep in the pit of the boy and then silence, nothing, just the muffled sounds of two people gasping for breath.

Instinctively, I dropped my chin to my chest, which caused the first punch to miss my jaw and land squarely on the side of my head. It hurt like hell but at least I had the satisfaction of hearing the guy yell "Goddammit!" about three times because he must have broken or sprained either his hand or his wrist. The chair toppled on two legs and I went with it as it fell to the floor, hoping that playing dead might at least delay the impending fun.

It didn't work. Someone grabbed my shoulders and righted the chair and I was all set for round two. A pair of hands grabbed my nylon warmup jacket at the neck and ripped it open, never mind the fact they could've just as easily zipped it down.

I'd been told once before how to beat the pain. Staff Sergeant Rick Webb was on his way back to the World when I met him, and to this day I've never come across anyone who came close to him in terms of sheer courage. He'd been taken prisoner on his second tour, during an operation in the Central Highlands. When he told me some of the things the VC had done to him it made my blood curdle: fingernails ripped off, electrodes up his ass, daily beatings and unthinkable torture. When I asked how he got through it he just shook his head and said that when deep shit happens, sometimes it's possible to go outside your own body, thereby removing yourself from the pain of the physical realm.

"If you can do that," he said, "you can beat the pain. At that point they either have to kill you or quit."

I felt the cold metal of the alligator clip on my nipple as a blue streak of electricity shot through my heart and out my ass. Blood rushed out my nose and I tried to go out of body, but it seemed as if the hood was keeping me trapped in the flesh. I remember screaming and pleading and for a moment I thought they were listening, but they were just getting ready to work on the other nipple.

"Calling long distance," cackled a high-pitched voice, as the current tingled, then flashed hot as I twisted, jerked, and blacked out, but not before pissing my pants.

When I came to, the hood was off.

My head lay tilted on my shoulder, and I could see Truck and Brundidge to my side, slumped in their chairs, their hoods off as well. Both their faces were bloody pulps, and I had no reason to believe mine looked any different. My bones felt loose and soft under my skin and a damp, fecal stench hung in the air, making me think perhaps I hadn't been the only one to lose bodily control.

The room felt huge, like a conference room, with mauve colored walls and hardwood floors that shined with the patina of meticulous care. Two nondescript oil paintings decorated the walls to my left and right, and a large ceremonial flag display with the U.S. and all branches of the Armed Services lined the wall in front of us. Even in my addled state my mind automatically picked out the five branches: Army, Navy, Air Force, Marine Corps, Coast Guard- but a sixth flag had been subtly added to the cluster, bright red with a deep blue border, and large white initials in the center that the folds made indecipherable.

Directly in front of us stood two hard-looking young men in military khakis stained in dark, drying splotches. Both their heads were buzz-cut but something about them told me they weren't military, at least not any kind of service I was aware of. Even so, they were almost indiscriminate, one from the other, both looking to be in their late-twenties, both tall and wiry and both sets of silvery, slitted eyes twinkling with evil. One sported a bad bottle-blonde pelt along the top of his head, and the other was a redhead, with pasty white skin dotted with freckles.

Freckles smiled a mouthful of yellow teeth.

"Well now," he began, "Seeing as how all the proper introductions have been made, you dudes can start off by telling us what the fuck you're doing here."

No one spoke for several long beats. I glanced over at Truck and Brundidge as the blonde one took a step forward, pivoted on his left foot, and drove a roundhouse kick into Brundidge's chest. I heard the air rush out of the kid's mouth as his chair slammed over and skidded across the polished floor with him still strapped to it.

"Anyone in the mood for conversation now?" asked Freckles, as his buddy positioned himself in front of Truck.

Truck's head was slumped forward and I could see him blinking his eyes, his bloody lips bubbling with effort as he struggled to get the words out, his metal tooth barely visible behind the thick film of blood.

The blonde asshole took his first step and was about to pivot when a voice from the edge of nowhere came rushing up out of my throat.

"Wait-" I sputtered, and he stopped, his right foot cocked and hanging in mid-air.

"We're listening, Bitch," Freckles said.

For the life of me I don't know where the story came from. It just seemed to pour out of me on its own, born in my creative subconscious with life given from the breath of absolute fear and panic. Perhaps it was because I knew they would never believe the bit about us being crackheads, and I couldn't take the chance Truck might try to run it by them if only because it was the story we'd agreed on. But this time I did go out of body, at least in a sense. I felt I was watching myself tell this incredible lie, and I wanted a good seat so I could watch them kick the shit out of me for making it up.

"We...we're from Dalton," I began. "...worked the block before...closer into Buckhead. Seen this place a few times... wanted to check it out...see if maybe it was worth coming back. We were on our way to this other house, the one with the stone fence down the street...but we thought with the rain and all, might give us a chance to come in and look around. You know... guns, laptops...anything we could move quick."

Blondie eased his foot to the floor, but I was sure they didn't believe me.

"You boys are some brave sumbitches to break into a compound with armed guards. Not too many burglars would try something like that," Freckles said.

There was doubt in his voice. He hadn't bought it.

"Normally we wouldn't," I answered, too desperate to give up. "I guess the rain gave us big balls. We wanted a quick look and this just seemed like the right time."

He lit a cigarette, walking back and forth in front of us as his buddy righted Brundidge's chair and slid him back between Truck and myself.

"So, you're the ones who've been knocking over houses around here for the past few months? I've heard about you guys, but I would've bet good money you weren't dumb enough to hit this joint."

I wasn't sure if he was trying to trap me, but his yellow smile seemed to elicit some sort of backhanded criminal respect.

"Like I said, the rain must have given us ideas."

"Pretty fucking stupid ideas if you ask me."

The blonde turdhead laughed as if that were just the funniest thing he'd heard all day.

"So...you calling the cops or what?" I said.

He leaned over and put his face in front of mine.

"What makes you think we *ain't* the cops, Princess?"

Blondie quit laughing on that note and I mentally braced myself for another round of fun and games.

"Not too many cops throw a party like you just did," I said, trying not to show any more fear than necessary. "The way I look at it, you've got three choices: call the cops, let us go, or kill us. And to tell you the truth, I'm sitting here bleeding with pissed pants and my buddies are in worse shape than I am, so Goddammit, do something- if you're not calling the cops, then either let us go or kill us, one or the other, because I'm sick of looking at you two sweethearts."

Truck and Brundidge bellowed like sick calves, jerking around and glaring at me in total disbelief.

"Maybe we're not through having fun yet," Freckles deadpanned.

That's when I realized they really were going to kill us. I didn't want to die, though I could at least face it as long as it was quick. But I had damn sure had enough romance for one night.

"Fuck both you pissants," I blurted, as Brundidge shrieked in amazement, though I don't know why, because it was me Blondie was spinning towards like Jackie Chan in semi-slow motion as I watched the sole of his boot plant itself across my mouth, snapping my head back and sending me careening across the floor like a pilot trapped in his ejection seat. The sonofabitch succeeded in loosening about ten-thousand dollars' worth of porcelain caps, the only reasonable investment I'd made, besides the Caddy, with that first big royalty check all those years ago.

Blondie pirouetted and did the same thing to Truck and then to Brundidge and it seemed like both were on the floor beside me before I'd even stopped sliding. Brundidge's purple face turned toward me and tried to speak but couldn't, though I'm sure he meant to compliment me on my excellent negotiation skills. We lay there strapped to the chairs and gasping for breath, the collective stink of our soiled bodies permeating the air like a rancid fog.

I guess the smell was enough to disgust the two sadists.

"Let's cap these fuckers and take 'em to the mill," Blondie said. "Christ, the whole room smells like shit."

"Take 'em to the showers first," Freckles ordered. "I don't want 'em stinking up the van. And don't do anything til we get to the mill, for God's sake. I don't want to have to carry their nasty asses. I'll call ahead and tell 'em to get the chipper ready."

I watched from the floor as he opened the door to leave. He stopped momentarily, holding the door open, and I could see the door to the office directly across the hall was also open now, though I couldn't see anyone in the room, just a modern desk with a wall full of framed photos behind it. Some of the photos were in color and others were black and white, but my eyes were still too blurred to make out a distinct face.

"I'll have the van brought around back," he continued. "Hose 'em down, then walk 'em out back to the loading dock. I'll see you in ten minutes."

Blondie righted our chairs, lining us up side-by-side as if we were about to watch a movie. He stepped behind Brundidge, pulled his arms back until the kid grunted in pain, then cut the plastic ties with a buck knife. He did the same with Truck and me, then moved around front and leveled an Uzi at us to let us know who was in charge, as if any of us might have doubts at this point.

"Heads up. When I open this door, you're gonna walk side by side down the hall and make a series of turns until you get to the john. Try anything dumb and I'll kill all three of you so fast you won't know what happened 'til you're kissing God's feet."

"Now move," he ordered, backing out the door and clicking the safety off the Uzi.

We walked close together, the three of us, bloody and beaten, down the catacombed hallway, turning as he directed until we reached the men's room.

"Inside," he motioned. "Hit the showers."

It was a large, white-tiled room with a row of toilets on one wall and a row of sinks on the other, like in a health club. At the end, an open tiled doorway led into a large stall with six showers.

We stripped and showered without dignity, heads down, watching the floor as the rippling water pooling into the center drain took on a muddy, crimson color while the blood and stink washed from our bodies. Blondie stood against the row of sinks smoking a cigarette, the Uzi cradled in his arms, trying his best to find something to look at besides us.

Truck was farthest away, on the end, his stumpy legs spread and both hands pressed against the wall for balance, the water jetting onto his pale, balding head and down his hairy back. He'd obviously had the worst of it, or maybe he was just less able to handle the kicks and punches at his age. Who's to say where one man's level of tolerance begins and another's ends? I was just about to start feeling more sorry for him than myself when he turned his head slightly toward me, then glanced about for a fix on Blondie before turning back and making what appeared to be a feeble attempt at winking through his puffy, purple eye.

'What?' I mouthed silently.

He half-smiled, and the light from the bright tile seemed to bounce off his shiny steel tooth that glistened like a false ray of hope at the front of his bruised mouth. Turning away, he lowered his head, then put his hand to his lips and began to jerk and convulse as if he were having trouble breathing. His old head bobbed back and forth a couple of times before he grunted with some kind of supreme effort and lunged forward at the knees, still standing but clutching his chest with balled fists.

I was about to reach out for him when he turned back to me, crouched like Quasimodo, his mouth dripping blood in a thin trickle through the dark gap where the chrome tooth had been. He cut his eyes in the direction of Blondie, who was still occupied with his cigarette, or else having enough doubts about his own masculinity to prevent him from paying too close attention to three naked men showering just a few feet away.

Looking down at Truck's hands, where he clutched the stainless-steel tooth between his thumb and forefinger, I wondered for a moment if this is what happens when we stand on the brink of death and insanity. Poised to fall either this way or that, do we look out across the chasm of the unknown and suddenly decide it's best to just pull out all our teeth, just jerk them out one by one in a fierce and final act of Kiss My Ass defiance before spitting a bloody wad in Death's face?

I took a half-step out to see where this madness was going and saw him working away with the tooth at the center of the four-pronged cold-water knob in a desperate effort to loosen the lone screw that held it in place. I tried to position myself in the line of vision between Blondie and him as he worked away, though I had no idea what his intentions were, unless he planned to use the sprocket like some kind of karate throwing star, and I was pretty sure that, even in desperation, Truck's aim and arm wouldn't be up to the task. Brundidge was closest to Blondie and he gave me a 'what's going on' look but I only half-nodded in Truck's direction.

"Hurry up in there," Blondie snapped, as I turned back toward Truck, who suddenly let out a loud "Unghh," as he dropped to his knees and pitched forward on the wet, tiled floor, the stream of blood still trickling from his mouth as his body kicked and bucked in spasmodic jerks.

"This man's dying- he's having a heart attack," I yelled.

The guard rushed into the shower, waving the Uzi at Brundidge and me.

"Up against the back wall. Turn around and face it. Put your hands up high and spread 'em."

I glanced quickly at Truck's shower as I moved to the wall, noting the missing cold-water knob. If Truck screwed this up I knew for a fact Blondie would kill us all right there which, truth be known, seemed to me a much better death than being fed to a woodchipper.

Truck lay still and limp now, the showers still running and spraying over his lifeless body. He was on his side, his right arm tucked under his ample belly and his left arm flaccid on the floor.

I turned slightly and yelled at Blondie to distract him. "Are you happy now, you sonofabitch? You've killed him. How does it feel to kill an old man? You feel like a Bad Ass?"

"Open your mouth one more time and you'll be lying here with him," he snapped, kneeling at Truck's head and feeling his neck for a pulse.

What happened next happened so fast I almost missed it. Still on his knees, with the Uzi cradled in the crook of his arm, Blondie put a hand on Truck's shoulder to roll him over onto his back. Just as he began to roll, Truck's left arm came up behind the boy's neck, pulling him down hard as his right hand shot up and plunged the shower sprocket into Blondie's eye with a squishy, steel thud, sending a wave of shock that caused him to lose the Uzi and instinctively grab at the embedded sprocket with both hands.

I heard him gasp and saw Truck roll him over until he was on top of him, the gun lying beside the guard's head. A high-pitched rattle was beginning to form in Blondie's throat, but it never made it to the top because Truck quickly grabbed the Uzi, jammed the barrel into the guard's mouth and instantly painted the floor crimson as the back of Blondie's head exploded in a flash of blood and pieces.

Brundidge suddenly came to life, bouncing off the wall and planting both feet on the dead guard's chest, kicking, cursing, crying and hysterical. He snatched the gun from Truck and pumped a half-dozen rounds into the body before we could pull him off.

"Get your shit together now!" Truck commanded. "We're going out the front door in a dead run. Son, if you want to keep that Uzi, then you gotta lead and shoot anything that moves. If not, you need to give it to me right now."

"Let's go," said Brundidge, and out the door we went, racing back down the carpeted maze of long hallways, the three of us still naked and wet, Brundidge leading with the Uzi, Truck and I behind him in single file.

Rounding a corner, a door suddenly flew open about thirty feet in front of us. Brundidge skidded to a halt and readied the

Uzi, but his jaw dropped when a girl stumbled out into the hallway, a very beautiful blonde girl in bra and panties, waving a glass of champagne. We stood frozen and dumbfounded as she weaved and fought for balance, giggling uncontrollably with the laugh of the happy drunk. I remember thinking her face looked familiar, though I couldn't place it.

When she finally saw us, she had to blink a couple times to make sure she wasn't hallucinating, then raised her glass to the three naked men in front of her.

"Hot Damn," she gushed, "you dudes are some partying motherfuckers."

But when she saw the Uzi in Brundidge's hands and looked closer at the blood now beginning to reappear on our faces, she dropped her champagne glass and gasped, then darted back through the door she'd tumbled out of.

Quickly, we doubled back and found the right turn, but as we came near the room with the open door, Freckles stepped out into the hall, still wearing the dingy smile that disappeared the moment he saw the Uzi. He reached for the Glock holstered at his side but stopped his hand in mid-air when he realized he didn't have a chance. He looked at Brundidge and flashed his yellow teeth.

"You shouldn't have stopped," Brundidge said, before spraying a short burst into his crotch. Freckles fell backwards, clutching at the remnants of his scrotum as we ran past him, Truck stopping just long enough to take his pistol. Brundidge sprayed a round of fire through the open door of the office as the three of us stared in awe at the wall of framed, autographed photos: all of them beautiful women and some of the faces recognizable: beauty queens, actresses, models, entertainers.

"Looks like we found the PR firm," observed Brundidge.

"I wish we had time to stay and figure this shit out," said Truck, "but we got maybe ten seconds before this whole fuckin' army comes down on us. Let's go!"

We hit the front door in a dead run and I grabbed the poncho I'd dropped on the way in. Out across the long yard, which had suddenly become illuminated by spotlights, the three of us sprinted in the direction of the guard shack. As we neared the gate, the sentry stepped out with his piece at the ready and his mouth open, but whatever he was about to say, Brundidge shot the words right off his tongue.

Through the guard shack and out onto the sidewalk we ran without looking back until we reached the car and jumped in. Speeding away toward Buckhead, I looked back to see if anyone was following. Strangely, there wasn't a soul in sight.

We'd already driven about two miles before we remembered the guy in the trunk.

CHAPTER 20

After driving around Buckhead and then north on Peachtree for a few miles, we finally decided no one had followed us. At a small, darkened strip center I turned in and cut the lights, then quickly pulled around back to a row of parked semi-trailers and loading ramps. The rain had stopped and the air felt thick enough to comb.

Still clad in the poncho, I opened the trunk and with considerable effort, managed to lift the bound sentry out of the well and onto his feet, then led him up a concrete rise and braced him against the railing several feet above a loading dock. His broken nose lay against his right cheek like putty and a thick stream of caked blood trailed down over the corner of his mouth to the bottom of his chin. He winced when I yanked the duct tape from his lips.

"Hush," I ordered. "Now pay attention. Three of your buddies are dead, and if you don't come up with some good answers, I'll gladly add you to the count." I nudged his ear with the barrel of Freckles' Glock. "You've got thirty seconds to tell me everything you know about that place back there. Start talking."

"I don't know shit," he said, a bit calm for a guy with a shattered nose and a gun at his head. "I've only been there a week. Everyone pulls outside guard duty for the first sixty days until they get final clearance. I'm still taking tests, still restricted to outside and ground floor only. I don't know what else to tell you. I mean...who are you guys anyway?"

I popped him across the forehead with the gun barrel, resisting the urge to yank at his ruined nose.

"I'm the guy asking the questions, and your time is fast running out. Now, one last time, what the hell is going on back there?"

"T-Double-A," he snapped, and I half-expected him to follow that with his name, rank, and serial number.

"Which is what, Dipshit?" I pushed the barrel of the Glock under his chin.

"Tactical Auxiliary Alliance. That's all I know."

I yanked at the collar of his khaki shirt.

"What kind of military bullshit is this? Who's your Commanding Officer?"

"Nothing military about it," he replied. "I'm private security, and I work for TAA. Like I said, I've been there a week. I don't know shit, Pal."

"You mean to tell me you're a rent-a-cop? Who hired you?"

I pulled the gun from under his chin and put the barrel against his eye, then clicked off the safety.

"Contractor. I got recruited, friend of a friend. And don't insult me, Asshole, just because you've got the gun. I did twelve years as a Navy Seal, and I piss on worse than you before breakfast. So whatever you gotta do- do it, because I'm through talking. Now fuck off."

He was looking at me with his one free eye, but there was a world of determination in it. I kept thinking to myself, what kind of private security force would beat three guys half to death and then make plans to kill them and turn their bodies into mulch? And now here was this idiot, banged up and bleeding, yet ready to die rather than talk. Unless he thought I was bluffing.

"Navy Seal, huh?"

"That's right," he growled, with a little too much bravado for my taste.

"I hate the fucking Navy," I said, then stepped back and put a round through his left kneecap. He fell to the pavement squirming and gritting his teeth.

"Son...of...a...bitch," he gnashed, his face biting at the asphalt. I bent down close to his ear.

"Feel like talking now?"

"Fuck you," he spit back.

And that's when I shot the other kneecap. I mashed the tape back across his gaping mouth, then lifted him up and heaved him over the railing and let him drop the ten feet or so to the bottom of the concrete ramp below. I thought I heard him moaning as I walked back to the car.

Back behind the wheel, I drove slowly to the front of the

little shopping center and hung a left on Peachtree, taking great pains not to speed.

"Well?" asked Truck. He was slumped low beside me in the passenger seat, his eyes alternating between the rear-view mirror and the back window.

"Not much of a talker," I said.

Brundidge lay in the back seat, his labored breathing occasionally punctuated by short chokes and sobs. It was hard to tell just how badly the kid was hurt, too early to separate the real pain from the fear still gripping at his gut.

The worst part was knowing I was responsible for all of it. Two days ago, he'd been a gung-ho rookie with high ideals and a strong sense of ethics. Then he went to bat for me and I'd shown my gratitude by putting him in a situation where he was tortured, nearly executed, and forced to kill two people in the bargain.

Nothing else was said as we drove through the muggy Atlanta night, desperately hoping the pain, horror, and humiliation of the past few hours would somehow be lifted from us like some dark, evil fog burned off by the light of morning sun.

The fact that no one had followed us led me to believe we were at least safe from the police. And even though we weren't being chased at that very moment, I felt pretty sure we weren't out of it, that it wouldn't be forgotten, and somewhere down the road, payback would be the veritable bitch.

I took the I-285 perimeter and got us back to the motel before daylight, which was fortunate because even though this was Atlanta, the sight of two naked men and another clad only in a poncho might still raise an eyebrow. Then again, maybe not.

Truck and I helped Brundidge into bed, where he passed out as soon as he hit the sheets, his breathing still alternating between a series of short coughs and urgent gasps. In the morning we could figure out the next move, but as it was, we both turned away from the sleeping boy and headed for our own rooms without saying anything.

Once inside I collapsed into bed but couldn't sleep, tossing and turning, helpless as the bloody ghosts and mental flotsam began crawling from the muddy ditches of my conscience. Finally, I gave up and closed my eyes as the familiar old movie began re-playing itself in my head again, the same reel that had been running two and three nights a week for as long as I could remember. And even though Cassidy's death may have added a double feature, it was Benny Watts who still commanded top billing in the horror show of my psyche.

Always the opening soundtrack of drenching monsoon rain, the distant thunder of artillery, and the scent of a wet jungle stinking with the sulphur smell of death and mildew. Roll titles. Music up...

We started the patrol with eight, counting myself and Benny Watts, both of us having recently transferred in. I'd been blown out of Third Recon at Quang Tri and Benny had only been in country a couple of weeks. I was half-way through my tour and seasoned, but Benny was a green kid who had no business being that far north so early on.

We'd pulled a few watches together, a couple of short details, and I soon became genuinely impressed with the kid, with his eagerness and his all-around good nature. A dirt-poor black boy from Florida, he'd been a high school track star with terrible grades and no shot at college, so he joined the Marines out of some naïve and patriotic sense of duty and pride. Now here he was on the other side of the world, scared shitless, both of us tossed into a dirt-bag patrol of short-timers, militants, and psychos.

Race problems were rampant in the military in those days, though recent histories of our beleaguered Asian campaign make little or no mention of it. Most incidents occurred back in the States, or at least way back in the rear, small riots quickly extinguished, occasional beatings on both sides, much of it carried over from the general unrest that fermented back home in the World but somehow managed to drift back across the ocean to add yet another brick to our sack of shitty morale.

There were the usual tales of fragging and lynchings, most of which could usually be dismissed as rumor, but I knew for a fact that two days after I landed, a band of militant blacks had hung a white airman from the tail of an A-1 bomber. I was still processing in when it happened, and four black sailors were arrested and awaiting court-martial. Nevertheless, tension hung in the air like guilt, even after the brass had labeled it an "isolated incident."

To me it all seemed senseless, especially given the fact that Charlie shot at us with bullets that weren't labeled 'black,' 'brown,' or 'white,' but rather 'to whom it may concern.'

I hadn't been around a lot of prejudice in my life. Where I came from everybody was black- the coal mines saw to that. But Benny was no stranger to the ways of hate, and once we became friends and he felt he could trust me, almost all our conversations were either peppered with or ended in the same reassuring exchange.

"You be watchin' my back, Bro, 'cause I sho' be watchin' yours, Okay?"

"Right on, Man," I'd always answer.

The eight of us numbered five whites and three blacks, including Benny. I should've known what we were in for because we hadn't gone three klicks until a white short-timer and a Black Panther wanna-be got into a knife fight right there on the trail, in the middle of the steaming jungle. The squad leader, a bad-ass Polack named Okraski, managed to get them separated, though at that point the mood was pretty well set. Benny shot me a wide-eyed look, but I shook my head and gave him a palm down to let him know to take it easy and that it would be all right, that we were way too deep in the badlands for any more crazy shit to take place.

But an hour later, with the dense jungle ceiling blocking out the sun, all hell suddenly broke loose with the sound of gunfire all around us.

"Ambush," someone screamed, as Benny and I, near the rear of the column, fell out and began firing into the trees on our left flank. It was impossible to tell where the fire was coming from, but we kept blasting away blindly into the thickness.

The whole thing lasted less than a minute. Finally, someone yelled, "Hold your fire," and the jungle got deathly quiet again as the smell of burnt gunpowder filled our senses. Then a voice I recognized as the radio man, an Italian Corporal who was simply called Dago, sang out:

"Who's breathin'? Call it out."

"Summers." One of the short-timers.

"Martin." The machine gunner.

"Shepherd," I hollered.

"Watts," I heard Benny say.

"Washington...I'm hit," came a faint voice way across the trail. One of the militants.

Then I heard Dago call out again.

"Ski, you alright?" But there was no answer. "Ingram, you cocksucker...you breathing?" Again, no answer.

"All right, everybody stay where you are," Dago ordered. "Washington, where are you?"

"Over here," was the dim reply.

"Sit tight, Washington, I'm coming," Dago soothed, and I could hear him wrestling his way through the foliage.

"Washington? That you?"

"Yeah, man...shit...it hurts bad."

"Here...Lemme give you something for the pain."

Bip-Bip-Bip-a quick burst. Then nothing for several breaths as we listened in stunned silence.

"Everybody move slow, back down the trail to the river," Dago barked. "Let's get checked. Keep your fuckin' eyes open and pay attention. Stay quiet, no chit-chat."

We moved quickly, if not quietly, back down the trail to the river bed, not far from the spot where the fight between Washington and Summers had taken place earlier.

I was the first one to speak as we dropped our gear. "What the Hell-"

"Washington didn't make it," Dago shrugged, then immediately walked over to Benny Watts and cold-cocked him under the chin with the butt of his M-16. Benny fell to the ground in a heap.

"No you don't-," was all I managed to get out before I felt the warm steel of Martin's M-60 nudge into my neck.

"Washington and Ingram killed Ski," charged Dago. "Shot the poor sonofabitch in the back. If you don't believe me go see for yourself. Ski managed to get Ingram as he went down. I saw Washington light up Ski's pack and that's when I shot the motherfucker the first time. He didn't think I knew what was going on, but I didn't buy that ambush shit for a minute."

"You bastards are gonna rot in the brig," I said, then immediately wished I hadn't.

"No-fucking-body is going to any-fucking-brig," said Martin, still holding the machine gun at my head. "The way I look at it, we're all in this together, if you know what I mean. Sem-per Fi, Mo-ther-fuck-er."

Dago reached into his backpack and brought out a roll of thick, hemp rope, the same kind carried by the VC. He tossed it to Summers, who immediately fashioned a slip knot, then threw the long end over a tree branch at the edge of the trail.

"Bring the nigger over here," said Summers, as coldly as if he were ordering coffee. Dago yanked Benny to his feet and shoved him under the rope.

But then the knocking started, faintly at first, like the distant thwapping of helicopter blades, then gradually becoming distinct as Benny, Dago, and the others began to lose their shape and break apart, disappearing, the jungle itself turning to mist with each knock that was bringing the movie to an early end...

I opened my eyes and looked up at the ceiling of the motel room, finally realizing where I was. More knocking, louder now.

"Housekeeping," came a female voice outside the door.

"Come back later," I hollered, then went into the bathroom and stuck my head under the cold shower, the water knifing over me with the force of a monsoon rain.

CHAPTER 21

I lay in bed drinking coffee and smoking, trying to forget the dream and refusing to allow Benny Watts any part of my conscious, waking life. Brundidge needed medical attention but there was no way we could take him to a local hospital without raising a lot of questions. At the same time, I also wasn't sure he could handle a four-hour ride back to Nashville.

Getting the Eskews involved in our mess was the last thing I wanted to do, and I went back and forth in my thinking for a long time before making the call. Mrs. Eskew answered the phone and after a brief exchange, in which she assured me that we would be both welcome and safe, she gave me simple directions to the town of Ellijay, in the north Georgia mountains at the tip of the Chattahoochee National Forest.

We loaded a sore but rested Brundidge into the back seat and headed out, riding in silence until finally I could stand it no longer and turned on the radio. Lloyd Price sang about Stagger Lee's early demise as we traveled north on I-75 until we caught the 575 connector that took us into the tiny hamlet of Ball Ground. From there we rode a two-lane highway through the old marble mining town of Tate, through Talking Rock and finally on into Ellijay, where Walter Eskew sat waiting in the gravel parking lot of the Dairy Dip just inside the city limits. The muddy Chrysler looked as though it hadn't been washed since his trip to Nashville a few weeks back.

As we pulled alongside, Walter nodded a greeting, then motioned for us to follow as he drove toward the town but then hung a sharp left onto a dirt road that seemed to wind itself like clay-colored thread through the lush, green hills and on into the mountains. After what seemed like ten miles of battered mobile homes with satellite dishes and cars on blocks, he turned right at a shiny red mailbox shaped like a barn, onto a pea gravel driveway that led us deep into the woods before spilling us out into a small clearing that served as the yard for the Eskew's two-story log home. There was a large covered porch complete with rocking chairs, one of which contained Esther Eskew, who appeared to be shelling butter beans as she rocked. She stood up and waved as we parked the cars and got out.

This time Walter Eskew shook my hand, then introduced himself to Truck as they both helped Brundidge out of the car and up the steps where his wife took over and led the kid into the house.

"I'll take care of this one," she said, opening the screen door. "Ya'll have a seat on the porch and I'll bring you some iced tea in a minute."

I found a spot at the top of the steps while Truck and Walter Eskew sat in the big wooden rockers. Walter took out his pipe and in a moment the fresh mountain air was complimented with the sharp, comforting smell of Prince Albert. I gave him a condensed version of our story, making sure to leave out the part about the three dead men. He listened quietly, drawing slowly on his pipe and nodding from time to time. When I finished, he sat for a few minutes staring out into the thick trees that started at the edge of his small yard and ran on forever into the beckoning woods. Finally, he spoke.

"Sounds to me like the three of you took a mighty big risk just to come away with nothing. And from the looks of it, I'd say you were lucky to get out at all."

"Just because we didn't find out anything last night doesn't mean we won't later on," Truck said. "I have no idea what goes on in that place, but I can promise you this, Mr. Eskew- we *will* find out about it, and if there's a connection to your daughter we'll find out what it is."

Walter folded both hands around his pipe and rested his elbows on the arms of the rocker.

"It ain't necessary for me to know everything she was involved in. To tell you the truth, I don't want to know. The only thing I need to know is who is responsible for what happened to my little girl. That's all I care about."

His wife brought out large glasses of iced tea and the three of us sat sipping our drinks and listening to the sounds of the woods until the quiet became uncomfortable and gave itself up to small talk.

"Beautiful country out here," said Truck.

Walter nodded and continued tamping at the worn pipe.

"It's all I know," he said. "I was born in this house. Me and my brothers and sisters was all raised here. They're all gone now, I'm the only one left. Except for two years in the Army, I've never really been away from here, just an overnight trip or two. I did go to Louisville once, to a church convention, and I got relations in Knoxville I visited one time years back.

"I sit out here and listen to the sounds in the trees, the same trees that's been talking to me since I was a boy. I tell you, there's not much could make me leave here. I'm a very blessed man, yes sir, very blessed. I've got a decent home, a good wife, Charlotte's a loving daughter, but I do know that sometimes the Lord needs to test his servants with trials."

He let out a tired breath and looked wistfully out into the dense trees, his long fingers kneading at his forehead as he went on.

"I've given it a lot of thought, and I really don't know what to make of Margaret Ellen. She was always free-spirited, maybe she was just bucking against me 'cause I was so hard on her and Charlotte when they was kids. I know I made mistakes with both of them but, I swear, I believe they both knew that I loved them. There ain't nothing I wouldn't have done for either one of those girls.

"But Margaret Ellen, she just wouldn't have it any other way 'cept her own. She was looking to get out of here since she could talk, always going on about Hollywood and such. I tell you, that girl had some big dreams, even for a kid."

His voice broke and for a moment I was able to see Walter Eskew in a different light: a loving, grieving father who was more than just a hard-headed backwoods preacher and no longer shielded in a blanket of wooded isolation and the surety of the love of the Lord.

"All kids have big dreams," I said. "It's part of being a kid to think anything in the world is possible."

Truck had been sitting quietly sipping his tea, listening back and forth to the woods and to Walter Eskew.

"That's because the world is a bigger place to a kid," he offered. "Everything is huge then and full of promise. It's not 'til you get older when you find out it's not so big after all, that there ain't much promise, and things ain't much different any place you go."

I was taken aback, at least momentarily, by Truck's philosophical bent. His work in the shower the night before had given me cause to look at him with newfound respect. I'd always thought of him as some kind of bumbling, befuddled loser, a bull-in-a-china-shop gumshoe long resigned to the fate of always being a couple of steps behind the big guys.

But the simple fact of the matter was, he'd saved my life and Brundidge's as well with some quick thinking and, when the time came, some damn fast and sure moves. So what if he had the moral code of a street shyster? The sonofagun had more guts than I would've ever given him credit for, and when it came time to make the tough call he did it, and he did it without blinking.

Some folks define character as doing the right thing when no one's looking, and I'm sure that's a workable definition. But if you ask me, character is also being able to put your head down and run straight and hard into the wall, knowing you're either gonna stick or slide off, so you'd damn well better give it a hundred and ten percent. I almost wished we were in a bar so I could buy him a drink and say thanks.

After a while Esther Eskew came back outside, her hands wrapped in her blue patterned apron.

"He'll be all right, he just needs to rest for a while. Somebody tore him up pretty good, if you ask me. And it looks like he wasn't the only one to get a whuppin." She nodded over at Truck, whose bruised and swollen face had actually begun to blend with the rest of his rumpled demeanor. She pulled something out of her apron pocket and walked over to where he sat in the rocker.

"This here is mallow root," she soothed. "It'll take most of the soreness out of your mouth. And I'm going to put some of this salve on your face to bring down the swelling and clear up some of those bruises." She touched his forehead with her fingers and Truck jerked his head back immediately.

"Whoa-" he whelped. "What's in that stuff?"

Mrs. Eskew smiled and went on working the salve into his face with her long dexterous fingers. "It's just a little something I put together to keep around the house for bumps and bruises. It's got a little of this and a smidgen of that." She stood for a moment and waved her arm toward the woods.

"I've got a pretty good drugstore out there: mustard for plasters and poultices, rhubarb for stomach trouble, poke berries for rheumatism, white oak for tender feet, and if I can get to it in time, I can whip stomach cancer with a steady dose of violet tea." She glanced at Walter Eskew, who blew a small cloud of smoke as he nodded in agreement, obviously proud of his beautiful and resourceful wife.

I remembered my conversation with her that first morning in the diner, how I'd nodded politely when she told me of her connection to the spirit world, and how quickly and wrong I'd been to dismiss Esther Eskew as just a backwoods woman with too much time on her hands.

A late afternoon breeze was winding its way through the trees, bringing with it a crystal hint of cool air, the woods at the edge of the dry yard already beginning to smell like fall. I closed my eyes and leaned my head back to breathe it all in and take a quick memory trip back to my youth when smells meant so much. I thought of sweaty football pads and helmets, rich green grass and burning lime. Hot dogs and marching bands, homecoming queens and innocence not yet lost. In my mind I was going deep for a touchdown pass when the rumble of a car coming up the gravel drive brought me out of my trance.

"Here she comes," Esther said.

"That'll be her," Walter nodded.

Charlotte's black Volvo was tearing up the drive, leaving a roostertail of dust and gravel in its wake. As she pulled into the yard she glanced at the strange car and then at the porch. When she saw me she broke into a smile and I felt something inside me start turning some old, familiar flips. The breeze caught her hair as she walked across the yard, lifting it gently to expose her soft neck. A vision in denim shirt, jeans and hiking boots, still I resisted the urge to run across the yard and wrap my arms around her.

"Well, talk about surprises," she said, as she marched up the steps and hugged both her father and mother before walking over to me and looking me dead in the eye.

"Hello, Jake. You look like a train wreck."

"It's good to see you, too, Charlotte."

I wasn't exactly sure how to react but then Charlotte reached down to plant a kiss on my bruised cheek, and I forgot about everything in the world except her standing right in front of me. She turned back toward her parents, who were both doing their best to appear nonchalant, as if I had just walked her home from church.

"What are you doing home?" I asked.

"It's Labor Day Weekend, Silly. No school 'til Tuesday. Besides, when I got up this morning something told me I needed to come home. I guess this is what I get for trusting my instincts, right Mama?" She winked, and I quickly realized Charlotte had both of them wrapped around her little finger as surely as she had me.

"Have either of you been to the mailbox today?"

Both the Eskews shook their heads.

"Walk with me, Jake. Let's go down and check the mail. Mama, Daddy, we'll be back in a few minutes."

She took my hand as we started down the steps and I turned to look at Walter and Esther as they gazed at each other in absolute wonder at what their darling daughter might be up to now. Mrs. Eskew managed an awkward smile and I thought I saw Walter shrug his shoulders as if that were the only explanation needed for the moment.

We walked the first few yards in silence, Charlotte squeezing my hand as she swung both our arms back and forth like a couple of school kids at recess. I resisted the urge to say anything. As far as I was concerned, it was still her move.

"I'm sorry about leaving the way I did," she finally said. And of course, that was all it took for me to forgive her completely.

"It's okay, Charlotte. Like you said in your letter- timing and all that. I understand, really I do."

"Thank you, Jake."

She reached up and lightly touched one of the bruises on my face with her fingers.

"Want to tell me about it?"

"Not much to tell," I said. "Three of us went down there and we're all three going home in the morning."

I was relieved when she let it go at that.

"Wait a sec-" she said, then stopped and pulled her eye drops and the foil packet of tissues from her shirt pocket.

"How are the eyes coming along?"

"Great," she said, dousing both eyes and then blotting with the blue tissue. "Twenty-twenty in my left and twenty- twenty-five in my right. I should've had it done years ago. I never understood why everyone in my family had perfect vision except me."

She reached out for my hand again as we continued down the drive.

"Your mother is an interesting woman."

Charlotte nodded her head, then looked up into the sheltering trees and laughed.

"Mama is in tune with things normal people can't fathom. That's the only way I know how to put it. She sees pictures in her head and meaning in everyday things other folks take for granted. The kicker is, she's almost always right. It's taken a while, but we've all finally learned to live with it."

"Did you inherit the gift?"

"No, thank God. And I wouldn't want it."

We made our way down the gravel and dirt drive as the pine trees, hickory, and live oaks that lined either side swayed in the gentle breeze. Just being near her made me giddy, and I thought about my first real kiss that late summer on Bluestone Lake, when I was fourteen and the girl a couple years older. We sat in her parents'

Plymouth Valiant while she slipped her tongue into my mouth as Chad and Jeremy sang of summer days and silver leaves.

Thirty years later I'm still the same wide-eyed kid as we round a curve and Charlotte suddenly tugs at my arm, pulling me off the gravel drive and into the woods, until we came to a small clearing covered by a thick ceiling of tall Georgia pines. Throwing her arms around me, she kissed me with total abandon as I braced myself against a thick pine and held her tight enough to almost pull her inside me.

"I'm sorry for leaving," she said, when she finally pulled away from my mouth.

"It's all right, Babe. Ancient history."

I pulled her back to me and kissed her again as I eased both hands down her back and cupped her firm ass while she ground herself into me.

"Are you my baby?" she whispered.

"You know I am, Charlotte."

"No, I mean are you *really* my baby?"

"More than you know."

"Promise?"

"I promise."

"Tell me what a bitch I am."

"No, you're not, you're the girl I-"

Charlotte slapped me so fast and so hard that my ears rang like high-hat cymbals.

"Tell me," she demanded.

The dichotomy of sex has always intrigued me. It took a second to figure out what she wanted, but then I caught on quickly, yanking her head back with a fistful of auburn hair and whispering a few select, decadent suggestions.

"Mmmmm...," was the sound she made as she pushed herself against me.

We played the game for a few more tense moments as she ground herself into me, denim against denim, until finally her eyes rolled back and she went limp against me, holding onto my neck as she gasped for breath. Then she slowly let herself slide down my body until her knees rested on the soft bed of pine needles. Unzipping my pants, she took me in her mouth and within seconds it was over, but she kept at it until there was nothing left and I dropped to my knees in front of her on the gentle pine floor. She kissed me again, hard and deep, as she unsnapped her jeans and pushed her hand inside, then brought it back out and smeared her wet, musky scent across my lips with her fingers.

"Good boy," she whispered.

"I love you," I said.

"You'd fucking better," she breathed.

We lay back as I held her close to me, breathing the sweet fragrance of her neck and kissing at her hair. Suddenly, she sat up and brushed the pine needles from her shirt and looked at me solemnly.

"There's something I need to tell you, Jake."

"Go ahead."

"I'm not sure this is something you'll understand," she began, "I'm not even sure I understand it myself."

"What is it?" I asked, curious now. "Charlotte, there's nothing you can say that will change the way I feel about you. Go ahead, tell me."

A few feet away, a brown squirrel was circling its way up the trunk of a persimmon tree, its tiny mouth stretched around a large acorn.

"Are you sure?"

"Positive," I answered. And I meant it.

She shifted her seat on the pine floor and folded her hands in her lap.

"Jake, I've...just recently ended a relationship," she began.

"Good," I injected.

"With a woman," she added.

My first reaction was one of incredible arousal, but I managed to stifle it long enough to reach for her hand and flash a gentle smile before saying, "So?"

"That doesn't bother you?" she asked.

"Not a bit." And I meant that too.

"It was just something that happened," she went on. "I'd never done anything like that before and can't picture myself doing it again."

"Someone from school I would guess," I said.

"No," she said, "not from school. I told you I had some investments. She and I became business partners and, before we knew it, one thing led to another. She's a little older than me, and I guess I just got caught up in the mystery of it all."

Mystery, I thought? As far as I was concerned, Charlotte Eskew had more mystery than the Sphinx. At this point nothing she could do or say would surprise me.

"Is it over?"

Charlotte looked at me and nodded her head.

"Yes...it is. I have a couple of loose ends to tie up, but yes, it's definitely over."

I assumed the loose ends had to do with business, so I let it slide without a reaction.

"You're mine now," I smiled. And I meant that more than anything in the world.

By the time we got back to the house with the mail, dusk was settling in. Walter was still smoking in his rocker with Truck taking my place on the steps as Brundidge rocked slowly back and forth in the other chair. The lights were on inside and the aroma that rode on the wings of the evening fireflies was the sweet smell of country cooking- biscuits, gravy, venison roast, butter beans, and all sorts of southern delights.

Soon we were all seated around the big oak table, holding hands as Walter Eskew said Grace, thanking God for all his many blessings and adding a special prayer for the safety of his guests. Afterwards we ate like famished soldiers and Esther Eskew seemed genuinely pleased at the way we put away the food. Even Brundidge seemed to be showing improvement. At least his appetite was healthy.

The dining room sat off to the side of the huge living room that had a great stone fireplace with an old-fashioned mantel stocked with pictures of generations of Eskews, many of which looked sepia-toned but were actually just faded yellow with age. Above the mantel, anchored by two small three-point deer antlers, rested an ancient deer rifle Truck had been eyeing throughout dinner.

"That's a fine old rifle you've got there," he finally said, nodding toward the fireplace.

"Thank you," Walter Eskew said. "I've had it since I was twelve years old. It's a single-shot Springfield 30.06, but it's been gathering a little dust these past couple of years. Except for this here deer we're eating right now that I took last fall, I don't get to hunt much anymore. My eyes ain't what they used to be and my knees just won't hold out for too long.

"I surely do love being in the woods though. As far back as I can remember, I've never seen a patch of woods that made me feel a stranger. If I've got the sun or the stars to guide me, I can usually find my way around just about anywhere."

"Don't let him kid you," said Charlotte, obviously proud of her old man. "Daddy can still shoot the eye out of a squirrel at a hundred yards. I've seen him do it.

"Daddy, remember that time you bet Paw Paw a quart of sorghum you could shoot the eye out of that squirrel? I was just a little girl and I couldn't even see the squirrel, it was so far away. But he did it, Jake, and even Paw Paw couldn't believe it. And not only that, I can't remember a single Thanksgiving that he didn't bring home a bird from the turkey shoot in Ellijay."

Walter Eskew blushed, delighted to still be the apple of his little girl's eye.

"It's just something I was always able to do," he admitted. "Some folks can play ball, some can paint pictures, I guess the Lord just saw fit to make me a good shot. That old rifle has put a lot of meat on this table over the years."

After dinner the Eskews offered to put us up for the night but we politely declined, opting instead to get rooms at the tiny motel in town. The three of us thanked them profusely for their hospitality, then left Walter and Esther standing and waving from the porch as Charlotte walked us across the yard to our car.

"When will I see you again?" I asked.

"In a couple of weeks, Jake, I promise. I'll come to Nashville for the weekend."

"I'm gonna hold you to that, Lady."

"I'll be there. Just one more thing though," she added, pulling me into the firefly-lit shadows at the edge of the yard. A symphony of crickets sounded from the woods, and in the distance a lone whippoorwill called.

"Jake, we think you've done enough. All of us: Mama, Daddy, and me. We believe Margaret Ellen was into something way out of her element, something bigger than any of us can imagine. You and I both know what a naive kid she was, and I doubt she had any idea what she was really into. But now we think it's time to leave all of it alone. Nothing is going to bring her back, and...well...if something were to happen to you at this point..."

She wrapped her arms around me and lay her head against my shoulder. I held her and made a point of not looking in the direction of the front porch although the wafting smell of Prince Albert assured me that Walter Eskew was standing there smoking and watching. Truck and Brundidge were already in the car waiting.

"Promise me you'll leave this alone," she went on. "Promise me you'll go back and forget about it so you and I can just work on spending the rest of our lives together. Will you promise me that? Please?"

Placing both hands on her shoulders, I eased her back and gazed at her. She looked like a gift from God. And more than anything in the world, I wanted to make that promise to her. But I knew I couldn't.

"I can't walk away from this now, Charlotte. Too much has happened to too many people. I've got to have some answers, if not for you and your family, then for me. I do promise that it'll be over soon and then we really can work on being together, if that's what you want."

She jerked away so fast it caught me by surprise.

"Quit being selfish, Jake," she snapped. "Trust me, you're going to end up dead."

Even in the dark I could see what was in her eyes. It wasn't fear, and it sure as hell wasn't love. It was more like rage, and the sound of her voice told me it was building. Still, I wasn't giving in.

"You see those two guys sitting over there in that car? Both nearly died last night, and both had to kill someone in order for me to be standing in front of you right now. You think I can just forget that-"

"-They had no business going down there with you in the first place," she interrupted. "Jake, just once, will you listen to reason, please? Leave it alone. You can keep the money-"

The word itself ignited a blaze of anger.

"Money? You think this is about money? Christ, Charlotte, I can't believe you even said that."

"Jake, you know that's not what I meant. I just-"

"Look Charlotte, I know I'm not the All-American Boy here. Twenty years ago I jumped off a star and landed in a bottle and I'll admit I haven't come up for air a whole helluva lot since. I've been pushed around, lied to, humiliated, ignored, and shit on for most of the past two decades. And maybe I deserved it, I don't know. One thing I do know- I was the only one who was getting hurt, so maybe that made it, if not right, then at least bearable.

"But this is different. Other people are involved: you, your family, your sister, not to even mention Truck and Brundidge. And you want me to just throw up my hands so you and I can waltz off into the sunset? I'm sorry, Charlotte, but I can't do that. And I can't really believe you'd want me to."

She stood there trembling with anger, biting her lip as tears streaked down her face. I took a step toward her but she held up her hand to stop me.

"You stupid sonofabitch," she hissed, then turned on her heels and walked back into the house.

I got behind the wheel and drove slowly back down the winding gravel drive. But when we hit the dirt road, I gunned the big Ford toward town like some crazed moonshiner, barreling down the straights and drifting through the clay-packed curves as Truck and Brundidge rode along in silence. We found the only motel in town and checked in for some needed, peaceful sleep. This time there were no dreams. Not of Cassidy, nor Charlotte, not even Benny Watts. Just the sweet, healing balm of slumber.

CHAPTER 22

The next morning, after going through the entire *Atlanta Journal* and finding no mention of our little episode at the West Paces Ferry compound, we were well into our second stack of pancakes when Walter Eskew joined us at our table in the motel cafe.

A steaming cup of coffee and sausage biscuit appeared almost instantly in front of him as we exchanged greetings and the three of us again thanked him for his family's hospitality the day before. He was dressed in clean overalls and khaki work shirt, and looked as though he could be headed for the fields or going hunting, although the area was too steep for farming and even I knew hunting season was still a few weeks away.

Yesterday he'd been the most congenial of hosts, laughing and telling stories about some of the mountain characters he'd known growing up in the area. Like so many preachers he was charismatic and a great storyteller, and the narratives he spun from his rocking chair had unfolded before us like tapestries, full of colorful scenes that played out like movies in our minds as Truck and I sat mesmerized at his wild and entertaining tales about the saints and sinners who inhabited this hardscrabble backwoods universe.

At some point in the evening, with the soft blanket of Prince Albert hovering around me, I'd begun to feel the pain and bloody memories of the night before rise out of me, billowing up into the healing smoke as Walter's voice became the voice of my great-grandfather, soothing, gently laughing, the sounds of the words every bit as meaningful as the words themselves, the wooden porch beneath me as solid and secure as the throne of God. I'd sat and listened, dozed and dreamed.

He took a long sip of coffee before pulling out the familiar tin of tobacco, speaking slowly and carefully as he hand-rolled a thin cigarette, just like he'd done that first morning we met. If anyone in the cafe minded the smoke, they didn't complain.

"You never did say what you plan on doing when you get back to Nashville," he began. "You gonna talk to the police, or what?"

I was about to tell him I didn't have the faintest idea when Brundidge spoke up.

"I think we need to look around a little more," he said. "Right now I'm not so sure we can't find some answers a lot quicker ourselves, not to take anything away from the police. But to tell you the truth, we don't know exactly who we're looking into or whether or not they've got ties to the force and if so, how far up they go." He glanced at Truck, who nodded agreement as he knifed at a piece of country ham.

"What makes you think them folks ain't followed you up here?" asked Walter. "And how do you know they're not waiting for you when you get back?"

"I'm pretty sure we weren't followed after we left Buckhead," I said. "If we had been, they would've had all night to make their move at the motel."

A young waitress made a lap around the table filling coffee cups and picking up plates.

"Well, I don't know," Walter continued, "I've had some time to think about it, and I'm just not sure it makes sense to keep digging around and stirring things up 'til somebody else gets hurt or maybe worse."

My thoughts flashed on the three dead guards.

"Vengeance belongs to the Lord, not to me," he went on. "I want to know who killed my baby girl, but I've also got Charlotte and Esther to think about. If something happened to either one of them, I don't think I could ever live with myself. I believe I'd feel a whole lot better if you'd just let things lie. The police may come up with something, but whether they do or don't doesn't matter. None of it'll bring Margaret Ellen back."

What he said made sense of course. But even though I'd only been around Walter Eskew on two occasions, the words didn't seem to come naturally from his mouth. I detected the strong, undeniable influence of Charlotte. She hadn't been able to change my mind the night before, so she'd sent her daddy to do the job.

"We'll let you know if anything else turns up," I said. "Right now, I just want to go back and get my name cleared."

"And you'll forget about the rest of it?"

"I can't make any promises, Mr. Eskew."

"I was afraid that's what you'd say," he sighed.

Truck paid the check and the four of us made our way out to our cars to once again say our goodbyes.

"I'm headed to Chatsworth to see a man about a shoat," Walter said. "Ya'll can follow me to the cutoff and then it's just a short piece over to Dalton and the interstate."

"Nothing like home-grown pork, is there," said Truck.

"Well, I don't raise 'em, I just buy half of one and let 'em butcher it come November. That and what little deer meat I bring home is about the only meat I eat these days."

I remembered the sweet, gamy taste of the venison roast the night before and pictured Walter Eskew sitting quietly in the woods, still as stone, leaned back against a hickory tree waiting for a buck to wander into view, the ancient deer rifle across his lap like a scepter.

We headed west on Highway 52 again, winding through the pine-covered North Georgia hills as Walter's dirty Chrysler led us out of the mountains toward home. Brundidge drove and Truck rode shotgun as I sat in the back wishing for a guitar in my grip, not so much to play but just to make me feel whole again.

I pushed Charlotte out of my mind and instead turned my attention to the roadside houses, trailers, and country stores that whizzed past the side window, caught in my eyes for a brief moment while I tried to imagine the lives that went on within each one. The steep hills made radio reception impossible, so we rode in relative silence with just the dinning harmony of the rubber and asphalt filling the car as the big Ford carried us on into late summer.

Just before we reached Chatsworth, Walter Eskew pulled over and we eased up alongside.

"Take a left at the big intersection about a half-mile up the road," he said. "You'll see a sign to Dalton, just follow that and it'll take you to 75."

"I'll talk to you soon," I promised.

He nodded and waved, then made a right onto a dirt road that no doubt led to the pig farm where he was headed. We found the turn and from there it was a short hop to Carpet Town and the Interstate. We made a pit stop for gas and a six-pack for Truck, then Brundidge begrudgingly handed me the keys after I insisted on driving, having had all I could stand of the back seat. But Truck wasn't so hard to please, and soon he was stretched out in back, a beer in hand and a blissful smile across his snaggle-toothed face.

I aimed us up I-75, taking our place in the long line of Labor Day traffic slowly snaking its way north.

"Are you almost back to fightin' weight?" I asked Brundidge.

"I feel better," he said, running a hand across his chest and ribs. "A little stiff but most of the soreness is going away. Mrs. Eskew is a heckuva doctor. How about you?"

"I'm Okay," I said. "Not too bad. I think you and Truck got the worst of it."

I glanced in the mirror at Truck, napping now with both hands still wrapped around the tall Budweiser.

"I'm curious, Brundidge. Whatever made you decide to become a cop?"

He shifted in the seat to get comfortable, then rolled the window down and half-closed his eyes against the breeze.

"I washed out of the FBI Academy and joined the force on

the rebound. I've been thinking about law school in a couple years. And I really would like to strike out on my own one of these days, maybe start a business. I figure there's no big rush. But for now, being a cop isn't the worst job in the world."

"That's true," I said. "Listen, Alvin, you've gone way beyond the call of duty here. And I'm really sorry for this whole mess. If I were you, I think I'd put all this behind me and just get back to work. Nothing is going to change what happened back there, but I want you to know that I truly appreciate everything you've done.

"You put your ass on the line just leaving town with me. I guess what I'm trying to say is, if you want to cut your losses now and get out while you can, then certainly no one would blame you."

I was hoping he'd do just that. Brundidge had changed, was different now, in the way we all rise up reborn when baptized by fire. He'd left something behind in that big, bloody house in Buckhead. Something he would never be able to get back.

"What about him?" he asked, nodding at Truck dozing in the back.

"He can get out anytime he wants, but I doubt he will because he's getting paid. That and partly because he still gets off on the rush. But you're different. You've got options, and you've got your whole life in front of you, whether it's law school, working a beat or whatever. Like I said, you've done enough. Go back to your job security, just put in a good word for me with Lyle when we get back."

"That's probably what I'll do," he said. "But today is Saturday and I don't have to be back at work until Tuesday. I've still got time to poke around some before I put the blues back on."

Nearing the Tennessee line, we slowed to a crawl as I-75 split north to Knoxville and we veered west on I-24.

"What kind of poking around are you talking about? You seemed to have some definite ideas back there at the cafe. Or were you just saying that for Walter Eskew's benefit?"

"A couple of guys I went to school with work for the Feds and they do a lot of snooping on the Web. If the Buckhead place has any kind of link to the net, they'll find out about it. I know we didn't get to see much, but so far nothing seems to point to Aleta Thomas. Even with three clubs running sixty to seventy percent cash business, I still don't put her in the same financial league with whoever owns that compound."

"I don't know," I said. "Something about that wall of framed photos made me think of her."

"Hell, Jake, anybody can hang a picture. Besides, wouldn't a PR firm have a wall of pictures like that? It's the gonzo security that doesn't fit the format."

"I know," I agreed. "And I keep thinking about that girl in the hall. I swear I've seen her before, but I can't place her."

"Well, whoever she was, she seemed to be having a helluva time 'til she saw us. I guess we crashed the wrong party."

The traffic was steady and tight as we twisted and turned our way through Chattanooga, once known as the Pittsburgh of the South because of its ugly steel mills and industry, but now on a commercial rebound. Through the city, with the Tennessee River to our right dotted with barges churning up river, we wound our way through the hills toward Monteagle Mountain. The line of cars stretched in front and behind us as far as I could see, both lanes packed but moving nonetheless.

We made a pit stop at an exit on top of Monteagle and stretched a bit, then kept our same positions when Truck again jumped into the back seat and resumed his nap. Coming down off the mountain we hit the long straightaway that led to Tullahoma and the traffic began to thin out little by little as I relaxed my driving and eased back into the seat to enjoy the beautiful afternoon.

Rolling over the mountain I'd noticed the leaves hadn't begun to turn just yet, but their green hue had dulled and it would only be a couple more weeks before the soft yellows and browns began taking their places against the picturesque mountainside. I imagined Charlotte's black Volvo driving past a vista of reds, purples, oranges, and golds, heading for Nashville some fine October morning.

"You never did tell me what it was that made you change your mind about me, Alvin."

"I don't know," he shrugged. "And I can't prove anything, but for some reason Lyle seemed really fired up to get you put away as quickly as possible, no matter what. I know Lyle pretty well. He's not a bad dude, and that just seemed out of character for him. Like maybe someone upstairs was putting the heat to his shoes."

Once on the flatlands I turned the radio to WSM 650- AM just in time to catch Charlie Pride singing "Just Between You and Me," one of my favorites of the many classics from the great "Cowboy" Jack Clement's pen. Truck snored from the back seat and Brundidge sipped at his beer, staring at the countryside as I drove along wondering why Cowboy had a truckload of hit songs to his credit and I only had one. Probably had something to do with hard work and discipline, two traits I'd long been short on.

Perhaps it was just a road buzz, but at that moment I could feel something beginning to stir around inside me, something that made me feel as though some kind of serious change was about to take place in my life. I made a promise to myself right then that, when all this business was over, I'd give it one more shot, one more hard and serious run at the brass ring. So what if the music business had changed? I'd changed quite a bit myself. I knew I was rusty and out of the loop, but I also knew I was smarter than most of those guys. I was a damn good writer, I just needed to get back in the game and show them. Was it Willie Nelson or George Bernard Shaw who said, "Youth and talent are no match for old age and treachery?"

Passing the Murfreesboro exit, which signaled the last thirty-mile stretch to Tunetown, I was lost in thought, day-dreaming about my acceptance speech for Song of the Year honors when- POW- the whole fantasy was shattered as a hole tore through the windshield, which then cracked and imploded, covering both Brundidge and myself with a swarm of glass pellets.

"Jesus Christ," Brundidge screamed, fighting at the glass shards as if they were hornets.

"What-the-Hell," yelled Truck, jumping up and turning around to shake off a blanket of crystalline splinters. "Shit, get moving Man- They're shooting at us."

I glanced in the rear-view mirror and couldn't believe what I was seeing. The back window was also gone and about seventy-five yards behind us was a flat black HumVee with two men in the front, one of whom was aiming a rifle at us. On instinct I whipped over into the left lane, just in time to see the passenger side mirror shatter with the brilliance of a shooting star.

I floored the big V-8 and immediately started putting some distance between us and the Hummer. Though not as close as before, he was still in sight and certainly within rifle range.

We'd stashed our captured weapons, the Uzi and the Glock, under the seats when we left Atlanta and now Truck and Brundidge were both in the floor frantically digging around for them. Truck found the Glock first and started throwing some fire back at the Hummer when traffic allowed. Brundidge came up with the Uzi.

"Stay on the Interstate," screamed Truck. "Go down the emergency lane if you have to. Use the median, but don't stop for anything and don't take an exit. They'll kill us the minute we stop. Our only hope is to outrun them or lose them in traffic."

"You think these guys followed us all the way from Georgia?" I shouted at either of them.

"You know anyone else who wants to kill us?" Brundidge said. He was cradling the Uzi and looking back but smart enough not to take a shot at that distance.

We flew past the Old Hickory Boulevard exit and started up the long hill toward Hickory Hollow when I spotted a Highway Patrol car up ahead in the distance, parked in the center of the grassy median. I breathed a half-sigh of relief and began slowing down.

"What the hell are you doing?" Truck hollered.

"There's a cop up there," I yelled back as I turned on my lights and began blinking them furiously before pulling off to the left emergency lane and slowing down. "They won't kill us in front of the police."

"The hell they won't!" Truck was carefully firing back at the Hummer, which by now was only about fifty yards behind us.

"Go! Go! Go, Dammit!"

The whole thing took only a couple seconds, though it seemed to unravel in slow motion, frame-by-frame. As we neared the parked patrol car, my heart stopped when it became obvious there was no one inside, just a dummy vehicle parked there to slow the holiday speeders. I hit the gas hard and looked over at Brundidge, crouched in his seat but raising his head for a quick look back at the Hummer. Behind me, I could hear Truck cursing and I glanced up at the rear-view mirror just as something went *phffft*, and flicked my ear lobe before splattering the dash with splotches of purple and red and pinkish gray. When I looked back up at the mirror Truck wasn't there and Brundidge was screaming something I couldn't, or didn't want to understand.

"Jesus Christ- they shot him," he gasped, total panic illuminating his eyes as he lay low in the seat clinging to the Uzi. "They blew his damn face off for Christ's sake. God, please...no...no..."

It was the same crying plea I'd heard all those years ago, grown men and young boys made equal in their fear, thrashing about in the dark, merciless jungle, helpless as the black night lit up around them in white streaks, their unanswered prayers wet and diluted by the relentless rain.

The blue vinyl dashboard looked as though it had been hit with a fistful of gumbo. The back of my shirt at the right shoulder was wet and I didn't want to imagine what was on there.

Brundidge had pulled himself together enough to start throwing select fire out the open back window but I stopped him when I saw the distance I'd gained in the last few seconds. He slumped down in the seat and started taking his breath in long, deep gasps. The Hummer was still with us, albeit a few hundred yards back, both of us zigging and zagging in and out of traffic as we barreled toward Nashville at ninety-miles-an-hour.

Passing Briley Parkway, I got a rush of an idea, a last-ditch, crazy notion to be sure, but in the heat of the moment it seemed to make about as much sense as anything else. I swung over to the right lane and jumped off on I-440, the perimeter highway that was a shortcut to Interstate 40, which runs west to Memphis. I checked the mirror to make sure the Hummer was still there. So be it. If they wanted a war, I'd take their asses to crazy Pat and let him show them what home-field advantage was all about.

Brundidge eased up into the seat again and almost lost it when he saw the direction we were heading.

"Where are we going? Are you nuts?"

"I'm taking these bastards to the only place I know where we'll have a fighting chance against them. Do you see Truck's gun back there anywhere?"

I made a quick swerve to the left lane to give him time to reach over the back seat. He came up with the bloody Glock and laid it in my lap.

"Jesus Christ, what a mess," he whispered. "I can't believe it."

I reached down and picked up the pistol, the grip slick with the blood of a man I'd come to appreciate and respect over the past few days. Placing the gun in the seat beside me, I wiped my bloody hand on my jeans, then spat into it and wiped it again.

The 440 connector dumped us into I-40 and we headed west for the Kingston Springs exit with the Hummer still behind us, but oddly maintaining the same distance. Maybe they were trying to see how far we'd get before we ran out of gas.

"Sonofabitch looks like a friggin' tank back there," said Brundidge, peering over the back seat at the Hummer.

And that's when it hit me: Tank...Tank... "Tank threw her away..." A second chill crawled up my spine.

"Brundidge, remember what the wino was saying about the tank? He saw the Hummer. He saw it. The poor guy just didn't know what it was. He thought it was a tank, don't you see?"

"Shepherd, at this point I'm up for believing anything, but get us somewhere that we can either make a run for it or fight those guys on even ground, I don't care which. Right now we're just ducks in a shooting gallery."

I took the Bellevue/Kingston Springs exit at a solid 75 mph and swung a hard right up Highway 70, heading for the old logging road that led to the big bluff and wondering what we'd do if we got to the top and there was no Pat to save us. It was Labor Day weekend and for all I knew he could've returned home to his wife and kids, his summer at Camp Harpeth just a warm, woodsy memory. If he was gone, then Brundidge and I were as good as dead.

"Shepherd, I hope to God you know what you're doing. If you ask me, you're heading right into the kind of territory those assholes would call home."

"Just hang on, Brundidge, and I'll be introducing you to one of the craziest dudes you'll ever meet. That is, if he's there."

"What do you mean, *if* he's there?"

"Just what I said- if he's there."

"And if he's not?"

"Then I guess you and I will just have to bend over and kiss our asses goodbye, because at that point we'll both be doing a swan dive into the Harpeth River from 200 feet."

"Shepherd," he groaned, like a man who had just heard his death sentence read aloud, "I can't swim."

"Not a problem, Brundidge. This time of the year the Harpeth is only about ten inches deep anyway."

Barreling down Highway 70, we flew through the sleepy little community of Pegram unnoticed and uninterrupted, as if speeding cars being chased by Hummers were just the natural order of the day around these parts. Off to my left, across the railroad tracks, was the town ballpark. It looked as though everyone in Pegram had turned out for some Labor Day barbeque and celebration, which explained the absence of other traffic. I had a quick notion of cutting across the railroad tracks to the park and trying to get lost in the crowd but dismissed it as a bad idea that might only serve to get some innocent citizens killed.

About a mile past the town, I spotted the logging road and made a hard left, burning up the dirt tracks, trying to straddle the worn ruts and not bottom out the big Ford. The thin, weedy path was dry and dusty but that made it easier to climb without four-wheel drive.

I wound out the car in low range and let the speed work in our favor to carry us up the steep switchbacks, praying to God we could make it, if not all the way to the top, then at least close enough to make a run for it. Brundidge sat in scared silence, resting the Uzi on the back of the seat and watching for the Hummer through the trailing cloud of red dust. I was trying to steer and honk the horn at the same time, hoping that if Pat were up there it might get his attention.

Somehow, through either sheer luck or blind faith, we made it to the top of the bluff and the edge of the deserted cornfield. I floored the gas and tore out across the rows of dead corn stalks and bought us about thirty more yards before the heavy car sank up to the frame in the soft earth.

"C'mon," I yelled to Brundidge, throwing open the door and taking off without even cutting the engine.

Stumbling through the field toward the woods with both of us calling out for Pat at the top of our lungs, we hit a thick patch of tall, brown corn stalks and stopped to catch our breath. In the momentary stillness I could hear the Hummer methodically making its way up the trail, getting nearer with every second.

"He's not here, is he?"

"I don't know," I panted, then took off again along the edge of the field that led to the bluff, Brundidge following blindly.

Once there I looked to the left, upstream, to where the cliffs began their ascent that led them to the majestic height we were standing on. If we ran in that direction, away from Pat's camp, we could follow the bluff down until it became just a riverbank. At that point we could cross the shallow river and maybe hide in the trees on the other side.

I was just about to go for it when the Hummer crested the trail in a cloud of dust, the front wheels rising off the ground as it bounced to the top of the plateau. Without speaking, we took off again, back in the direction of Pat's camp, me leading the way as we ran through the tall, decaying rows of corn, the dry stalks and paper-thin husks slicing at our arms and faces like razor blades.

I heard Brundidge stumble, then curse as he fell a few feet behind me, and for a split second I wanted to keep going without turning around. But I didn't, and instead ran back to help the kid to his feet. His face and arms were covered in fine strips of bright red blood.

"We can't stop...keep moving."

He merely nodded as we turned back down the rows toward the woods. But before we'd gone thirty feet, Pat stepped out into our path a few yards in front of us, both hands on his hips like Superman, and looking like an answered prayer.

"Pat...Thank God...You've got to...help us," I wheezed, out of breath. "There's some...people...following us...they've got guns...please..."

Pat smiled and raised both hands, palms out in a show of peace like some crazy, hip, gonzo Jesus who could probably talk the bad guys out of any ill intentions. Brundidge and I both fought for breath as we waited for the Avenging Angel to speak. But before he spoke, he unholstered his 9mm and pointed it at us.

"Put your hands behind your head and turn around. Lace your fingers."

Brundidge looked up at me and winced as I stood there bewildered. Pat took our guns, then herded us down the path in the direction we'd been heading, warning that he'd shoot both of us if either tried to run.

"What about those other guys?" Brundidge asked.

"Don't worry about them," Pat said. "They'll be along in a bit."

As we reached the end of the cornfield, we turned left into the small clearing that I almost didn't recognize from before. All the camouflaged nets had been raised, revealing more crude picnic tables and several large wooden crates. In the center of it all the big stone fireplace was already stacked with wood for the coming night's blaze.

Near the edge of the clearing stood a small flagpole, its blue-bordered red flag outstretched in the river breeze. It was identical to the one in the Buckhead compound, only this time I could read the letters TAA at the center emblazoned in white. Beneath it in a semi-circle sat a dozen or so men, all of whom had their attention focused on a tall man in camo fatigues who was standing in front of them engaged in a spirited lecture.

When Brundidge recognized Carter Robinson, you could almost hear his heart hit the pit of his stomach.

CHAPTER 23

Within minutes, Brundidge and I were both securely trussed and seated on a picnic table to the right of Carter Robinson, who'd begun using us as props for the dog-and-pony show he was putting on for the other men.

"Gentlemen, this is what happens when you take your eyes off your objective. It's what happens when you don't take your job or an adversary seriously," he warned, pointing at us with his cigar.

"Someone didn't follow procedure. They underestimated the need for security, which is in itself unforgivable because security is what we are all about. Now three men are dead and we're facing a world of trouble unless we take care of business right now."

"You're out of your mind, Robinson," I blurted, just seconds before Pat executed a spinning, Okinawan roundhouse kick to the side of my head, sending me flying off the table into the dirt.

"Perfect example right there," Robinson observed. "We tend to give a worthy opponent plenty of respect, and yet we'll turn right around and take a fool lightly. And that's a fatal mistake, Gentlemen, because, as we've all learned, the only thing a fool needs to bring you down is a little bit of blind luck."

I wanted to argue the 'luck' issue with him but at that moment I was content to have just one side of my head throbbing.

"You men are professionals," he continued. "You were chosen for this unit because of your courage, your experience, and your unbridled discipline. As a result, you are now members of the finest, and I might add, the highest paid security force on the planet.

"When you signed on with The Alliance you signed on for the duration. Every one of you stands to retire a rich man one day, but until that day comes you must understand that one simple little mistake, a single breach of security, can have catastrophic effects. With that in mind, mistakes *cannot and will not* be tolerated."

I heard a noise from the woods off to my left and turned to see three men approaching, two of whom I assumed to be from the Hummer, and a third, on crutches, vaguely familiar. As they got nearer, I recognized the guard I'd shot and dumped down the loading ramp.

"Come in and take a seat," ordered Robinson.

The two HumVee dudes found a spot down front and the

wounded guard started to follow, until Pat put his hand on the man's shoulder.

"Gentlemen, this is Purvis," Robinson said, as Pat began leading the crippled man to the front of the clearing.

"As far as I'm concerned, Purvis had the most important job in the whole compound: Purvis guarded the front gate. Purvis was our first line of defense and Purvis let his attention falter just long enough for these clowns to come into our house, shit on everything, and leave three men dead in their wake."

Purvis seemed suddenly aware of his situation. His eyes went wide and his crutches began to wobble nervously.

Robinson wiped at his forehead with a red bandana, then lowered his voice and shook his head solemnly.

"Gentlemen, I wish I could give everyone a second chance, but circumstances will not allow it. From here on out the stakes are just too high." He nodded at Pat, who unholstered his 9mm in a single motion.

"Wait," I screamed, suddenly aware of what was about to happen. "He never told me anything. There's no reason to-"

But Purvis took it a lot better than I did. He never said a word, simply closed his eyes as Pat brought the barrel of the gun up to his temple and pulled the trigger, the other side of his head exploding in a crimson spray. He fell limp to the ground with one of the crutches still under his arm.

Pat walked over to a locker and pulled something out, then tossed it to one of the HumVee guys.

"Bag him and drag him," he said.

In less than a minute Purvis was wrapped in a body bag and being transported back through the woods by the two men in the direction from which they'd arrived.

I looked over at the gathering of disciples. Two rows of blank faces. I couldn't tell if they were in shock or if watching a man die was just business-as-usual.

"This country is under siege," Robinson went on. "And the American people are in danger of losing a way of life they'll never see again. We have enemies, Gentlemen, both beyond and within our borders, and the average American is totally unaware, so preoccupied with trying to make a living they can't see the enemy encroaching, invading, better still *infesting* our neighborhoods and our culture in a way that threatens to destroy everything our ancestors fought and died for."

He struck at the air with his fist and was answered by a wave of nodding heads and muttering.

"Take a ride down any busy street in any town in America and you'll see what I'm talking about. Whole neighborhoods have been taken over, property values driven down, I'm telling you, America looks like a third world country these days.

"But it's much, much more than that," he went on. "Now they've begun to take over our economy: gas stations, motels, fast food, housing- 85% of this nation's service industry is foreign-owned. And yet people just turn their heads and pretend not to notice, or worse— not to think about it, never realizing that one day there will be no more jobs to be had and the American Dream will be nothing more than a vague memory of times gone by.

"Gentlemen, the American people deserve to once again have the same great country they had for the first two-hundred years-"

A chorus of cheers and applause interrupted him.

"Well, by God, we're gonna give it back to them. And we're

gonna start by taking the Statue of Liberty and turning that bitch around and pointing her inward!"

Another round of Hoo-ahs rang out.

I watched as Robinson continued working the small gathering, pushing their emotional buttons and reveling in the expected response.

"For the past two decades we've opened the gates and given a free pass to every illiterate, felonious, disease-infested indigent who wants in, with the only requirement being that they have enough energy to climb onto a boat or crawl under a fence. The Mid-East, Africa, South America- they ship us the sediment of their society and we fall all over ourselves putting out a Welcome mat.

"We let 'em in, give 'em aid, educate their kids and give 'em free healthcare. Then we pay for their extended families to come over and join them. Then we give 'em loans so they can go into business and get an even bigger swig off America's tit."

He leaned over and spit into the fire amidst an eruption of yells and raised fists.

"Gentlemen, it's no secret the middle-class American is fast becoming a minority. But I'm afraid it's much, much worse than that. Indeed, the middle-class American is on his way to becoming an endangered species," he went on, tilting his head to receive the resounding bank of applause.

"But trust me, gentlemen, the worst is yet to come. At this very moment we are being invaded from the south in numbers that are nothing less than staggering. Illegals are pouring across the border by the hundreds every day and they are doing it in broad daylight. And if you think the federal government is going to do anything about it you are dead wrong. As we near the end of this century, I shudder to think what our beloved country is going to look like in fifteen or twenty years. I'm telling you, it breaks my Goddamn heart.

"T-A-A," he choked, wiping at his eyes and turning to salute the red flag at the edge of the clearing.

"T-A-A," they echoed.

"T-Double-A," he said louder. "Turn America Around!"

"Amen," someone yelled from the pack.

"You give us the word, by God, and we'll take it to the streets!" another voice called out.

"Give the order, General," came a shout.

Robinson had begun pacing back and forth frenetically, tossing in quotes from Thoreau, Thomas Payne, the Bible, underscoring the fine points of his sermon with a wave of his lit cigar. It was hardline oratory blessed by God, and I wouldn't have been surprised if he'd begun chant preaching.

"I know we've got a lot of work to do. And I know we're just getting started. But we are going to do what Washington refuses to do. We've got a long way to go, but trust me, Gentlemen, we will get there. The groundwork is in place and our numbers are growing every day."

And then, once he had them filled with the spirit, he began talking softly to bring them back down, almost like an alter call.

"Right now the only thing we can do is be patient. We are building our war chest, and we must continue to do our jobs while the plan is being put into place, knowing that one wrong move, one slip, could be fatal for all. Patience, Gentlemen. Diligence, and Trust."

With that, Robinson raised his hand in salute as they all stood and snapped to attention, saluting him in irregular motion.

"Now turn-to for some R&R," he barked, as the men fell out of formation and the hum of conversation and laughter began to fill the woods.

Robinson motioned to Pat, who drew a K-Bar knife from a hip scabbard, then walked over and cut the thick plastic bands that held our feet.

"Secure these prisoners away from the immediate area," he ordered, as Pat herded us toward a hickory tree at the rear of the clearing.

We stood with our backs to the tree while Pat circled us several times with a heavy gauge link chain that cut into our chests and made breathing almost impossible. When he finished, he secured the chain with a padlock and walked back to the group who were now passing around bottles of whiskey. With the tree between us, Brundidge and I viewed the goings-on from our respective sides.

"Just like I always wanted to die," he coughed, "At the hands of a bunch of whiskey-filled, racist peckerwoods, out in the middle of nowhere."

"Don't fight the chain," I gasped, struggling for air. "When one of us moves, the other can't breathe. Stand still and try to be calm. They can only kill us once, Alvin, and I'll be damned if I'm giving these bastards the satisfaction of seeing us beg for our lives."

"I can't believe he just shot that guy in front of everybody," he whispered.

"Hell, I'm still trying to figure out what this is all about," I said. "I'm as clueless now as I was when we left Atlanta."

Night had begun to fall as the men built a roaring fire that lit up the small clearing and the edge of the woods. Their mood seemed joyous, as if the Purvis incident had never occurred.

The whiskey-tinged laughter carried through the trees and on down the cliffs to the bed of the slow rolling river.

"I had a feeling this was some kind of militia bullshit," Brundidge said. "What I don't understand is why Robinson would get involved in something like that. It just doesn't make sense. He's got too much to lose."

After the fire had burned down to a bed of hot coals, a big grill was thrown across the top of the stone fireplace and a designated cook began unloading steaks from a large plastic cooler. The whole scene seemed eerie, and if not for the rack of automatic weapons stacked off to the side, take away the camo fatigues and these guys could just as easily have been the local Rotary club getting together for camping and a cookout.

As the cool night air became thick with the hickory smell of burning meat, Robinson, cigar in mouth and a bottle of Cutty Sark in hand, made his way over to our tree, but not before stopping at the edge of the clearing and pissing into the dense, black woods. When he finished, he walked over and stood a couple of feet in front of me.

"I just want you to know, Son, there's nothing personal in any of this. You were just the sacrificial goat that got out of the pen and wound up tearing up the barnyard."

"You killed Cassidy, didn't you, Robinson?"

The question hung in the air between us.

"Well...yes and no," he finally admitted. "The fact of the matter is something had to be done about her." He looked up at the stars as if he half-expected God to nod in agreement.

"I still don't understand what all this means," I said, gesturing toward the troops gathered around the fire.

He cocked his head and eyed me quizzically.

"No, Shepherd, I don't suppose you would understand. Or even if you *could*, for that matter."

"Try me."

He smiled and took a long pull on the Cutty Sark, then blew a cloud of smoke at me with the assurance of a man who'd finally come to terms with his own destiny.

"It's about power, Son. Plain and simple. But more power than most folks ever imagine."

"You're telling me this is your idea of the road to the White House? Is that what you're saying?

Robinson looked at me as if I'd been speaking Swahili.

"Who the hell wants to be President?" he laughed. "Hell, I've already *got* more power than the President." He said it as if everyone knew that but me.

"So what's all this bullshit in the papers every day?"

"Just that," he chortled. "Bullshit. I mean, why would I want to be President when I can get things done the President can't even dream of doing. Oh sure, I can get a bill pushed through, or a law passed. But then I can get a law passed in fucking China if I need to. Or Russia. Half the countries in the Mid-East. I've got heads of state, Chancellors, Dictators, Shahs- Hell, I've even got Kings in my pocket, and they're all there when I need 'em."

He saw the blank look on my face and shook his head.

"You still don't get it do you, Shepherd?"

"I guess not."

"It's *Pussy*, Son," he grinned. "It's about the one thing power is most vulnerable to, the thing that power attracts. Hell, it's what power is *for*."

"Come again?" I said, dumbfounded at the least, and wondering if maybe I'd misheard him.

He laughed and took a step closer.

"Listen, I spent twenty-five years in the Army, ten of 'em in Washington, and if I learned anything in all that time, it's that Cooter truly does rule the world. All the guns, bombs, artillery- they're nothing compared to the power of one tiny little jelly roll. You hook a guy up with the right action- you're holding his marker for life. That's *Power*."

My jaw hung open in disbelief. Surely he was just drunk and shooting off his mouth.

"Let me tell you a story," he said. "Back in the Nam, I had this VC general we'd captured in the highlands and, after several rounds of rather serious interrogation involving some minor electrical appliances, he decided to tell us damn near anything we wanted to know and a few things we didn't give a rat's rectum about. Anyway, as we're driving his rice-fartin' ass back to the rear for incarceration, we stopped the Jeep to take a leak beside this huge rice paddy. I'd barely zipped up when he turns and speaks to me in English."

"Do you know the difference between your philosophy and ours?" he asks me.

"No," I says, "Why don't you tell me."

"The difference between us," he says, "is that you would want to own the rice field; we would rather own the *man* who owns the rice field."

"Well, boy, let me tell you- That made more sense to me than damn near anything I'd ever heard. Who'd ever think you'd get a life lesson from a gook?"

"You mean Ho Chi Minh is responsible for all this?"

Robinson coughed at that, almost choking on his scotch.

"You can joke if you want to, Son," he boasted. "But I've got the Chocha, and the juice that goes with it- I can get a Sultan laid by a movie star. I've got beauty queens standing in line to knock boots with world rulers. I've got playmates and celebrities who'll party hard with a sheik or senator, just as long as the money is right. And believe me, the money is *Right*."

I nodded over at the troops chowing down around the campfire. "So how does all this fit in with that philosophy? And what about that flag-waving, reactionary speech you just gave, what was that all about?"

"Aw Hell, just something for the benefit of the boys," he shrugged. "I pay 'em well, but true loyalty only comes when people feel they're working for a just and righteous cause, preferably one that will benefit the greater good. Tell you what though- fifteen or twenty years from now that 'Turn America Around' slogan might make a good platform. You never know."

"So there really is no 'movement'?"

"Just the movement of a lot of cash," he grinned. "And most of it is moving in my direction."

"You're absolutely crazy," I laughed. "And the sad part is, you make it sound so...so simple."

"Hell, Boy, it is simple. Let me try to explain. Ever wonder what happens to all the beauty queens and runners up from two or three years back? I'll tell you what happens to 'em. They either get married, or they try to be an actress or model or singer for about fifteen minutes, and when that bottoms out, they're faced with the dim prospect of going back to whatever podunk place they came from and marrying the local car dealer or chiropractor.

"Now, most of 'em don't like that idea a whole lot. At that point, it ain't too hard to get 'em to drop panty for some foreign dignitary, especially when they come away with fifty large for their efforts. You'd be surprised at the number of guys who'll pay a couple hundred grand to do the horizontal mambo with Miss Universe."

"Nobody pays that kind of money for sex," I argued.

"Oh, really? Well, I've got about fifteen offshore bank accounts that beg to differ."

A tidal wave of disappointment washed over me. I slumped against the chain and heard Brundidge gasp for breath on the other side.

"Robinson, do you mean to tell me I've been chained to a tree all this time, thinking I was going to be offed by some revolutionary madman, only to find out I'm dying at the hands of a sleazy, white-trash pimp?"

Flicking the ashes from his cigar, he cleared his throat and spat into the woods.

"Everybody sells out sooner or later, Shepherd. You just have to pick your shot. But as far as being dead goes, I wouldn't worry about that too much. I've seen a lot more of it than you, and there ain't nothing noble about it."

The light from the fire danced off his white porcelain caps up into his eyes, and for a moment it seemed as if I was face to face with the devil himself. And yet for some strange reason, I wasn't afraid. Hell, I'd gotten down in the dirt and wrestled with the devil a time or two before. I wanted answers.

"So you had Cassidy killed, is that right?"

He stood still and quiet for a minute, as if measuring his words.

"I'll tell you this much, Son. I didn't want to. Truly I didn't. But she left me no choice. I had a plan...a program... and I was going to make her a big star in it. The idea was... there'd be a small contingent of about ten to twenty girls, mostly unknowns, but all beautiful, and all of them from different countries: Miss Spain, Miss Denmark, Miss China- you get the idea. Your girl was going to be Miss America. Hell, I baited her for weeks, telling her how I could help her become Miss America. She was like a kid at Christmas, and I thought she'd be thrilled.

"But when I finally laid it all out, she went ballistic. Just totally fucking nuts- threatened to blow the whistle on the whole thing. I tried every way in the world to reason with her but No-Way-José "

He took another long pull on the scotch, then wiped his mouth with the sleeve of his shirt.

"Even if I could understand that, Robinson, what I can't figure out is, with all the money you're talking about, why get into porn on the Internet? That doesn't make sense to me. Seems rather small-time for a man of your vision."

The condescension went right over his head.

"There was never any website," he admitted. "I sent one of our guys up to talk your girl into taking some pictures, thinking I might be able to use 'em as leverage when the time came to bring her into the program. A lot of girls do the first trick for shits and giggles, as well as the money. But you need leverage to keep 'em in the stable for any length of time."

"You mean leverage, as in blackmail?" I corrected.

He shot back a thin smile.

"Let's just say we deal with some very rich and powerful people, and they all trust me with their anonymity. That kind of power demands discretion, and leverage just helps keep the lips sealed. I can't afford for some bimbo to get all jacked up and start talking to the media. Besides, as you just witnessed a little earlier, I'm a stickler for security."

Suddenly, my memory flashed on the news bulletin I'd read about the missing Hollywood actress. I shook it off and kept at him.

"But you couldn't blackmail Cassidy because she'd worn the wig and couldn't be recognized, right?"

"That's part of it."

"And because she had so little to lose."

"Bingo. And that was a serious error on my part. I underestimated her. I mean, Hell, she'd lickety-split on the Internet for *One* grand, but she wouldn't lick a senator for *Fifty*. I tell you, Boy, strippers have a warped sense of values, that's for damn sure."

What a bastard, I thought. Only a politician could admit murder and prostitution and then talk about values in the same breath.

"So when you couldn't turn her out, you had her killed."

"Like I said, Shepherd, I didn't want to, but Christ, what else could I do? I tried paying her off, even sent the bitch a hundred grand and she responds by trying to ruin me- Hell, I wanted to kill her myself at that point, but thankfully, Pat talked me into using my head. And then I remembered your little scene that night in the club and it all seemed to just fall into place."

My brain was spinning, and even though I'd never been much at math, I suddenly realized there was eighty-thousand dollars floating around somewhere unaccounted for. The question was, what had Cassidy done with it?

"It's a damn shame, is what it is," he went on. "You could've done five or six years and been out, gotten on with your life.

But Hell no, you gotta play John Wayne and cause a bunch of other people to get killed too. Stupid sonofabitch- running off to Atlanta- Hell, I was all for killing you the first time you ran off down there. I wish now I had."

Robinson couldn't have hit me any harder if he'd used a Louisville Slugger.

"How'd you know about that?" I demanded, although I already knew the answer. I felt the blood draining from my head, my heart, my gut, on down to my feet where it all settled and turned solid.

I realized in that moment that Cassidy had never seen the money nor written the note Charlotte had handed me that morning in the diner. Carter Robinson was smarter than even he knew. With those few words he'd stripped away any will to live I might have clung to.

"Charlotte." I finally managed to say the name.

"What about her?" he challenged.

"Charlotte," I said again.

"Charlotte is very special to me. We go back a long time, ever since she was a coed in college. She was a big fan of my books. Katherine had been sick for a while before we met, and Charlotte was a lot of comfort to me for a few years."

I remembered the story Charlotte had told me at lunch.

"And I know all about the bullshit that's been going on between you and her," he went on. "But Charlotte isn't going anywhere. She's in way too deep to get out now. Besides, she could never give up the money, she likes it too much. Not to mention the fact that Charlotte likes power too, plus- she's got her own pussy- Hah!" He slapped his leg and cackled at his joke.

"You sonofabitch... you mean you've even got Charlotte turning tricks?"

Robinson's expression became incredulous.

"Don't kid yourself, Romeo," he laughed. "Charlotte only gives it up when there's something to be gained by it, for an edge. You'd be better off looking for true love with a pawnbroker than with that gal."

He laughed again, then cleared his throat and spit toward the fire.

"Charlotte helped me put the whole scheme together in the first place. I tell you, the girl does have a head for business. And somebody has to be the go-between, Hell, I certainly can't do it.

"That whole Miss America thing was pretty much her idea. It seemed like such a big deal to her, like it was tailor-made for her sister. Unfortunately, it backfired."

My tongue felt thick as a wave of nausea began rising in my throat. I wasn't sure I wanted to hear the answer to my next question, but I knew I had to ask it anyway.

"Are you saying Charlotte was involved in Cassidy's murder?"

He worked his mouth as if he were chewing the words, then paused a moment before speaking carefully.

"Not directly. But the girl was Charlotte's responsibility, so I'm sure she knew in the back of her mind that it was inevitable. She tried to intervene but by then it was out of her hands. I guess you could say Charlotte got caught in her *own web*," he roared, "Damn, I'm hot tonight, ain't I, Sport?"

"What a sick fuck," I heard Brundidge say behind me.

"And the compound in Atlanta?" I inquired, although I was only half-interested anymore.

Robinson composed himself with a sip of Cutty.

"It ain't nothing but the biggest, most expensive, lavish hi-tech whorehouse in the world, that's all," he chuckled.

"Of course, we've got a couple of fronts downstairs. Got a dummy investment group, and we've got a legitimate PR firm that handles some of the better-known girls. Keeps their name out there and makes them a lot more marketable to the clients, which of course translates into more money. Most of these guys like chicks that have some kind of title or fame attached to them."

"Now I remember," said Brundidge from behind me. "That girl in the hall- I've seen her on television."

"Could be," said Robinson.

"So, whose phone number was Cassidy calling?" I asked.

"Why, Charlotte's of course. It was her office, til she got pissed off and moved out."

"I thought she was teaching," I argued.

"Oh, she was," Robinson winked. "But two classes a week ain't a helluva workload."

I figured the longer I kept him talking, the longer Brundidge and I had to live.

"Why Atlanta?" I continued.

The look on his face suggested he knew what I was up to, but he went on anyway.

"Logistics, mostly. It's close, convenient, big city, bigger airport. And we needed someplace secure to handle the limo traffic. You put an armed guard in front of a building in Nashville, people start asking questions. But there's so much international shit in Atlanta that nobody notices something like that. Plus, all these transactions are cash, so we need some damn good security around there. Hell, I'll bet there's three or four million in cash going in and out of there every week."

"Not to mention that Aleta has a club there, right?"

The tip of his cigar burned bright red as he puffed at it absently before waving off the accusation.

"Aleta is family," he said. "And the caliber of girl needed in this kind of operation ain't likely to be found in a strip joint. Your gal was one-in-a-million. There was just something special about her, you know?"

Like I hadn't heard that before.

"Alita's clubs are handy for washing money, and she owes me a couple of favors."

"You mean for killing her husband?"

Robinson coughed hard, then spit at the ground but hit the toe of his boot. He ground at it with his other foot, realized how foolish he looked, and then glared at me.

"We're done here, Hoss," he growled. "I try to give you a little closure and you want to turn it into a gab fest. Maybe you haven't noticed but I'm the one with the cigar here and you're the one tied to the tree."

"You know, Robinson," I said, "the really sad part of all this is that you probably *could* have been president if you'd really wanted to. You could've helped write history."

He nodded, then turned his gaze to the dark woods.

"Trust me, boy, we got problems coming over the next few years gonna take decades to straighten out. And I don't fuckin' envy the ones who attempt to do it.

"Being president is highly overrated. And I don't give a black cat's ass about history. I've served this country since I was twenty years old- that's history enough for me. Now it's *my* turn. I'm gonna take my money and get the hell out before the whole country turns into a diseased slum."

The rage that had been smoldering inside me suddenly burst like napalm.

"You're a bastard for killing Cassidy, Robinson. And you're a bastard for hiding behind your sick wife so you could play pimp."

I'd barely gotten those last words out when he stepped in and shoved his palm up under my chin, pushing my head up and into the bark of the tree.

"Listen to me, you jive-ass-jiffy-pop-mother-fucker," he hissed. "Katherine was the love of my life. We had everything, and I worshipped the very ground she walked on. But when she got sick and started dying, everything I ever hoped to be just died right along with her. You think it's easy to watch the woman you love waste away, day by day, for years?"

His breath was hot, stinking of whiskey and smoke. I tried to turn my face and in a moment he eased his grip and stepped back.

"I did everything I could for her but nothing helped. Pretty soon none of it mattered anymore, at least until Charlotte came along. And you have no idea how much it cost to keep running Katherine in and out of hospitals- Nurses round the clock- I'd spent my whole life in service to my country and had zip to show for it."

"Her family had money," I countered.

"Are you kidding? Aleta and I have been floating that family for years. Her doctor daddy and both her brothers are plungers- all of 'em owe money to every bookie and casino this side of the Rockies. If it hadn't been for Aleta and me, they'd all be in double-wides today. Either that or hobbling around on busted knee-caps. Nothing but a bunch of spoiled, inept trash.

307

And poor Katherine never even had a clue, not ever, God rest her soul."

A tired sadness began to fill his eyes, a weariness that seemed to dull the whiskey glow illuminating his face.

"I don't expect you to understand," he said. "But without Katherine, the rest of it meant nothing. Sure, I could've made a run for the White House, let the media destroy Katherine's family and good name, then get beat and come home broke. Charlotte just showed me a way out, that's all. And in the process, I was able to take care of my darling baby girl. I saw daylight and I ran for it."

When he leaned in closer, I could see the thin trickle of a tear sliding down his cheek.

"I'll tell you one thing, Son," he half-smiled, "Katherine would've made one beautiful First Lady."

Loaded on the scotch, he turned to survey his troops but had to blink his eyes several times to focus. The men were quieter now, busy gnawing on bloody steaks and corn-on- the-cob, washing it all down with intermittent gulps of whiskey and beer. I watched his face as he eyeballed them, saw his expression turn from drunken pride to curious, then to anger before he unholstered his sidearm and fired a shot into the air, killing the picnic atmosphere quicker than a swarm of yellow jackets.

"Fuckin' Mess Hall's closed," he yelled. "We got business to tend to."

A rumble of small grumbling could be heard as the troops abandoned their meal, some quickly, others not so quickly, some tearing off a piece of steak to take with them. Pat came over and, without speaking, unlocked the padlock that held the chain taut around us. Circling the tree, he unwrapped the steel links that had worked their way into our skin, both Brundidge and myself writhing in pain but taking deep breaths as the chain fell away.

"So much for Tet and Khe Sanh, huh?" I chided.

"War's over, Jarhead. Welcome to the World."

"Who killed Cassidy?" I asked again, as Pat went on with his task.

Robinson shook his head in exasperation. "Jesus H. Christ, Son, it don't matter who killed her. A soldier killed her, that's who."

Pat was still walking in circles around the tree, coiling the heavy chain in his arms. When he came around again, he spoke.

"You mean the stripper? That was my work."

It was the matter-of-fact way he said it, flatly, with no emotion, that left no doubt in my mind it was true.

He was passing to my left, heading around the tree toward Brundidge, the link of chain dragging across his shoulder. Suddenly, a fiery rage came over me and I knew I had nothing to lose. With my cuffed hands I managed to grab the chain and pull Pat into me before he knew what happened. Pinned against me, he couldn't move his arms so I quickly set about using the only weapon I had available: my teeth.

I bit down hard on his nose, feeling his dirty flesh soften and then go damp as I came away with a good half-inch plug, and when he stepped back to swing at me, I spit it in his face, grinning as a deep red trickle dripped onto his chin from the ragged wound above his mouth.

"Aaarrghh," he screeched.

But before he could follow through with some exotic Asian death blow, Robinson stepped in and laid his pistol upside my head so hard I almost lost consciousness.

"Take 'em to the killing floor," he bellowed, and in my addled state I half-wondered if he was a big Howlin' Wolf fan, but then someone shoved us across the clearing to a larger, more ominous tree with a huge, low-hanging limb overlooking the river below.

The rest of the men gathered in a sloppy semi-circle, drinks in hand, as though they were about to watch a sporting event. Brundidge and I stood defeated with our backs to the bluff, facing our drunken executioners.

I first thought they were just going to shoot us and let us fall backwards over the cliff, and for a split-second I wondered if I'd feel anything as I bounced down the rocks and into the shallow water. But when Pat came through the circle carrying a long coil of nylon rope with a noose at one end, I knew the trip down the rocky bluff would be nothing more than an afterthought.

"Whatta-ya-say we let his little buddy do the honors," Pat said, his nose still a bleeding bubble and the chest of his shirt a spreading, crimson stain. He took a step toward Brundidge and cut the ties that bound his wrists with the K-Bar.

"Why didn't you kill me the first time I was here?" I asked, at the same time wondering what kind of perverse Providence had led me there in the first place, much less twice.

"Two reasons," snapped Pat. "One, nobody gave the order. And two, I couldn't figure out what the hell you were doing here. I wasn't sure if you were on to us or if you'd just stumbled in like the supreme dumbass you turned out to be. Plus, we still needed you to take the rap for the girl."

Robinson was doing his best to stand up straight. Pistol in one hand, whiskey bottle in the other, the ever-present cigar clenched firmly in his teeth, he staggered over to stand beside Pat, who had placed the noose in Brundidge's hands.

Pat threw the end of the rope over the thick tree limb above my head, as one of the men picked up the slack and pulled until Brundidge felt the rope tug in his hands. He looked up at me with tears in his eyes, his mouth trembling.

Up until that moment I'd never put much stock in the notion that our lives flash before us in the last few microseconds before death. I'd spent the greater part of my life trying to make things rhyme, if for no other reason than it was always easier to make it rhyme than to try and make it make sense. I'd been driving on an expired poetic license, living a life of platitudes, metaphors, and sad irony, chasing the bitch-goddess of art at a dead run, with my emotional baggage tied to the back bumper like tin cans at a wedding.

And all that time I'd fooled myself into thinking I'd been running toward something when all along, my heart and my soul both knew I'd really just been running away from the lie that had been my life for longer than I could remember.

As Brundidge held the circle of nylon rope in front of my face, I looked into it, through it, as though looking into another dimension, another world, a shadowy place in the past where I had once lived and where, by all rights, I should have died. In the scant seconds it took him to reach up and hold the noose over my head, I left those woods and went way back, to another wooded night and a rain-soaked jungle that stunk with the sulphur smell of death and rot. But there was another foul stink in the air that night- a black, bloody, pungent odor that only I could smell. It was the stink of my own shame...

"Bring the nigger over here," Summers barked, as Dago yanked Benny Watts to his feet and shoved him under the rope.

"Time you made your bones, Hero," said Martin, as he buried the warm barrel of the M-60 in my back, nudging me forward until Summers handed me the noose.

"No..no way," I stammered, "I'm not doing it." I tossed the rope back at Summers.

"Fine," said Dago, "We'll hang you first and then him. Float your dead asses down the river and everybody'll think Charles did it. No sweat off my ass."

I tried to call out to Benny but his name caught in my throat.

And that's when Benny Watts spoke the words I would carry with me for the rest of my life. I remember the white brilliance of his teeth and eyes, white as the full Asian moon that hung almost hidden overhead, watching it all with total indifference.

"It's all right, Brother," Benny said slowly,"...It's all right...it all comes back around."

My hands were shaking so badly that Summers had to keep putting the rope back in them. At some point Dago stepped in and jammed my gut with the butt of his rifle, dropping me to my knees where I immediately started puking, either from pain or self-disgust or both. They pulled me back up and this time I managed to drop the loop over Benny's head where it barely hit his shoulders before Summers yanked it tight around his neck and under his dark chin.

I fell back as Dago and Summers began to pull, feeling every bit the craven coward I knew myself to be. Benny Watts began to rise from the riverbed, feet kicking spasmodically, hands digging at his neck for a moment before turning loose and jerking up and down at his sides like some strange, black angel trying

312

to take wing, to lift off from the floor of the jungle and soar up, up and away.

When it was over, and he was still, Dago and Summers let go the rope and Benny fell lifeless to the ground. A hollow quiet hung in the dank, merciless air as I felt Martin's machine gun ease out of my back. Slowly, I reached down and picked up my M-16 and, without saying anything, fired three quick rounds into Benny Watts' unbreathing chest.

"There you go," said Dago. "Now he'll go home to a hero's burial."

But Benny hadn't left us, at least not entirely. Just like he'd promised so many times, he was still watching my back. A couple of klicks down the trail we were ambushed, for real this time, the four of us in slow-moving single file. Summers, on point, tripped a wire and instantly became separated from both legs. A spray of machine gun fire lethalized Martin and Dago, then blasted my rifle from my hands as I rolled off the trail and into the bush.

I lay face down, playing dead, trying not to breathe and listening to the smoky silence surrounding me. Nothing. Once again Charlie had hit and run without bothering to check for damages. I lay in the muddy weeds until dark, afraid to open my eyes, and when I finally did, I was looking into the face of Benny Watts, with his neck tilted at an odd angle and his bulging ping-pong ball eyes almost popping out as the hanging played over and over in my mind.

I watched as Benny struggled to fly, and then I *became* him as he looked up at me, at my face, until that too, began to change, and I realized the face I was looking into was Brundidge's. As he let the rope fall loosely around my neck, I heard the laughter and taunts of Dago and Summers, only now their faces had been replaced by those of Carter Robinson and Pat. I saw the helpless look in Brundidge's eyes and I wanted so badly to say the brave words Benny Watts had spoken to me that fateful night. But once again the fear in my heart held me silent.

Robinson staggered in front of me and cinched the rope tight around my neck, cutting off my air and yanking me completely into the present.

"Let's get on with it," he grunted, his eyes glistening behind the cigar.

But then something strange happened. Robinson took a sudden half-step back and his cigar exploded in a burst of sparks like something from an old Marx Brothers movie. Except his head exploded along with it.

He fell straight back like a big oak timber just as the lone rifle shot sounded in the distance. Everything froze for a split second before Pat dove to the ground, his bush hat flying from his head as if pulled by a string, the second shot ringing from across the river and into the woods around us. I felt the rope go slack and I reached up and yanked it from around my neck, then fell to the ground looking for cover.

Brundidge disappeared over the side of the bluff, as Pat and the others began scurrying toward the stack of rifles at the edge of the clearing. The first man there grabbed a weapon just as the back of his shirt blew open and he dropped face first into the dirt. The others began firing into the woods in a panic, but actually doing a lot more running than shooting, running away from the camp and the bluff in the direction of the cornfield.

"Get back here, you bunch of chickenshits," Pat called after them. He yelled again but when no one turned around he shot

314

the last two in the back. So much for courage and unbridled discipline.

He turned and began firing across the river into the woods that lined the other side. I thought he'd forgotten about me, so I bellied toward Robinson's body and the .45 holstered on his hip. When I was about three feet away Pat spotted me. He whipped the rifle around, aimed quickly and pulled the trigger twice. Click- Click....

"*BANG*!" he yelled, and I froze momentarily, giving him a split-second advantage as he threw the empty gun down and we both lunged at once for Robinson's pistol.

Hand-to-hand combat with someone like Pat is unthinkable, even under the best conditions. But with both my hands tied it was simply futile. I reached the gun first, but he was on me before I could lock and load, the two of us rolling around on the ground like school kids with the .45 caught between us.

It wasn't much of a fight.

Before I knew it, he had me flat on my back with his knees in my stomach and my head and shoulders hanging over the edge of the cliff. He tore the pistol from my hands, but it slipped out of his grasp and fell clacking down the rocks. We went on wrestling at the edge of the cliff, with me doing little more than flailing my tied arms at him to keep him from choking me. I jerked to my side to try to throw him off and still he hung on, but as he pulled me back over I spotted the K-Bar sheathed in the scabbard at his side. His hands tightened around my throat and I felt my windpipe starting to give, the air forced out of my mouth.

"So..long..jar..head," he grunted.

In a desperate, last-ditch effort, I shoved both fists up and into the bleeding stub of Pat's nose. He screamed, grabbing at the wound, and sat up straight. Just long enough for me to grab the K-Bar.

When he came back down I was waiting for him, catching him under the chin with the point and holding steady, letting his angry weight do the work as he came down hard, the blade already through his tongue and deep into the roof of his mouth before he realized what had happened.

He sat back, still in shock, staring out across the chasm at the riverbank in the distance, his mouth held open by the knife. He jerked slightly, and for a moment I thought he had winked at me, but it was just his left eye disappearing, shot through and out the back of his head, the trickle of warm blood washing my neck as he fell over me, the distant crack of a rifle ringing down the canyon a half-second later.

I lay breathless in total silence, the top half of my body hanging over the rocky cliff, the rest of me pinned by Pat's dead weight. Looking up at the stars it seemed I'd never seen them shine so brilliantly. I tried to pull myself up but all I succeeded in doing was inching myself closer to the edge of the cliff. I thought about trying to roll Pat off me, but his body was the only thing keeping me from going over onto the rocks below. Then I felt myself gently sliding, inch by inch, the heels of my boots digging but unable to hold me down.

I remember looking up at the stars and wondering where the shots had come from. Some farmer maybe, who'd been watching the whole thing from across the river? The cops? The FBI?

Just as my thighs began slipping over the edge, I dug my heels in one last time, hanging head down for a long moment before the deep drop to the craggy rocks and the shallow water.

I hung there upside down, breathing in the damp night air, listening to the stunned silence of the woods around me. I hung there and smelled the river and the late summer pastures on the other side, rich with the promise of fat cattle and slick horses.

And then, just as I was going over, I smelled something else, something unmistakable: the warm, harsh, familiar aroma of Prince Albert...

CHAPTER 24

The nurses tell me I was semi-comatose for several days, though I think they may be given to exaggeration. I do know that I came and went, drifting in and out of consciousness long enough to either recognize or imagine a familiar face: Brundidge, Walter Eskew, maybe Lyle once, Angie for sure. Then I'd fall away back down the long dark tunnel where there were more faces: Cassidy, Truck Bennett, Carter Robinson. Ironically, Benny Watts never showed.

When I went over the cliff I took everything with me, and any events that happened afterwards had to be filled in by Brundidge, who'd somehow managed to slip down the bluff that night without breaking his neck.

Walter Eskew had followed us at the urging of his wife, who claimed to have been warned in a dream the night before. Once again Esther Eskew had amazed me with her talents, and my initial skepticism was now replaced by the conviction of the true believer.

Walter was behind us when the business with the Hummer started, saw it all, and simply kept his distance until it all unraveled at the bluff. Together, he and Brundidge pulled my broken body from the rocks and carried me up the river beyond the cliffs and back down the road to Walter's car. They dumped me in front of an emergency room, then Brundidge hid out in Truck's old office while Walter Eskew beat a path back to the Georgia pines.

Instead of calling Lyle and the rest of Nashville's Finest, Brundidge made a call to Washington that night, to an old fraternity brother at the FBI who flew down with a mop-and-clean-up team the next day. As it turned out, Robinson and his operation were in the initial stages of an investigation, thanks to an anonymous phone tip by someone offering an international laundry list of prominent participants. It was all buried in the interest of national security, and a few days later the *Tennessean* ran a front-page story on the apparent suicide of Carter Robinson, a beloved statesman obviously overwhelmed by the passing of his wife and the pressures of the political arena.

Truck Bennett had no family and few friends, and it would be a long time before anyone noticed he was missing, though Brundidge had taken steps to cover that as well.

What they did with the bodies of Truck, Pat, and the others I didn't want to know, which was good because Brundidge wasn't talking about it anymore, only that he had resigned from the force and set himself up in Truck's old office, telling anyone who might ask that Truck had gone out West for a while to dry out. He wasn't sure when, or if, the old man was coming back.

And that's right where I found him when the cab dropped me off the morning they let me out of Baptist Hospital. I had freshly taped ribs and a brand-new cane to help me get around, and although I was moving slow, I was at least moving. Brundidge came out the door smiling, then helped me up the steps and inside where we both sat down to a fresh pot of coffee.

"You don't look so bad," he said, grinning at my bruised and bandaged face.

"I don't know," I answered, "I think this pretty much eighty-sixes the modeling career."

We both laughed a second before he turned serious.

"Jake, we're two very lucky guys. You know that don't you?"

"That I do, Brundidge. That I do."

He still had the same boyish face but here and there, around the corners of his eyes, faint creases were beginning to take their place among his features.

"I know I don't have to tell you," he went on, "but as far as anyone is concerned, none of this ever happened, capiche? We need to be together on this."

"I have no idea what you're talking about, Alvin. I got jumped by a bunch of bikers a few weeks back and can't remember a thing. Is Gerald Ford still President? Did they find Patty Hearst?"

He nodded agreement and got up to pour fresh coffee.

"Make mine with a dash of cream, no sugar," came a voice from the front door, as Detective Lyle strode into the room like the King of Denmark.

"Just poured the last drop," Brundidge said, "but I can make more if you're planning to stay and help clean up this dump."

"Don't bother," Lyle said. "Where's Bennett?"

"On vacation, somewhere out West."

"Really? He missed a court date last week and nobody's heard from him. He leave a number?"

"Nope, but you can leave a message and I'll give it to him when he calls."

Lyle looked at Brundidge, then at me, then around the cluttered room and back at the two of us again.

"You boys think I've been in this racket for twenty-two years and don't know when something smells? Is that it?"

"Let's face it, Sergeant," I smirked, "you were born way too late. Joe McCarthy could've used you back in the Fifties for the congressional witch hunts."

He walked over to where I sat and propped his ass on Truck's old desk.

"Son, you think because you've been in the hospital a few days that you're out from under the lamp?" He leaned towards me but this time I saw through it. I knew he was just posing.

"I don't know, Lyle. You tell me. Whatcha got?"

He sat back and pulled a cigarette from a pack of Pall Malls Truck had left on the desk.

"You know, Shepherd," he said, trying but failing to blow a smoke ring. "Civilians sit home watching movies and TV, they think all the crimes get solved. Unfortunately, that ain't the case. People get away with shit every day. At first, I liked you for the girl's murder but now I'm not so sure. To be honest, Shepherd, I don't really think you've got the stones to kill anybody."

"I can live with that," I said.

"I don't doubt it," he agreed, then rose and started for the door before turning back to Brundidge. "You tell Bennett to call me as soon as he checks in, you hear?"

"Will do, Sergeant."

"You know, Brundidge," Lyle added, "You might've made a good cop if you'd given yourself a little time. Takes time, you know."

"I doubt it," Brundidge shook his head. "Probably didn't have the stones."

Lyle left then, letting our collective sighs of relief fill the room like fresh air. Afterwards, Brundidge drove me across the river to my apartment. As I walked unsteadily across the parking lot I saw the survey team surrounding the feed store, plotting lines and jotting notes, staking out the final frontier in the name of downtown progress. A crew of Hispanic guys were lugging instruments and marking lines.

Mr. Pitts and a well-dressed man were standing on the sidewalk, laughing and talking animatedly like new best friends. He saw me out of the corner of his eye, noticed the cane, and waved. I gave him a big, knowing smile and waved back, pointing at the old building. He just grinned and shrugged his shoulders as if to say, "Oh Well," then stepped off the sidewalk into a sleek new, midnight blue 7-Series BMW and drove away.

Hell, I wasn't all that surprised. It had always been just a matter of time before this town finally drove me into the river. Only now I was newly baptized and born-again-hard, and I wasn't afraid of the water anymore.

My place was just like I left it except for the new Martin D-28 guitar Brundidge had dropped off, along with a note saying it might help me with my recovery. Most of the money the Eskews had given me was still there, though most of it would go to cover hospital bills.

Like an old drunk clinging to the last shreds of denial, I found the note Charlotte had left for me at the hotel and compared it to the one she had given me in the diner that first morning, the one supposedly written by Cassidy to her parents. I held them side by side for a long time, although the simplest fool could see the handwriting was identical.

It took a while before I came up with a working explanation: Unable to save Cassidy, even at the risk of her own life, Charlotte had been as helpless as I'd been the night I slipped the noose around Benny Watts' neck. Her only recourse had been to use whatever means she had to bring Robinson down and try, in some small way, to avenge her sister's death. So she used me to get to him, knowing I'd have no choice but to go after him, and never dreaming that a little thing like love would throw a monkey wrench in the plan. And when that happened, she called the FBI.

I liked that story. I liked it a lot. It didn't matter whether it was true, I just needed something I could live with.

Maybe Robinson was right. Maybe we all sell out sooner or later. Charlotte sold out her sister, Robinson sold out the whole country, and God knows I'd hustled everything near and dear to me for the better part of my life, beginning with the night I sold out Benny Watts. In the end, even an old stalwart like Mr. Pitts found it hard not to nibble at the fruit of temptation.

But then I remembered Cassidy and Angie and Toad, and I knew that wasn't the case, that there will always be those among us who refuse to compromise, who would break rather than bend: the Shadrachs, Meshachs, and Abednigos of our time, who get through the day on equal parts will and stubborn pride.

As for Benny Watts, only time would tell if he'd been satisfied with my meager deliverance. Still, I had the feeling that somehow things had been squared between us. At the very least I felt I finally understood what he meant when he said it all comes back around, that justice is much more concerned with those who cause the noose to be drawn than with those who merely place it there.

Cassidy was another story, however, and one that still awaited an ending. But if she decided to pick up where Benny left off, then so be it. I'd grown accustomed to the demons in my life and could not imagine it otherwise.

That evening I hitched down the steps to the parking lot and climbed behind the wheel of the dusty, black Eldorado. The car had been sitting for a long time and I wasn't even sure she would start, but when I hit the switch, the big engine turned over once and roared to life as though she'd been waiting for me with the patience of a seaman's wife.

I knew there was still one place where I might find the last few answers, one last stop to make to put all the events of the past weeks in perspective. Once on Interstate 65 and heading south, I opened up the Caddy to blow out the cobwebs, my palms wringing with the thrill of raw power pulsing through the wheel.

I took the Old Hickory Boulevard exit in Brentwood and drove west two blocks before making a right and driving past the wooden-fenced compound where Waylon and Jessi lived.

Aleta's house was nestled back in the woods at the end of a long, dead-end street. A tall, wrought-iron fence surrounded the property and led off on both sides into the dark, expensive Brentwood forest. A cold shudder swept over me when I remembered the brick and iron fence of the mansion in Atlanta, but I shook it off and turned into the driveway.

I was surprised to find the gate open, and I drove slowly down the tree-lined drive until the big, two-story glass and cedar chateau came into view. Bear's truck was parked in the driveway and the front door of the house stood open. I eased out of the Caddy and used my cane to climb the wide, stone steps leading up to the porch. For some strange reason, it never occurred to me to ring the bell or knock on the open door. I stepped into the foyer and began hobbling down the dark hall toward the living room, the tip of my cane burying itself in the deep-piled, cream-colored carpet. As my eyes became focused I heard, or thought I heard, the soft, indistinct sounds of mumbling. Then I stepped out into the open, glass-walled living room that was lit with the last remaining rays of the evening sun.

Bear was sitting on the floor in red shorts and tank top, his back braced against the sofa, his black, thick muscles softer in the pale light, his arms cradling the gray, rigored body of Aleta Thomas.

"Why...why...?" he was sobbing, as he held her and rocked back and forth against the sofa. On the floor by the glass coffee table, a crimson stain the size of a throw pillow had soaked deep into the carpet.

The blood on the front of Aleta's white blouse had long since dried, and it was obvious she'd been dead for a while. I moved closer and could see three modest, bead-sized holes in the center of her chest that looked like the signature of a small caliber handgun.

When he was finally aware of my presence, Bear looked up at me, his eyes brimming with the tears of a little boy.

"Look what they did," he whispered, more to the world than to me.

"We need to call the police, Marcellus." It was the first time I'd ever used his given name.

"She never did nothing to nobody," he railed. "Why anybody want to hurt her?" He gritted his teeth and rocked harder, holding her stiff body like a bruised mannequin.

I found the phone, called 911, and gave them the address.

"I been calling her for three days," Bear went on. "Finally, I just say I'm gonna come out here and see what's the matter with her...see why she all-of-a-sudden ain't taking my calls... and then this..."

He looked up at me again from the floor, his eyes full of questions I could never answer.

"She loved me," he went on. "I know that much. Now somebody gone and done this ...and I can't help her."

I struggled but couldn't find anything to say to ease his pain. What I wanted to tell him was that it was all just someone's way of tying up loose ends, that none of it had anything to do with him, and that he had never really been a part of the equation. But of course, I didn't. Instead, I did the only thing I could do, which was to leave him alone with her.

I started for the front porch to wait for the police, turning on the hall light as I hobbled back down the long stretch of thick carpet. And that's when I saw it.

It would've been easy enough to miss but, passing the open door of the tiny half-bathroom, I glanced at the base of the sink and the small wicker waste basket that sat on the floor between it and the toilet. Resting on the white carpet outside the wicker basket was a crumpled, thin blue tissue. I picked it up and held it between my fingers, the moisture gone now, only the soft, silky feel of a familiar towelette. Slipping the tissue into my pocket, I went out onto the porch to wait for Lyle.

I was determined to make the most of my latest second chance, so I went through my apartment and tossed out all the remaining alcohol, then spent the next few days just lying around, getting stronger, eating well, and playing my new guitar. At some point the words began to take shape again, materializing out of the air almost, so that pretty soon I was writing, this time with a renewed sense of purpose that surprised even myself.

Once I could move about, I started going through my things, trying to decide what to hold onto and what to let go. It's amazing at the junk you can accumulate in twenty years, but by the end of the week I had it all down to six large boxes neatly packed and taped, stacked in the middle of the living room floor.

Angie dropped by once, bringing me a fresh-pressed copy of her new CD.

"I think it's the best thing I've ever done, Jake," she said, tears welling up in her eyes. "Thanks for helping me get another shot."

"Heck, Angie, all I did was write the song. Besides, I think we all deserve more than one shot. Don't you?"

"Yeah, Jake, I truly do. And you know what? I'm betting your next shot is just around the corner."

"Honey," I laughed, "My next shot has always been just around the corner."

When she left I called my old buddy, Charlie, from the radio station, and he came by later that night to pick up the CD and some other mementos I wanted him to have. We struck a deal, and I knew he'd live up to his part.

On Friday morning I loaded the Eldorado, then called Brundidge to come pick up the key and the storage instructions for my boxes.

"How long will you be gone?" he asked.

"Can't say. Six months, maybe a year, who knows? I need a good long rest before I climb back into the ring with Tunetown again."

"You take care of yourself, Jake. You know you've always got a place to come back to."

"Believe me, that's good to know, Alvin. But are you sure this is really what you want to do? Being a private eye can get mighty boring sometimes."

"Right now boring sounds just fine to me," he smiled. "I've been doing some research lately and I think there may be some money in this. People are starting to pay a lot for information and security these days. Who knows where it'll lead?"

We shook hands in the parking lot and he drove away in the big, battered Ford. I stood for a moment and looked up at the old building that had been my home for the past ten years, then across the river where the new football stadium was under construction. Music City had grown up a lot since I first blew into town all those years ago. And finally, I guess, so had I.

It was almost eleven o'clock, so I drove over to Odyssey Studios where I knew Papa would be mixing tracks on the lovely and talented Yolanda Sweet. I managed to catch him taking a break, then hustled him outside to the car under the premise that we needed to talk about publishing rights to my song. Once in the car, I started the engine for the AC, the radio already set on WSM.

"I'm telling you, Jake, we've got big money behind this. The people at Sony are interested big-time and there's more offers waiting in the wings. This is our shot, Boy- "Sheet Music" is gonna put us over the top."

"That's great, Papa," I said. "I'm glad somebody is finally doing something with that old song. Hell, it's been floating around town for years, been cut two or three times but nothing ever came of it."

"Well, by God, something's gonna come of it now," he laughed, slapping the dashboard with his big thick hand.

Just then Charlie's voice came over the radio:

"Here's a hot new release from someone we haven't heard from in quite some time- Miss Angie Lefevre. It just debuted at Number Twenty-four on the Billboard charts and folks are loving it. Let's give it a listen."

I watched Papa's reaction as the steel guitar slid out of the intro, then tried to keep a straight face as Angie began singing "Sheet Music." And even though it was all a big hoax, I'd be lying if I said it didn't thrill me just a little to hear one of my songs on the radio again. Nevertheless, I was cool as the color quickly drained from the old man's face.

"Sonofabitch..." he gasped.

"I'll be damned," I said, feigning surprise. "Can you believe it? Now I'm gonna have *two* cuts of my song out at the same time."

"The Hell you preach," he stammered.

"What do you mean, Papa?"

"Shepherd, are you crazy? No record label will release that song now. That old gal has already gone and released it and it won't stay on the charts three weeks at best. You, me, and Yolanda Sweet are all officially screwed, blued and tattooed."

"Wait a minute, Papa," I pleaded. "Won't it at least make a good album cut?"

"No way," he hollered, as he got out and slammed the door, then opened it again and stuck his head back in.

"It's like I always said, Shepherd- You're jinxed! Jinxed, God-dammit! I don't want nothing else to do with you. You're the worst kind of bad luck. Now get the hell outta here before you jinx the whole damn block."

He slammed the door again and walked back into the studio, shaking his grizzled head all the way. I drove away laughing, happy that at least one of my meager schemes had finally gone right.

Of course, the odds were stacked way against Angie ever really having another hit, whether with my song or anyone else's. But if I had to bet on anyone beating the odds, I'd sure as heck bet on her. I hoped my buddy at WSM didn't get fired for playing her song that one time, but I figured he'd been around long enough to cover his backside. And who knows, some folks might like it and call in to hear it again. The one thing the music business has taught me is to never say "never."

I took the long way out of town, winding through the shady streets and sidewalks of the quiet neighborhoods where kids played and dogs barked and snapped at the first golden leaves dropping like feathers to the ground.

As for me, right now I'm blowing down I-24 East with the cool September breeze washing my face and fanning through my hair. I've got the tape deck cranked up and Guy Clark is singing about leaving the concrete behind in search of a good dirt-road back street.

I've been told the north Georgia mountains are a sight to behold in the Fall, so I figure I'll find out for myself if that's true.

And as for Charlotte, I'm not really sure what I'll do when I find her. But I want to hear her side of the story, see if it comes close to the one I invented. If it does, I just might throw my arms around her and sing her one of the songs I've written over the past few days. But if not, well... I guess I'll just have to deal with it the only way I know how.

Either way, I've got my guitar in the trunk and my gun under the seat. I guess I'll know when I get there.

THE END

ABOUT THE AUTHOR

Pharoah Cain has been a Marine, a musician and the Writer/
Producer of several hundred country music television shows.
His songs have been performed and recorded by various artists,
including members of the Grand Ole Opry, and the Country
Music Hall of Fame. He lives in Tennessee.

Other Books by Pharoah Cain:
Clyde's Ride
Dupree's Delta Double-Down

For more on Pharoah Cain go to DuckRiverPress.com,
Facebook, and PharoahCain.com.

ACKNOWLEDGEMENT

Thunder in the Hole, by Harvey Keene, Kiwi Music, BMI. Lyrics reprinted by permission.